WE'LL MEET AGAIN *on* ·CORONATION ST.·

Maggie Sullivan writes Northern family dramas, including the bestselling *Coronation Street* series, that have taken her into the bestseller lists and have garnered her legions of fans and readers around the globe.

Maggie was born and brought up in Manchester where the award-winning soap was compulsory family viewing, and she acquired a lifelong passion for its legendary characters. She won't admit to having a favourite but can't deny a soft spot for feisty, strong-willed Elsie Tanner who, despite hard times, always managed to have some fun.

Maggie has a love of travelling, is a freelance lecturer, and an active member of the Romantic Novelist's Association. Maggie lived in Canada for several years, but she now lives in London.

Also by Maggie Sullivan

Christmas on Coronation Street
Mother's Day on Coronation Street
Snow on the Cobbles
The Land Girls from Coronation Street

Our Street at War series

The Postmistress

WE'LL MEET AGAIN *on* CORONATION ST.

MAGGIE SULLIVAN

HarperCollins*Publishers*

HarperCollins*Publishers* Ltd
1 London Bridge Street,
London SE1 9GF

www.harpercollins.co.uk

HarperCollins*Publishers*
1st Floor, Watermarque Building, Ringsend Road
Dublin 4, Ireland

First published by HarperCollins*Publishers* 2022
1

A catalogue record for this book is available from the British Library

ISBN: 978-0-00-849931-0

Typeset in Sabon LT Std by Palimpsest Book Production Ltd, Falkirk, Stirlingshire

Printed and bound in the UK using 100% Renewable Electricity by CPI Group (UK) Ltd

In fond memory of Richard Alexander

Part One

August 1949

Chapter 1

Weatherfield

Wendy Collins stood in the middle of the tiny bedroom, struggling to hold back the tears as she wondered what she had let herself in for. This was not quite what she had expected when she had agreed to come to Weatherfield, and she suddenly felt sad and alone, though she was trying her best to put on a brave front. There was certainly no point in crying about it, now that her friend Ada had married and gone off to Australia. The atmosphere in the house was gloomy enough without her adding to it, though the offer of accommodation by Esther, Ada's sister, that Wendy should take Ada's place, had been sincerely made, Wendy thought. And Coronation Street was an ideal place to live because it was so close to the Bessie Street County Primary school where she was about to take up her new teaching post.

At least I don't have to share a bed with Esther, she thought with relief. Kind as it was of Ada's sister to offer her a home, she hardly knew her. And from what she'd seen of the way the Hayes family lived, she realized she hadn't known Ada as well as she'd thought. She lifted her small suitcase onto the bed by the window which Esther had told her was to be hers, and stared down at the well-worn leather. It was one of the few things she had managed to salvage all those years ago when the family home in Blackpool had been shattered by a bomb but she was thankful she didn't have much to unpack because it took no more than a quick glance for her to realize how limited the space was in the cupboards and drawers. Before she could even snap open the locks on the shabby case that had once been her mother's, she heard Esther's voice call up the stairs, 'I've a cup of tea waiting when you're ready.'

Wendy glanced in the mirror on the wall above the chest of drawers and registered with horror how pale she looked. She pinched her cheeks and rewound the curls on the top of her head, trying to give them a boost by lifting them away from her face. She stepped out onto the tiny square of landing to call to Esther that she would be down in a minute, but when she saw the closed door of the bedroom opposite which no doubt belonged to Esther's mother Alice, she changed her mind about shouting, in case the old woman might be sleeping.

Alice had reputedly taken to her bed several years previously when her husband had died, and her son Tom had been caught breaking and entering. He'd been taken back into prison, and she had remained there in bed, in a deep depression, expecting to be waited on by one or the other of her daughters. Wendy shut her own door and went as quietly as was possible in Cuban-heeled shoes down the carpetless stairs.

'You don't have to worry too much about my mam,' Esther said as Wendy crept into the living room. 'She can sleep through anything when she's a mind.' She laughed. 'Unless she deliberately decides to get testy. But never mind her for now, she'll shout if she needs anything. Let us have some tea while we've got the chance.'

'Thanks,' Wendy said, suddenly realizing that it was some time since she had eaten or drunk anything, 'that sounds like a good idea.'

'I've put a spot of milk in,' Esther said, 'I hope that was all right, but I've no sugar, I'm afraid, what with rationing and all. Mam finished out the last bit of honey that was left,' she added, arranging her face in an attitude of resignation.

'Oh, that's all right,' Wendy assured her. 'I've almost forgotten what sweet stuff tastes like.' It was true; she hardly could remember a time when sugar and sweets were in plentiful supply. While Esther went into the kitchen for the cups and saucers, Wendy looked around the shabby but cosy living room of the house where she would be lodging for the foreseeable future. It wasn't as spacious and didn't have as much furniture as the house where she had rented a room in Blackpool, but at least she only had to share the bathroom and the outside privy with two other people.

She picked up a photograph that was standing on a shelf of the whatnot in the corner of the room. It was a slightly out-of-focus picture of a young couple in their Sunday best, grinning sheepishly.

'That's our Ada, as you can see,' Esther said.

Wendy smiled. 'I almost didn't recognize her. I suppose that must be Matthew then? I never actually met him.'

Esther nodded. 'It's the only wedding picture we've got. Some kind neighbour snapped them as they came back to the house from the Mission Hall where they got wed.'

'They certainly look very happy,' Wendy said.

'I think they are,' Esther said. 'In their own way.' Her voice sounded cheerful enough, though Wendy couldn't help noticing that her eyes had misted. 'But then, so would I be, escaping this nightmare,' Esther said. She had spoken the words softly, but her hand shot out quickly to cover her mouth and she gave a sort of muffled giggle. 'I'm sorry,' she said, 'that's hardly the thing to be saying to a new lodger is it? I apologize. Let me assure you I didn't mean there's anything wrong with the accommodation, only with my situation.'

'And that's what I understood, Esther. It was kind of you to offer Ada's bed to me when she decided to get married and emigrate and I knew her well enough to understand your family circumstances, so you don't have to apologize for that. If there's anything I can do to help . . .' Wendy said, and she put her hand on Esther's arm for a moment.

Esther smiled. 'That's very kind, thanks. What I really meant was the nightmare of having to look after a sick mother, which of course is my problem not yours,' she said. 'It . . . it just feels like carrying a dead weight, having all that responsibility sometimes,' and she patted Wendy's hand gratefully. Then she gave a little laugh. 'Although, as you probably know, both Ada and I are convinced there's nothing actually wrong with her. Nothing that some fresh air and a brisk walk won't fix.'

'Oh, really? I thought she actually did have a bad heart?' Wendy said.

'I very much doubt it, though she's got a bad

everything if you listen to her, but the doctor's never said. He just keeps on giving her something he calls a tonic to make her happy and a load of different coloured pills that to my mind may as well be dolly mixtures.'

'Have you heard from Ada since they left?' Wendy felt it safer to change the subject.

'We had a telegram to say the ship had finally docked in Sydney and they were waiting for some kind of transport to take them to this farm where they'll be staying for the moment. But there's been nothing since. Never a great one for letter writing, my sister. I doubt we had more than a handful of notes in the four years she spent working in Blackpool during the war, so I reckon that's possibly the last we'll hear for quite some time.' She paused, her cheeks colouring slightly as she added, 'And in case you're wondering, I don't expect to hear from our Tom again either; at least, not until he comes out and needs money,' she said and she glanced up at Wendy. 'I'm sure you knew Ada long enough to have heard all about our wayward brother.'

Wendy nodded and kept a straight face, though it had always made her want to smile when Ada referred to her brother as being 'a guest of His Majesty'. But she could sense Esther's discomfort and she let the matter drop.

Esther sighed as she sat down. 'I'm glad you

applied for Ada's old job here in Weatherfield, Wendy,' she said. 'And I thought it would make sense for you to live locally if you're to teach at Bessie Street, what with Ada's bed going spare . . .'

Wendy smiled. 'Your kind offer gave me the chance to get away from Blackpool for a bit, which is what I really needed to do.'

'Has life been tough recently for you too?' Esther asked.

Wendy could feel her throat tighten as she had a sudden vision of Andrew and how he had looked on the day that he had walked out of her life, and she had to swallow hard.

'Afraid so,' she said, almost in a whisper. 'I'm sure that's true for lots of other people too, but I know for me it was definitely time for a change.'

They were clearing away the remains of what Esther had called their high tea, beans on toast with extra dripping, when there was a loud knocking on the front door and Esther and Wendy both jumped.

'Who can that be at this hour?' Esther said.

Wendy glanced at the garniture clock on the mantelpiece that was registering six thirty. 'Well, as I don't know anyone in Weatherfield,' she said, 'it must be for you.'

Esther didn't say anything but she dried her hands on the tea towel and went to answer it.

Wendy heard the sound of muffled voices in the hallway and when Esther reappeared, her rather dowdy appearance was overshadowed by the striking woman who was following in her wake. The woman wore a low-cut wrapover dress in a silk-like material that clung to her shapely figure. The rust and white design of the fabric set off the redness of her hair which hung in curls to her shoulders and she had generously applied make-up to her eyes and lips so that her face seemed to light up when she smiled, as she did now when she looked directly at Wendy. She thrust out an arm.

'Hi! I hear you've just arrived in Coronation Street. I'm Elsie Tanner and I thought I'd be one of the first to drop in to say welcome.' She sat down at the table without waiting to be asked.

Esther went through to the kitchen and, quickly emerging with a clean cup and saucer, poured another cup of tea. 'You are very definitely the first, Elsie,' she said. 'Wendy only arrived this afternoon.'

'School doesn't start for another couple of days, so it gives me a chance to settle in,' Wendy said.

'To help you do that I thought you might like to meet some of the neighbours, Wendy,' Elsie said, 'and see what's on offer in the vicinity. I know that Esther can't easily get away so I reckoned I might be the very person for the job. Wouldn't you agree, Esther?'

Esther forced a smile. 'I couldn't have put it better myself,' she said, then, 'Elsie sees it as her mission to cheer us all up and I must admit she does a pretty good job, especially when I get to feeling down about . . .' She jerked her thumb in the direction of the stairs.

'A little birdie told me you're going to teach at the county primary school now that Ada's left?' Elsie turned to Wendy. 'Is that right? That's where my kids go.'

Wendy nodded. 'I'll be taking one of the junior classes,' she said.

'Well, if you'd like to meet some of the locals before you start then I could take you to the Rovers Return a bit later on tonight, introduce you to some of the residents.'

Wendy wasn't sure what to say, uncertain how Esther would feel about being left behind, but as if she read her mind Elsie said, 'I'm sure Esther's not bothered, are you, chuck?' she asked Esther directly.

Esther shrugged. 'I'm used to it. Someone has to be here with Mum in case she needs anything. She goes into a flat panic if she thinks she's alone in the house. I'm afraid I definitely won't be able to take you anywhere, Wendy, so you may as well take up Elsie's offer while you can.'

Elsie gulped down the rest of her tea and stood up. 'I'll knock about eight if that suits you, Wendy?' she said. 'Give you a chance to get unpacked first.'

Wendy turned to look at Esther. It was as if the reality of the situation was striking her for the first time and she was becoming aware of what she was taking on, leaving everything she knew and starting afresh like this. Naturally she was keen to make a good first impression in her new job but she was not sure how it would look if the first meeting with the parents of many of the children she'd be working with was to take place in the local pub and she fancied it would feel more like walking into a lion's den. But the offer had been made warmly and sincerely and it seemed churlish to refuse.

'Thanks,' Wendy said, and she gave an uncertain smile, thinking it might be better if Elsie's children were not in her class.

'Elsie's a good sort, Wendy, so don't let her rather offhand manner put you off,' Esther said when Elsie had gone, promising to call back later. 'In fact, that goes for several of the neighbours round here.'

'Where does she live?' Wendy wanted to know.

'Number 11, a few doors further down Coronation Street.' She pointed in the opposite direction to the pub.

'Is she on her own? She said she's got kids.'

'Yes, she's got two, a girl and a boy. Linda is nine and Dennis is about seven, I think. They're both a bit of a handful but she's managing to bring them up on her own, if that's what you mean. You've got to admire her.'

'What happened to her husband?'

'She got married to Arnold Tanner when she was about sixteen, I believe, and he had a bit of a reputation in these parts. I'm sure she'll tell you about him some day; but he went into the navy during the war and never came back,' Esther said.

'Oh dear, I'm sorry.' A look of sadness crossed Wendy's face as she thought for a moment of the people she had loved and lost during the wretched war.

'Oh no, it was nothing like that,' Esther said hastily. 'He ran off somewhere with another woman. Elsie reckons she's well rid of him, although as far as I know, they aren't actually officially divorced. Whichever way, he's long gone from Weatherfield. But Elsie's quite a character.'

'Is there anyone else I should know about if I'm going to the pub? Anyone I need to look out for?'

'I'm sure those with kids will soon introduce themselves,' Esther said. 'They always used to like getting to know Ada. Apart from that, Ena Sharples is the only other person most people in this street manage to have a barney with at some point, though she doesn't actually have any kids at school any more.' Esther laughed. 'She's the caretaker at the Mission of Glad Tidings down by the viaduct, where our Ada got married, and she can be very – how shall I say? – bossy. But I would never speak ill of her, especially not in front of Elsie, unless you want to start a local war; they don't always see eye to eye. But actually I don't want to prejudice you against Ena because I have to say she's always been very nice to me, particularly since Dad died. Anyways, you're bound to meet her soon so I'll let you make up your own mind.'

When Elsie called to pick her up on her way down to the Rovers Return as she had promised, the first thing Wendy noticed was her make-up. Her lipstick seemed to be more vibrant than before so had obviously been replenished and the kohl markings that picked out her eyes were more pronounced than they had been earlier. It was hard not to be drawn by Elsie's striking appearance and Wendy felt palely insignificant standing next to her, glad that they only had to walk a very short distance to the pub. Elsie was dressed in the same outfit she had been wearing that afternoon and when Wendy joined her in the hallway she was patting down her flame-coloured curls that had been pinned back, not entirely successfully, into a French pleat.

Wendy had wondered whether the clothes that she had in her suitcase were more suitable for standing up in front of a classroom of children than propping up a bar in a Weatherfield pub, but she had little choice. She had settled on a simple rayon skirt and matching top with pale-blue and white polka dots splashed onto a navy background and hoped it would be all right. She had tied her blonde ringlets back away from her face and they rested in the nape of her neck on the Peter Pan collar of the blouse that she had neatly tucked in at the waist. She knew the outfit made her look younger than she was, but at thirty-five that was perhaps no bad thing and she hoped she would pass muster.

'Will I do?' Wendy asked as she came down the stairs and she was disconcerted when Elsie laughed.

'Of course you'll do,' Elsie said. 'That outfit's perfect for you. You look very nice. And in case you're worried, I'd say I'm happy for you to come to the Rovers with me and to teach either of my kids at any time. I don't know why you look so nervous.'

Wendy shrugged. She could feel the tears she had hoped to avoid amassing behind her eyelids. 'It's hard to explain,' she said, cross that her voice was already giving her away.

'No one round here bites,' Elsie said, still in a jocular manner. 'Except maybe Ena Sharples on occasion, but I'll make sure she doesn't bother you tonight.' Elsie laughed and shook her head. 'I don't know,' she said, 'anyone would think you've not been to a pub before.'

There was an awkward pause before Wendy admitted, 'Actually, I've not been all that often. Not that I see anything wrong with women drinking in a bar,' she added hastily, when she saw the expression on Elsie's face, 'but it wasn't something either of my parents did often and they didn't like the idea of young women going into a pub without an escort, so I suppose I never really got into the habit. Not while I was still living at home.'

'Well, perhaps it's just as well that neither of them are here right now,' Elsie joked. 'They'll never know, I promise.' She put her finger to her lips as if they were sharing a playground secret.

Wendy's eyes suddenly filled with tears that were in danger of spilling over. She felt the usual rush of emotion that threatened to overwhelm her whenever she thought of her parents and she turned away to look for her jacket, busily rummaging through the variety of items that had been flung at various times across the newel post at the bottom of the stairs.

Now Elsie looked alarmed. 'I'm sorry, Wendy. Have I spoken out of turn? I didn't mean to upset you, chuck.' Elsie came over to her, her voice full of concern. 'Don't tell me I've put my foot in it again?'

'It's all right, you weren't to know,' Wendy said softly. 'Even I never know when something might catch me unawares like that. You can guarantee it's when I'm least expecting it.' She tried to laugh, but this was followed by an awkward silence and for a moment none of them moved.

'Why don't you sit down for a minute, there's no rush is there, Elsie?' Esther said eventually.

'None at all,' Elsie said as she led them into the kitchen.

'Is it anything you want to talk about?' Esther asked.

Wendy shrugged. 'I'm sorry, it's no great mystery, but it might make it easier in the future for you both to know that – that I lost my entire family in Blackpool. They were killed quite early on in the war. Nine years ago!' She exhaled noisily. 'You'd think I'd have got over it by now.'

'I don't know that you ever really get over these things,' Elsie said, a surprisingly wistful look on her face.

'The irony is,' Wendy said, 'Blackpool didn't really suffer any serious bomb damage. Just one stray bomb on one particular night.' She stared off into space as if she could see the bomb falling, then shut her eyes tight. 'It was dropped by a German aircraft flying home from a Manchester raid and it hit Seed Street where we lived. Eight people died.' She looked from Esther to Elsie before she said, 'It not only destroyed my entire family, my mum, my dad and my younger brother, but it demolished the house and damaged almost all of our belongings. I'd been staying overnight with a friend and by the time I got home next morning, most of the fires were out but there wasn't much left to salvage.'

Nobody spoke and Wendy was aware of the clock clearly ticking the minutes away on the other side of the room.

'I had to move into digs and that was where I met Ada, who'd been evacuated to Blackpool from Weatherfield with all the kids from Bessie Street School. She became a good friend.' Wendy stared down into her lap wrapped up in her memories, but then she suddenly looked up and, breaking the tension, grinned. 'It was because of her challenge that I first saw the inside of a pub,' she said. 'She was billeted for at bit at the Rose and Crown, behind Central Pier. And the one and only time I've ever been drunk was there.' She giggled now. 'It felt so daring. Ada was becoming concerned about me getting depressed and she thought it might help cheer me up if I drank neat whisky, but all I got out of it was a sore head.'

'And you haven't been inside a pub since?' Now Elsie sounded anxious. 'Maybe the Rovers isn't such a good idea after all. I don't want to be accused of leading you astray.'

Wendy smiled. 'Of course I've been in a pub since, you don't have to worry about that; though I've never been drunk again. But I do have to confess that every time I go into a pub my stomach does a backflip and I can't help thinking of my mum and dad.'

'So how are you feeling now?' Elsie asked anxiously.

Wendy stood up. 'I'm fine,' she said. 'All the better now that you both know so I won't have to keep explaining.' She reached out and squeezed Esther's fingers, winking at her and giving her a warm smile. Then she put her hand on Elsie's arm. 'So, come on, Elsie, let's get going to the Rovers.'

Chapter 2

It was still bright daylight when Elsie and Wendy approached the Rovers Return, light enough to see that the outside of the pub was badly in need of a fresh lick of paint, and as they pushed open the swing doors Wendy was not surprised to see that the interior was also in need of some refurbishment. The most heartening thing for her was that there were so many people, although the initial illusion of gaiety was soon shattered. They were standing and sitting together in small groups and seemed to be engaged in animated conversation, with the occasional triumphant shout from the direction of the dartboard, but as her eyes adjusted to the smoky haze she became aware that there was little actual laughter to be heard and that the general atmosphere was subdued.

'What can I get you?' Elsie asked as they approached the bar.

'I'll have a lager and lime, please, but you don't have to . . . I can . . .'

Wendy began to rummage for her purse in her capacious handbag but Elsie put her hands over the metal clasp. 'I know I don't have to but I'd like to as a kind of welcome.'

'I'd make the most of it if I were you, for that's not an offer you'll get every day of the week.'

A strident voice cut in before Wendy could respond to Elsie, and she could feel Elsie stiffening as she glared at the speaker. It was an older-looking woman who had spoken and she was wearing a double-breasted black coat buttoned up to the neck as if it were winter. But it was the large-gauge hairnet that was the giveaway to Wendy and she recognized Ena Sharples from Esther's earlier description.

'Wendy, allow me to introduce you to Mrs Sharples, she's the caretaker of the Mission of Glad Tidings as you'll no doubt be hearing.' Elsie confirmed Wendy's guess through clenched teeth. 'Mrs Sharples, this is Wendy Collins. It's her first night in Weatherfield so be nice to her if you can find it in yourself; she's from Blackpool.'

'We won't hold that against her,' Ena said as she eyed Wendy with some disdain.

'She's lodging at number 5 with the Hayes,' Elsie said, ignoring Ena's remark.

'What? Come to babysit Alice? That'll please young Esther now that Ada's deserted her.'

'I'll have you know that Miss Collins – Wendy – is one of the new teachers who'll be starting at Bessie Street County Primary.' Elsie spoke loudly so that others could hear and Wendy was touched that there seemed to be more than a hint of pride in her voice as she made the introduction.

'Is that right?' Ena said. 'Well, maybe she can teach you a thing or two,' she added pointedly. Then she turned to Wendy. 'And all I can say to you is that I wish you luck if either of her two horrors are in your class,' she said. 'Like mother like kids, I always say.' She nodded towards Elsie then deliberately turned her back and gave a half-smile in Wendy's direction. 'Nice to meet you. Wendy, was it? No doubt we'll be seeing more of you in here of a night when the kids get to be too much for you during the day.' She chuckled then looked serious again. 'Maybe you can persuade young Esther to come in here with you some time. I'm always telling her it would do her the world of good to get out for a bit. She deserves a night off. But I'd watch yerself with this one if I were you.' She turned back and pointed her finger at Elsie. 'You don't want to be seen around with her too often.' She switched her gaze for a moment then she picked up a bottle of milk stout from the counter, nodded to her two friends who seemed to be waiting patiently for her to take the lead and headed for the door marked Snug.

'Cheers, Wendy!' 'Welcome to Coronation Street, Miss Collins!' There were several shouts of greeting as more people came to the bar and Wendy was introduced as she and Elsie waited for their drinks.

'I wish you luck trying to stuff anything useful in the way of education into my lad,' someone called from the other side of the counter and everyone laughed, then there were a variety of calls from several of the women who raised their glasses in her direction. Even one or two of the men at the nearby tables looked up from their game of dominoes with appraising glances and Wendy felt quite the local celebrity.

'Indeed, welcome to Coronation Street.' The woman behind the bar placed their drinks on the metal tray on the countertop and flashed what looked like a prearranged fixed smile. 'Please, have this one on the house,' she said and she projected her fingers between the glasses so that Wendy could grasp their tips instead of a handshake. 'I'm Mrs

Walker,' the woman said, 'the landlady here,' and she carefully picked out half of the coins that were in Elsie's hand as she proffered payment for the drinks.

'Thanks, thanks very much,' Wendy said, not sure which direction to look in first, and she followed Elsie to one of the corner booths where the faded, felt-like material looked as if it had once been velveteen though it had long since lost its plush pile.

'I don't suppose you know yet which class you'll be taking?' A woman with short dark curling hair and a pretty, if somewhat hesitant, smile leaned across the table as Wendy and Elsie passed by and offered her hand for shaking.

'No, I've not been told that yet, Mrs . . . ?'

'It's Mrs Barlow, Ida Barlow,' the woman said.

'I won't find out until I actually go down to the school for the inaugural staff meeting,' Wendy said.

The woman smiled more confidently now. 'I believe we're next-door neighbours,' she said. 'I live at number 3. Only I've two boys in the school and I'm sure you'll come across them once term starts. Kenneth's nine and David's seven. They're both good boys. David's a bit young, of course, but Kenneth's eleven-plus is on the horizon next year and he needs a bit of encouragement, like. Only my husband—'

'That's a nice way to greet a new teacher I must say! And term's not even started yet. I'm sure Miss Collins has not come here on her first night in town to discuss school matters with complete strangers or to be mithered about your family problems,' a strident voice Wendy instantly recognized snapped behind her and she looked up to see Mrs Sharples glaring down at Ida, flanked on either side by what were obviously her two followers, all three of them clutching bottles of milk stout. They put in an order for another round but seemed disinclined to go back into the Snug. Instead they found a vacant table close to the bar.

'What's up, Mrs Sharples? Frightened you're missing summat?' Elsie challenged, but Ena ignored her as she set down her new bottle firmly on the table.

Wendy heard Elsie's deep-throated laugh. 'You should be flattered, Wendy,' Elsie said, 'You're providing the kind of entertainment this place has been missing for a long while – someone new and interesting to talk to.'

'Or talk *about*,' someone muttered behind her but Elsie pretended not to hear.

'You're obviously the star turn tonight,' she said. 'And no one wants to miss out.'

Wendy stared at her. She could feel a blush rising from her neck until she was sure that by now it must have passed through her pale cheeks as far as her cheekbones. A part of her was still wondering if she had done the right thing by coming to a pub that so many of the parents frequented and she wasn't sure whether to be flattered or not by Elsie's remark.

'I, personally, am very delighted to welcome some new teachers into the school at last,' Ida Barlow said. 'Though I am sorry to be losing Ada. She was always so good about helping my Kenneth, you know,' she confided. 'Next year is to be his eleven-plus year, did I say?' She beamed at Wendy.

'Am I to be the only new teacher?' Wendy couldn't resist asking. 'Or are there to be others too?'

'There's a newly qualified lass and a young man coming from down south, I believe, though I don't know much else about either of them,' Ida said.

Wendy's heart sank. She had presumed for some reason that any other new teachers would also be women.

'No doubt we'll get to meet him in due course,' Ena Sharples said. 'Most folk eventually find their way to the Rovers when they move into Weatherfield. Even if they don't all find their way to the Mission.'

'We should be thankful it's that way around,' Elsie said pointedly. 'Give me teachers over missionaries any day of the week.' She lifted her glass. 'Here's hoping some of the new stock might be able to stir things up a bit and put a bit of life back into this place.'

'Stir things up? What do you mean, Mrs Tanner.' Everyone nearby looked surprised when softly spoken Minnie Caldwell, one of Ena Sharples' cronies, suddenly spoke up. They turned to look at her and Ena glared at her friend as if she was surprised to hear that Minnie had a voice; but for once Minnie didn't seem fazed.

'You know what I mean,' Elsie said. 'I think we all need summat to get excited about. Let's face it, there's nowt much happened in Weatherfield since the war ended.'

'I don't know about that,' Minnie said. 'I thought things were beginning to brighten up a bit.'

'Like what?' Elsie sneered.

'Well, for starters . . .' Minnie considered her answer. 'There's lots of things that aren't rationed any more so we can go shopping again as often as we want,' she said eventually. 'And we can even go out at night without worrying about the blackout.'

Elsie looked scornful. 'I'm sorry, Mrs Caldwell, but I don't find any of that terribly exciting. For starters, there's still lots of things we can't get hold of. My kids have still never set eyes on a banana or an orange.'

'What?' Ena sounded surprised. 'You mean you haven't managed to get hold of any under the counter? You must be losing your touch, Elsie Tanner. You never had any trouble when your Yankee friends were stationed nearby during the war. It was amazing what you managed to get hold of then.' Ena flashed a spiteful glance in Elsie's direction. 'Perhaps it's the GIs you're hankering after, not the bananas!'

'Oh, I know there's still plenty of things we can't get,' Minnie piped up as if trying not to let Ena have her usual last word. 'Like sweets, for one. I can't get any fruit gums or pear drops and I do miss them,' she said and Elsie couldn't help smiling.

'And you can't get a decent joint for a Sunday even if you *are* registered with a butcher.' Martha Longhurst, wedged as usual between her friends Ena and Minnie suddenly joined in, addressing her words generally to the room but the only responses were a series of heavy groans and grunts.

'I agree with Elsie,' Ida Barlow said eventually. 'I haven't found any fresh fruit at any of my regular haunts.'

'Oh, I'm afraid there's still plenty to grumble about,' Elsie said. 'But there is one thing we can be thankful for: we can finally get some new clothes. I've had quite enough of making do and mending, thank you very much, or at least having stuff mended by someone like Ida here. I don't know what I'd have done without you, Ida.' She gave a mock salute and addressed her words directly to Ida Barlow who was sitting on the other side of the table.

Ida smiled back for a moment before she gently

pressed her elbow into the ribs of the large lady sitting beside her. 'Bessie's the one you should really thank,' Ida said. 'She's the one who turned "make do and mend" into a business, didn't you, Bessie love? I just went along with it.'

'And a jolly good business it's turned out to be,' Ena said before Bessie could respond. Her tone was halfway between admiration and jealousy.

'We work hard for our money,' Ida said indignantly. 'Even you can't begrudge us a decent reward for our efforts, Mrs Sharples.'

Bessie smiled. 'And for anyone who's interested in topping up their wardrobe, we'll be having some fancy new fabrics in next week and be making things from scratch.'

Elsie jumped to her feet and grinned. 'Shall I be an advertisement for you?' she said indicating the brown and white dress she was wearing and she did a few twirls and took up several different positions to show off the shape and style from all sides.

'I don't think you've met Bessie properly, have you, Wendy?' Elsie said as she sat down again. 'You'll no doubt be meeting her husband, Albert Tatlock, when the men can tear themselves away from their game.' She pointed across to where a group of men were playing darts and paying no heed to anyone else in the room. 'But for now let me introduce you to Mrs Tatlock. They live at number 1.'

'Pleased to meet you, Wendy,' Bessie said. 'I'd already guessed who you was and I was admiring your lovely trim figure when you came in, if you don't mind my remarking. So if you fancy some new clothes, we'll be happy to help.' Bessie's face creased into smiles.

'At least some things are beginning to shift,' Ida said. 'And I understand petrol will be coming off rationing pretty soon.'

Now it was Elsie's turn to smile. 'How does that help me? I haven't got a car and I'm not likely to be getting one. For my money, even when things are changing, it's happening far too slowly. I don't know about anyone else but I reckon we need to put some fun back into our lives right now!' Elsie said and she took a long gulp from her gin and tonic as if to indicate that she was ready to start. 'When did we last do anything you could call fun?' she challenged. 'Like, what's happening about the new Essoldo cinema they keep promising us, or the new dance hall they've talked about building for years? That would be more my idea of fun.'

At that moment there was a shout from the other side of the room where the men who'd been involved in the game had suddenly surrounded the dartboard and were slapping one other on the back with a mix of cheers and jeers and gales of laughter.

Ida sighed. 'Maybe we're doing something wrong,'

she said, 'cos it sounds to me like the men at least are having fun right now.'

Elsie looked across and was suddenly thoughtful. 'You might have a point there, Ida. Maybe that's the answer,' she said.

Ida's brow furrowed into a question.

'Perhaps we should muscle in on what they're doing,' Elsie said, 'and think about starting up a women's darts team.'

Chapter 3

Ida Barlow and her husband Frank left the Rovers together shortly after the end of the darts match and it was fortunate they didn't have far to walk because after Frank's momentary elation at his team's victory he seemed to clam up and they covered the rest of the short distance in frosty silence. Ida could not believe how quickly they came to be at loggerheads these days – and usually about something trivial, as it was tonight.

'You looked to be having a good time,' Frank said as Ida paused for a few moments beyond the swing doors to breathe in the fresh balm of the cooling air. She sensed from the tone of his voice that some kind of argument might be brewing. 'Who was that you were talking to?' Frank said. 'Not someone I recognized.'

'That's cos she's new to Weatherfield,' Ida said. 'Her name's Wendy Collins and she's been appointed to one of them vacant posts at the county primary.'

Frank visibly stiffened. 'And you were cosying up to her, I suppose?' he flashed. 'Getting ahead of yourself again, no doubt?' He shook his head. 'She'll be our Kenneth's private tutor next! And I'll be forking out again for summat that's totally unnecessary.'

'Don't be so daft, Frank! How could she think of tutoring him when she doesn't even know him, or know what he is and isn't capable of? Besides which it was hardly the time or the place in the pub to be having that kind of conversation.' She was disconcerted by his perception but she managed to sound indignant and couldn't resist adding, 'Though I can see nowt wrong with me just talking to the lass.' She paused. 'And now that you've raised the subject, why shouldn't she help Kenneth? Ada Hayes always felt he had great . . . what did she call it? . . . great potential.' Ida could see the veins on Frank's neck had begun to stand out though he didn't say anything as he strode on ahead and opened the front door.

Ida sighed, astonished at how quickly the tension between them had flared up again. She thought back to the time, several years previously, when she had been worried sick about Frank because of his delayed repatriation after the war was over. She had an overexercised imagination and had almost made herself ill, convinced that he had actually been hurt or even killed and that the authorities were avoiding telling her. At that point she would have given anything to have him safely home and so convinced was she that something was wrong that she had felt it necessary to prepare the boys for their father not coming back. That was why she had welcomed the distraction when her neighbour, Bessie Tatlock, had suggested they set up the mending business together. It had not only taken her mind off things but had provided a source of extra cash that she had been very grateful for. And that had enabled her to enjoy a new level of freedom and independence she had never had before. When Frank had finally arrived home, she had, of course, been overjoyed to see him and had given him a hero's welcome, but he hadn't been home long before cracks started to show and it was only now that she realized how much she had changed in recent years. They had both changed, but she was the first to recognize that she needed more from her marriage and that things at number 3 could never return to how they had been before the war.

Unfortunately, Frank seemed to expect things to fall back into the same place they had been when he had left and seemed unable and unwilling to embrace the changes. Ida, on the other hand, having been forced to bring up the boys virtually single-handed for several years, had had the opportunity to develop ideas of her own. The amount of time she had spent learning to cope alone had given her the confidence to express those ideas, and that was something that Frank was now finding difficult to accept. Which was why they had reached the stage now that when Frank found Ida idly chatting to a new teacher he assumed they must be talking about his son's prospects and saw it as a threat to their everyday lives.

Frank stepped into the narrow dark hallway ahead of Ida and the first thing he saw at the end of the passage was Kenneth and his school friend, Lionel Brown, both fully dressed, stretched out on the living room floor leafing through a stack of *The Beano* and *The Dandy* comics, while the embers from the last piece of coal were disintegrating to ash in the grate.

'What are you still doing up and dressed? I thought you were supposed to have got ready for bed before we left, Kenneth?' Kenneth jumped when Frank shouted and Lionel, looking startled, scrambled quickly to his feet. 'Where's our David?'

Frank yelled as he picked up and then discarded the cushions on the small sofa as if convinced his younger son must be hiding underneath.

'I was just leaving, honest, Mr Barlow,' Lionel stammered, and without further engagement he shot out of the back door.

'D-David's g-gone to bed, like you said he should,' Kenneth stammered.

'And what about you?' Frank turned on him. 'Shouldn't you be in bed by now too? How do you think you're going to get up for school when it starts?'

Kenneth stood up. 'We don't have to go in early on the first day. We don't have to go in until the afternoon and then we'll probably only do some reading and play a few games.' He looked down at his feet as he spoke.

'Play games? Did I hear you right? Then maybe it's time you left school, son, and started doing some real work?'

'Don't be so daft, Frank,' Ida mocked as she came into the room behind him. 'Apart from it not being legal for him to leave until he's fifteen, would you be wanting him to shin up chimneys? Or maybe you'd like to send him off down the mines?'

'I'm thinking about the money I let you talk me into shelling out to Ada Hayes for extra tutoring so that he can pass those precious exams that you're always going on about? Why are they suddenly not important?'

'They *are* important but I don't have to study for them right now. They're ages away' Kenneth mumbled.

'I'd have thought if they mean so much to you, you wouldn't want to be wasting any precious time playing games when you could be studying.' Frank's voice leaked sarcasm.

'For goodness' sake, Frank, stop talking rubbish! Can't you leave the lad alone for once?' Ida complained, pushing Kenneth towards the stairs.

'Sure, I'll leave him alone. It doesn't matter to me. As far as I'm concerned, so long as he learns to read and write and do his sums enough to handle his own money when he gets to earning some, he doesn't have to bother his head at all about exams. I've managed all my life without them and so have a hell of a lot of others I know around here.'

'That's not what I'm saying and you know it!' Ida sounded exasperated. 'Why shouldn't he take exams if it means he's got a chance of bettering himself?'

'Bettering himself? Frank mocked. 'You know very well that if it were up to me then he wouldn't be bothering with that blessed eleven-plus at all. For my money he certainly doesn't need to be going to any fancy grammar school.'

'Well, thank goodness it isn't up to you!' Ida was

almost shouting now. 'Cos if it were he'd be a blooming postman all his life and unless he's on the first shift he doesn't need to be going to bed early for that.'

There was a sudden silence as Ida stopped, wondering if she had gone too far.

Frank turned to face her, his face ashen. 'And what's wrong with being a blooming postman all his life as you so nicely put it? It's served me well enough and I never heard you complaining when it brings in a regular pay packet.'

'I'm not saying there's anything wrong with it.' Ida did her best to lower her voice in the hope that it might calm the situation, particularly as she could see that Frank's temper was beginning to roil.

'It's all your fault for filling his head with fancy ideas,' Frank snapped. 'A regular secondary school was good enough for me and it'll be good enough for him. There'll be no need for special exams and he won't have to have any kind of fancy uniform or special books to go there. But whichever way, for now he's still only a lad who needs his sleep and I said that he was to have been ready for bed by the time we got back.'

Kenneth had inched towards the stairs and when his father turned to throw his coat over the bannister, Kenneth raced upstairs not caring that the thud of his thick boots on the thinly carpeted wooden tread was making enough of a din to wake up the dead, let alone David. He hoped his brother had fallen asleep by now, in the double bed they shared.

Chapter 4

Wendy had only been inside Bessie Street County Primary school once before and that had been on the day when she had been called for an interview with the headmaster, Mr Lorian, and Counsellor James, who was the head of the Weatherfield education board. It had been a rushed affair, as the small panel had to fit in several interviews throughout the day for the different posts that were available and there had been little time for her to take in much about her surroundings. She had registered the austere nature of the once-red bricks that comprised the late-Victorian building and she couldn't help but notice that, overall, it was a forbidding looking construction with dozens of tiny windowpanes in the high arched frames that looked too small to be able to absorb much light. Once inside she had been struck by the coldness of the stone floors of the staircases and the extensive corridors, both upstairs and downstairs, that echoed eerily as they'd tramped through the long hallways to the headmaster's office.

Today she knew that she was early but, as she rattled the chain that looped through the heavy padlock, she was surprised to find the gates were still locked. However, through the railings she was glad to see some patches of pale-blue sky textured with white fluffy clouds, for her memory of the interview day was of mist, a dull gloom that had settled over everything, and the dismal, gunmetal-coloured clouds that had hung depressingly low in the grey sky. Her eyes filled when she thought about how far she was from her beloved Blackpool; she had never lived this far away from the sea and she missed the freshness of the air, the sharp tang of ozone and salt that was thrown up by the spray coming off the sea and the screeching of the seagulls as they followed the boats, hoping for food. She had worked hard to convince herself that Weatherfield, on the edges of the great northern metropolis that had once thrived on cotton mills, was the perfect place to escape to, one that offered her some real hope for the future; a place where she could forget about the heartbreak of losing her family and confine Andrew's betrayal to the past so that she could begin to build her new life. And now she was here, ready to start that new life, refusing to even consider that she might be making a mistake.

The job interview that she had attended several weeks previously had been short, considering the distance she had travelled to get there, and had not given her much time to scrutinize her new surroundings. In addition, she had been disappointed to receive a note from Esther Hayes apologizing that she had to take her mother to the hospital on that day and that she wouldn't be available to show Wendy her prospective new digs. When a letter arrived the day after the interview from Mr Lorian offering her the job, Wendy knew she had to make up her mind quickly, and she accepted his offer without even seeing the place that was to be her new home. And now here she was, about to embark on her first staff meeting in readiness for the autumn term that was about to begin.

She walked round the side of the building until she found an external flight of stone steps that led down to a single side door and she tapped timidly on what looked like a cellar window. She was pressing her nose to the glass and trying to peer inside when the door was suddenly wrenched open and she almost fell inside. She was confronted by a bearded, jovial-looking man she recognized as the caretaker. He turned back to quickly grind a glowing cigarette butt into the ashtray on the worktop and scratched his woolly white chin.

'It's Miss . . . Miss Collins, isn't it?' he said with a ready smile. 'I never forget a pretty face. Jed Barnes,' he said as he extended his hand.

'I'm afraid I'm a bit early,' she said 'but . . .'

'But you're here for the staff meeting and what I call the introductions.'

Wendy felt her cheeks redden as she nodded.

'Don't worry, you're not the first to arrive,' he said. 'There's another new 'un like yourself, and another one soon to follow no doubt, so it's obviously high time I opened the front gates, but if you'd like to follow me I'll show you directly to the staffroom. I tell you, the school's not seen this much upheaval since Miss Hayes marched off with them youngsters to the seaside when the war first started. Like the Pied Piper, she was.' He chuckled. 'I bet those kiddies never forgot them sea breezes,' he said with a grin.

'I don't know about them, but I'm certainly missing the sea air already,' Wendy said, 'and I've only been gone a couple of days.'

'Then I reckon you should get organizing a school trip.' Mr Barnes lowered his voice. 'Take all the kiddies there before the winter sets in and the old arthritis starts playing up.'

As he led the way down the main corridor Jed Barnes pointed to the double doors that led into a large assembly hall with a well-polished wooden floor. There were stacks of wooden benches down both sides and a raised stage that filled one entire wall. In her previous school Wendy had been responsible for the end-of-term concerts and plays that the children had always enjoyed and she hoped she might have similar opportunities here. She also noted the sturdy wooden bars that were attached to the walls, and the set of solidly plaited ropes that hung from the ceiling, indicating the room was also used as a gym. But on that front, she was happy to leave anything to do with physical education to the specialists who actually enjoyed doing that sort of thing.

They carried on down the corridor and stopped in front of a door that had a brass plate at head height, marked Staffroom.

'Here y'are Miss,' Jed Barnes said. 'I hope you settle in real quick and once you're into your own classroom, let me know if you need owt.'

'Thanks,' Wendy said. 'That's very kind.' Then she clicked the latch and gingerly pushed open the staffroom door.

The first thing that struck her was the stale smell of cigarette smoke and the telltale yellowing of the once-distempered walls. The fading scent of tobacco was diluted by disinfectant and the odour of dampness that arose from recently washed wooden floors, but the combination was nevertheless pungent and it hit her like a solid but invisible wall.

She was about to step outside again to fill her lungs with fresher air but she realized she had been spotted by a young man on the other side of the room who had been browsing through some exercise books that were piled on a small table and she didn't feel as if she could retreat quite so soon. He looked up as she entered, a guilty look on his face, and he quickly reshaped the books back into a neat stack.

He was still carrying a fawn raincoat and brown trilby hat in one hand as he smiled and strode over to her. 'Hello, I'm Richard Faulkner,' he said, his free arm outstretched. 'I'm new here.'

Wendy was shocked for a moment that her first instinct was to step back. He was much better looking than she had imagined and it took a few moments for her to catch her breath and steady her voice. Ever since her acrimonious break-up with Andrew she had tried to avoid any kind of physical contact with young men, particularly handsome ones like Richard Faulkner, but she could hardly ignore him when there were only the two of them in the room. She shook his hand, albeit diffidently.

'Wendy Collins,' she said, 'and I'm new too.' She

realized she was trembling and withdrew her hand as quickly as she could.

'Are you new to teaching, or only to the school?' Richard said pointing to the large blackboard that had been fitted to the wall at the far end of the room. It had been scrubbed clean of all its previously chalked messages and bore only the words, *To all BSCP staff, old and new, Welcome!*

'Very definitely new to the school,' Wendy said. 'But I've actually been teaching for several years now,' she added. She felt the heat prickle in her cheeks.

'And I presume you're here for the staff meeting?' Richard asked.

Wendy nodded.

'I've just moved into a room in Rosamund Street,' Richard said, 'and it didn't take me as long as I'd thought it might to walk here this morning. 'Do you live locally as well?'

'I'm renting a room in Coronation Street,' Wendy replied after a slight hesitation. 'With a family I sort of know.'

'I haven't fully got my bearings yet but I do believe that makes us neighbours then,' Richard said. 'Though I don't know anybody in Weatherfield, so you'll have to introduce me to some of the locals.'

Wendy looked at him sharply; he seemed to be grinning, but she looked away and didn't answer.

Since Andrew's departure she had avoided making what she considered to be any unnecessary disclosures of personal details to young men. But now she was overcome by a wave of self-consciousness and was unable to think of anything else to say. She needn't have worried because Richard was certainly not at a loss for words and he filled in the silence by asking pleasantly where she had come from and how long she had been in Weatherfield. At first it was all she could do to answer civilly, but she kept reminding herself that not all men were like Andrew and she began to relax a little.

A variety of upright wooden chairs had been strategically placed around the two large tables that stretched across the middle of the room and Richard threw his raincoat and hat onto one of the chairs to stake his claim to a seat. Wendy carefully peeled off her own jacket and threw it over the back of a chair several seats away.

'I must admit, I didn't think there would be that many staff,' Richard said indicating the chairs. 'The school is obviously bigger than I thought.'

'Same here,' Wendy said. 'I was astonished when I saw how many rows of pegs there were in the children's cloakrooms.'

'And that's only for the infants. I believe there are almost the same number again for the juniors upstairs,' Richard said. 'They're the age group I teach

– at least, the younger juniors who've just come up from the infants. How about you?'

'I usually teach the older juniors,' Wendy said.

'Are they your favourite age group?'

'Usually, but I'm not actually sure yet what group I'll be teaching here. Mr Lorian asked me at interview if I would be prepared to be flexible if I was offered the job.'

'And naturally you felt you had to say yes,' Richard filled in the answer with a laugh.

'Of course I did,' Wendy agreed, relaxing even more. 'I was hardly in a position to refuse.'

'No, of course not. I would have said the same thing in your shoes,' he said.

'I believe there's another new teacher starting today as well, who is actually new to teaching, so maybe he wanted to have some flexibility.'

'I only hope he appreciates what you're doing,' Richard said. 'Where I come from it's the most junior members of staff who are usually expected to make the sacrifices, not the other way round.'

'Yes, it was pretty much the same in my old school,' Wendy said, 'but I remember only too well what it's like being a new recruit.'

'That's very accommodating of you,' Richard said. 'Are you one of these who volunteer at exam time to run extra sessions for the kids after school?' he asked, and although he said it in a semi-jocular fashion, Wendy tried not to care when she felt the embarrassing blush rise from her neck that she knew wouldn't stop till it reached her cheeks.

'Yes, as a matter of fact I do like to help the kids where I can, particularly around exam time. Is there anything wrong with that?

'Nothing wrong at all,' Richard said. 'I admire your dedication.'

'Some of the children go into a blind panic and risk failing even though I know they've got the ability. So I will try to help if I think I can do some good.' She tried to speak casually, though she couldn't deny that she felt irritated that she should be made to feel so defensive. 'I find not all kids get the start in life they deserve,' she felt she had to add, 'and if I can give them a leg up then I don't see anything wrong in that.' She spoke as firmly as she could, wondering why she felt that she had to justify her actions and she hoped that she didn't sound too stuffy or self-righteous.

'I'm afraid my only contribution to out-of-hours activities is to supervise the odd game of football after school,' he said. 'And I might be persuaded to referee the odd match on a Saturday morning – so long as it's not raining!'

'Well, *I* hate anything that smacks of athleticism, so that probably makes us even,' Wendy said and this time she couldn't resist a smile. ' To her relief Richard laughed.

'Have you had the tour? Seen inside any of the classrooms yet?' Richard asked.

Wendy shook her head. 'I never got a chance on my interview day and the only thing I've seen so far today is the hall which looks like it's used for gym as well. How about you? Have you seen anything as you were here even earlier than me?'

'I managed to glance into a few rooms on my way down the corridor but that's all.'

'And?' Wendy raised her brows.

'And . . .' Richard made a wry face. 'I don't want to put you off, but I'm afraid the ones I've seen so far hardly look big enough to squash in the thirty plus kids I believe they have in most classes. It'll be interesting to see how they actually manage it without piling the desks one on top of the other.'

Wendy giggled. 'It seems to me that it's pretty much the same wherever you go nowadays. In my experience, it's always a tight squeeze,' she said and she made a hopeless gesture with her hands. 'But they're going to build an extension on the site very shortly, I believe. They've got a lot of land at the back and they should be starting building soon. Mr Lorian told me about it at interview,' Wendy said, 'and it certainly helped persuade me this would be a good place to come to.'

'Ah yes!' Richard said. 'Yes, the sound of that attracted me too.' He paused. 'Unfortunately,' he said slowly, 'I've since found out that this wonderful new extension is a bit of a myth. Apparently they've been promising to build it for several years now, since soon after the end of the war.'

Wendy raised her brows questioningly. 'But it all seemed so definite! It sounded as though they were only waiting for the ink to dry on the contract when Mr Lorian told me about the development plans.'

'I'm sure that's what he believed at the time.' Richard shrugged. 'And yet, sadly, it seems, everyone's still waiting.'

Wendy felt her spirits deflate as if she had been pricked by a pin. She hadn't realized how much she was looking forward to the promise that she would soon be working in a bright, new modern classroom. She opened her mouth to speak but then closed it again as Richard said, 'Unfortunately we are still living in fairly austere times and we have to be realistic. At least the council has managed to patch up most of the bomb damage in the neighbourhood but maybe it's expecting too much to hope for a new school as well.'

Wendy sighed. 'You could be right but that doesn't make it any less disappointing.'

'What made you want to come to a place like this in any case?' Richard said. 'It can't only have been the promise of a new building.'

That made Wendy smile. 'No, that was hardly the main reason,' she began. 'I was living in Blackpool—'

She stopped, suddenly realizing that she was not yet ready to talk to a comparative stranger about Andrew. 'I-I needed a change,' she added lamely, and she went on to explain about Ada and Esther's invitation instead.

Wendy was disconcerted when Richard laughed until he said, 'Did you never question why she wanted to get as far away as Australia?'

'You don't think—' she said, but Richard interrupted.

'I'm sorry, that was unkind,' he said. 'I was only teasing.'

'But it didn't stop *you* coming here. If you knew all this why did you still want to come?' Wendy challenged him.

'Unfortunately I found out too late about the council's turnaround and I'd already accepted the position. Besides, I was desperate to get away from the big smoke – too many memories – and while I know Weatherfield is full of outside privies and back-to-backs on cobbled terraces with only an alleyway between them, it's only a stone's throw from the moors and all that wonderful wild countryside.'

'You make it sound like a very depressing place when you describe it like that,' Wendy said.

'Apologies, but I don't always find it easy to be optimistic, these days,' Richard said.

'I like to think that every new term starts off full of hopes and dreams,' Wendy said. 'And we've then got the rest of the year to find out how far off the mark we were.' Her words were partly serious but she did her best to keep her voice light.

'I'm sorry, I didn't mean to put you off before we've even begun,' Richard laughed. 'I'm not usually a killjoy but I suppose I'm trying to be realistic and the school itself does have a decent reputation locally.'

'I suppose there are worse places than Weatherfield,' Wendy said as cheerfully as she could.

'I thought it would provide a solid stepping stone for moving up the ladder, if you can bear with me mixing metaphors.' He grinned and Wendy couldn't help smiling back. She hadn't heard anyone use that kind of talk since she had graduated from teachers' training college several years previously and now it sounded so pedantic it made her want to laugh.

'I suppose you've got your eye on a deputy headship already then?' she said.

'Am I that shallow?' Richard said. 'Though I suppose you've got to have your eye on the brass plate on the door and be ready to move quickly if you want to get anywhere fast in this profession,' he admitted.

'You mean move more quickly than usual? Why is that?' Wendy asked without thinking, then put her hand to her mouth. 'Sorry,' she said, 'I didn't mean to be nosey.'

'There's no real mystery. The fact is, I was a late starter,' Richard said, 'so I've got a lot of climbing to do in a short space of time.'

'Was that because of the war?' Wendy asked.

Richard nodded. 'I was called up right at the start and I was in the army for the duration. I was fighting on the European front at first then I was shipped off to Africa. I didn't get started on my teacher's training until after the war was over, when I got a grant because they were desperate to train new teachers quickly. I had to work for the local council afterwards in a sort of payback deal, and now I'm free to go wherever I want. But I can't afford to hang around if I want to get on.'

'You make it sound as if you're preparing to move off already!' Wendy said.

Richard rubbed his hands together. 'Well, I'm certainly ready to get cracking,' he said with a chuckle. 'and I'm really looking forward to meeting the kids.'

'They're what make this job worthwhile,' Wendy said. She glanced up at the large clock on the wall above the chalkboard and saw that Richard was smiling directly at her, his gaze so intense that she had to look away.

'That, and living on the doorstep of the moors,' he added with a grin. 'You came from Blackpool, you said?'

'Originally, yes, though not this morning.' Wendy gave a little laugh.

'Am I right in thinking that Blackpool's on the west coast?' Richard asked. 'Apologies for my ignorance, but I'm not too hot on northern geography, I'm afraid.'

Wendy's eyebrows shot up in surprise. 'It is indeed a west coast seaside town. Next stop America,' she joked. 'And I'm already missing the sea. Which bit of the country are you from originally? I know you've been living in London and you don't sound as though you come from anywhere near here.'

'Ten out of ten for that,' Richard said. 'I come from Hertfordshire, though I was living in London, but like you I wanted a change.' Richard was looking off into the distance and his eyes seemed to mist over. 'I'm looking forward to being able to get out onto the moors at the weekends for some good long walks and fresh country air,' he said after a few moments. 'Are you a walker?'

'I like to get out in the fresh air as much as possible, but I'm not sure I'd call myself a walker . . .' Wendy said cautiously.

'Prefer the nightlife, do you?' Richard said with a laugh.

Wendy felt her face suddenly suffuse with embarrassment. 'I'd hardly say that,' she said indignantly.

'Sorry! You'll have to learn not to take me too literally. I'm sure you've hardly had time to get to know much about the neighbourhood yet.'

'All I can say is that at the one pub I've been to in Coronation Street, the Rovers Return, the people were very nice and friendly,' Wendy said.

Richard spluttered with laughter. 'That's very diplomatic,' he said. 'I can see I'll have to sample it with you some time to make my own mind up. And maybe I'll be able to persuade you to come walking on the moors with me. Then we can fill in the missing bits about ourselves.'

Wendy looked at him quizzically. Richard smiled and lowered his voice as he said, 'If there's one thing the war has taught me, it's that every one of us has a story to tell . . .'

Wendy felt a sudden panic rise in her chest and she didn't know what to say but, to her relief, at that moment the door opened and she recognized Mr Lorian the headmaster as he entered the room carrying a handful of folders tucked under one arm. A white-haired, paunchy man trotted after him, a cigarette cupped in his right hand, and the rest of the teaching staff filed in behind him to claim a place at the table. Several nodded and smiled at Wendy and she politely responded. Then Mr Lorian greeted everyone in clipped, business-like tones. He particularly welcomed the new staff,

Wendy, Richard and newly qualified Denise Unwin who'd come hurrying in just before the meeting started, and invited everyone to sit down so that the business of the day could begin.

Chapter 5

The morning passed quickly enough although Wendy realized when she looked up at the clock that the proceedings had actually gone on for longer than she had expected. She was pleased to discover that she had been assigned the class she had hoped for, the older juniors. Mr Lorian made no reference to the cancellation of the new building when he allocated each teacher to their classroom and, with no further discussion, dismissed the group, wishing everyone good luck for a successful academic year.

The deputy head, Philip Jackson, who never seemed to be without a cigarette in his hand, offered to take the new staff on a guided tour of the school and to show them to their classrooms and he wasted no time in leading the way up and down the steep steps and through the long stone corridors of the two-storey building. When they came to the classrooms he consulted his clipboard.

'I believe this one is yours, Miss Collins,' he said.

Wendy peered into a room that was tightly packed with desks lined up neatly in rows with barely enough space for an adult to squeeze between them. All the desks had inkwells, although there was also a pile of small slates and some thin sticks of charcoal at the front. A blackboard filled one whole wall of the room and in one corner a tall desk that was more like a lectern stood on a raised dais. The room looked no different from any other classroom Wendy had ever worked in.

The afternoon session was short – there was barely time for Wendy to take the register and to distribute some books and exercises to be completed by the next day before the bell was rung and the children and staff were preparing to go home.

Wendy was feeling strangely exhausted, despite the shortness of the day, and when she reached the staffroom she was pleased to see that she was not the only one who was looking tired. All she wanted to do was to go home and put her feet up and, if she had sufficient energy, add some further touches to the week's lesson plans she'd already begun preparing.

'I hope there's no hard feelings that I was given the older age group in the end?' Wendy turned to Denise Unwin with a smile as the younger woman was about to depart. 'I understand the two of us were actually in competition for that particular class,' she said, and she extended her hand in a peace offering.

'Were we? I didn't realize.' Denise half-heartedly put out her own limp hand in return. 'But I really didn't expect to get my first choice. After all, you've got *years* of seniority.'

Wendy smarted at the way Denise emphasized the word *years* but she had no time to brood on it for the younger woman quickly said, 'Sorry, but I can't stand here gossiping, I've got a bus to catch. I'll see you tomorrow,' and without so much as a wave she grabbed her jacket from the back of one of the chairs and ran out.

Astonished by her abrupt departure, Wendy wondered if Richard Faulkner, who'd been standing nearby, might have something to say, but he was busy shrugging his arms into his raincoat, trying to shake out the creases that made it look like he'd been sitting on it all day and he didn't seem to have noticed the exchange.

'It's been a long day, considering we've hardly seen the children,' he said eventually as he buttoned up his coat, still trying to smooth out some of the deeper wrinkles. 'I dread to think what we're going to feel like tomorrow when we'll have had a whole day of them running us ragged!' He snapped the brim of his hat with a practised hand as he put on his trilby without the aid of a mirror. 'I suppose I'd best be off then,' he said. He gave Wendy a long, lingering look and then his whole face suddenly creased into a smile. 'Unless you'd like me to see you home?' he said. 'I believe we're heading in much the same direction.'

His eyes seemed to be beckoning her and Wendy knew she should be flattered, but she looked away immediately. Not only did she feel the heat of an annoying blush rising from her neck to her face, and upwards into her forehead and scalp, but she found her breath was coming in short gasps and for a moment she was unable to speak.

She made no attempt to engage, even though she was aware that he was trying to make eye contact, for she had already begun to feel the prickle of tears behind her eyes and she didn't want to risk them spilling down her cheeks. She felt cross with herself that, after all the years she had spent teaching, she had never worked out how best to deal with the kind of light flirtatiousness she had come to expect from her male colleagues. It was harmless enough, as was the banter that went with it, she knew that, but since her painful parting from Andrew she had found it best to avoid being in the sole company of any attractive young man because in that way she could sidestep even the gentlest of advances. Some form of flirting seemed to be second nature to young men like Richard – and if his line of questioning was anything to go by, there was the danger that any further conversation between them might automatically lead to topics she was not prepared to discuss.

Images of Andrew kept flashing through her mind as she tried to control her breathing but the subject was still far too raw and painful to think about, even though it had been more than a year since the man she had thought of as her fiancé, the man she thought she was going to marry, had crashed out of her flat and disappeared out of her life.

Wendy felt the familiar lump rise in her throat as the memory of his betrayal stabbed at her heart once more and she tried to swallow down the hurt that remained. Would she ever be able to talk about what Andrew had done and acknowledge out loud what she had for so long failed to recognize? Richard seemed nice enough on the surface, but would she ever be able to trust a man again?

Wendy grasped hold of the chair that was closest to her and Richard looked immediately concerned. 'Are you all right?' he asked, leaning towards her as if about to take her arm.

Wendy stepped back and closed her eyes for a brief moment, then she took a deep breath. 'Yes, I'm fine, thanks,' she said, 'and th-thank you, that's a very kind offer,' Wendy wavered as she tried to meet his gaze, for the truth was she wasn't sure she remembered the way home. Then she said, as firmly as she could, 'But I'm not actually going straight home tonight. I promised Esther that I would call in at the corner shop and pick up something we can have for our tea.' This all came out in a rush and Richard took a step back looking surprised.

'Esther's older sister Ada used to work here, and Esther's technically my landlady now.' She felt she had better explain when he looked puzzled. 'She works at the council offices and her mother's an invalid, so she doesn't get much time to shop.'

'That's fine, you don't have to apologize,' Richard said. 'Perhaps some other time?' He touched the brim of his hat.

'Of course,' Wendy said, 'that would be nice,' and before she could change her mind she set off at a brisk pace in what she hoped was the right direction.

Richard watched her go and made no attempt to follow her. He was disappointed that she seemed to be so wary of him, though he refused to blame himself entirely. Something must have happened in Blackpool that had made her so guarded, he thought, and he wondered what he could do or say to make her trust him. The only positive note in his favour was that he would be seeing her again soon when he could try again. In fact, he thought, I shall be meeting up with her tomorrow, and the next day, and the one after that, and that made him smile.

He had been attracted to her from the moment he first saw her and even in their very brief acquaintance he acknowledged that there was something about Wendy Collins that he found very appealing. He couldn't put his finger on exactly what it was, but he hoped he might be able to find out in the ensuing weeks. It wasn't just her looks, though she was certainly pretty with her blonde curls and winningly alert blue eyes; no, there was something about the way she blushed from her neck right up to the roots of her hair that he found attractive and which seemed to highlight her vulnerability. He was sure that she was equally attracted to him though he doubted she was aware of it yet, but he felt he could read something into the way that she looked at him, listened to him intently, and seemed genuinely interested in what he had to say. *I'll most likely learn a lot more about her when I see how the children respond to her*, he thought, for he always maintained that children were good judges of character, and not as easily fooled by poseurs as many adults were.

Richard set off walking in the direction of Rosamund Street, thinking about how much his life had changed in the last few years, and how much he had grown. *Maybe it's time for me to take the next logical step, to take a chance on life and consider making even bigger changes*, he thought as he kicked idly at some stones on the pavement. *After all, if anyone had told me that after the war was over I'd be teaching at a primary school in a place like Weatherfield I wouldn't have believed them.*

He had been embroiled in the war from the beginning, having been shipped off first to the Mediterranean and then to Africa almost as soon as the fighting had begun there. All he'd been able to think about then was staying alive and worrying about how soon he could get home to marry his fiancée, refusing to marry while the threat of hostilities continued to hang over their heads. But it was not to be. Richard stopped walking as a picture of Susanne popped into his head and he wiped the back of his hand across his forehead which had suddenly grown hot.

He stood perfectly still, wondering if he had actually groaned out loud and he slammed his fist into the palm of his other hand, thinking about how things had eventually turned out.

Everyone has a story, Richard thought. Wasn't that what he had told Wendy? It had been easy to say but he wondered if he would ever be able to tell her his.

Might Wendy be capable of reintroducing that old spark into his life? He scratched his chin which was beginning to show signs of late-afternoon stubble, glad that there was no one else in the street to witness his broad smile.

Chapter 6

Wendy settled in to the school routine faster than she could have imagined and she was soon convinced that she had never before taught such a deserving group of children. They made her want to go that extra mile although sometimes she was disappointed when her hard work didn't always trigger the response from them that she hoped for. 'Rough and tough', were the words used by Mr Jackson the deputy headmaster to describe them, but she preferred words like 'vulnerable' and 'at risk'.

Having all been born during the war, most of the children in her class had had a difficult start in life and so, to Wendy's way of thinking, warranted more empathy than the disciplinary approach the school seemed to favour. Despite their tender years many of the children had already had to contend with more grief and bereavement than many adults, and in some cases had suffered the destruction of their homes. What did surprise her, however, was to find how irrepressible their spirits were and their incorrigibility helped her to put her own misfortunes in perspective. Unfortunately, their survival instinct did not always go hand in hand with an interest in education. Even some of the brighter children had lost their competitive edge as they worked their way up the school and Wendy had to acknowledge how difficult it was to keep them keen and well-motivated.

'I imagine you had a different class of children in Blackpool, if you'll pardon the pun?' Mr Jackson challenged her, one dinnertime in the staffroom when she ventured an opinion about her charges. 'Well, let me tell you, these kids are survivors.'

Wendy couldn't disagree and, as several other staff members also nodded their agreement, Wendy wondered what Richard made of the children's fortitude, for she suspected he came from a very different background from these working-class children. But she didn't get a chance to ask him for whenever she tried to float a specific question in his direction, Denise Unwin intervened and spoke over her in a way that was becoming increasingly irritating as she had begun to feel that she would have liked the opportunity to talk to him again. Elsie was always telling her that she should learn to be more open and she now regretted having turned down his offer to walk her home and had even contemplated that maybe he was someone she could learn to trust.

Esther was usually exhausted by the end of the working day and it was all she could do to make tea for them and tidy the living room before putting her feet up. She tried her best not to lose patience with her mother for she did still love her, but it wasn't always easy to be generous and understanding with someone who thought of little else but herself. At the same time, she tried to suppress her resentment towards Ada, who despite predictions that she would end up living with her mother as a wizened old maid, had somehow managed to find a way to escape the sisters' dire situation. Unfortunately, that prediction had now been passed on to Esther.

Everyone had been astonished when Matt Harvey had come along and no one had blamed Ada for grabbing the opportunity for marriage with both hands and skipping the country the first chance she got. But what chance did Esther have of doing something similar? Apart from going to work – which she had no choice about if they were to keep their heads above water – Esther could rarely get out of the house in the evenings. She had to admit things had improved a little since Wendy's arrival as she could now get out on the odd occasion, even if it was only to go to the Rovers. But it was when she contemplated her long-term situation that Esther became upset, almost depressed, about the future and she couldn't help feeling some resentment when she considered what little hope she had of ever having a life herself. So far she had contented herself with doing nothing more than putting her feet up and reading a book most evenings, but she could hardly be expected to do that forever.

Wendy was content to stay home with Esther most evenings and they would listen to the radio together as they ate their tea and cleared away the dishes. Afterwards, Wendy would carry on knitting the hot water bottle cover or the bed jacket that she had promised Alice, or Esther would get out Tom's old pack of playing cards and they would play Gin Rummy or Whist. The two of them were getting along well together, better than Wendy might have hoped, considering the ten-year difference in their ages, but while Esther might be younger, she was mature in her ways. She was well-educated and held down a responsible job so that they always seemed to have something to talk about. Wendy would listen to tales about Esther's work on the libraries board and some of the more interesting characters she met at the town hall, and

Wendy would regale Esther with stories about the children's escapades.

They could pass whole evenings fairly pleasurably in this way, but whenever there was a knock at the door Wendy couldn't help noticing how Esther's face would light up and she would hurry to answer it, welcoming any new visitor who might want to come in and keep them company.

Wendy admired the younger girl's selfless devotion to her mother since Ada's departure and knew she would really enjoy it if they could go out together.

'It's bad enough that I have to leave her during the day to go to work,' Esther said when Wendy had suggested it. 'Though she does have everything to hand that she might need, and I know she can always knock on the wall for Bessie Tatlock to come in an emergency, but somehow I feel it's worse leaving her alone at night. Being stuck in bed is a pretty miserable place to be, even if it is, as I strongly suspect, mostly of her own doing. And it's not as though there's anywhere special that I'm dying to go.'

Wendy didn't push it. She knew she would have said the same thing in Esther's position, only she had never been given that chance.

'Do you know,' Esther said suddenly, 'sometimes I can't believe that the war's been over for four years now and that . . . Well, I suppose all those who are coming back are back.' Her voice suddenly cracked and she paused for a moment as a sob caught at the back of her throat. Wendy was shocked as she saw a tear trickle down her friend's cheek and didn't respond immediately. She had heard rumours about Esther having been engaged to a young man when the war began, but why had that suddenly come up now? She waited for Esther to say something more.

'I don't know if Ada ever told you anything about my Jack?' Esther went on. 'Sadly, he was one of those who didn't come back.' Then she lowered her voice and almost whispered, 'It would have been his birthday today.'

Wendy didn't say anything as Esther haltingly explained, her tears flowing freely as she talked. 'He was a pilot in the RAF,' Esther said, 'but his plane was shot down.'

'Was there no hope that . . . ?' Wendy asked, though she immediately wished she had kept quiet.

'There was no hope about anything,' Esther said, 'not according to the standard form letter I received, and his squadron leader had added a personal note at the bottom to make sure that I wasn't harbouring any false hopes. Apparently, there was sufficient evidence to prove that Jack would never come home.'

Esther had been pacing restlessly as she told Wendy this, but now she sat on the sofa to compose herself and she gradually became still. Wendy reached out and briefly put her hand on Esther's arm, wondering what she could say but, it was Esther who spoke softly, saying, 'It was a long time ago. There's nothing left to say,' as if she had read Wendy's mind.

Wendy withdrew her arm and nodded her understanding. She sat back in her chair without comment.

'You wouldn't think the war had been over that long,' Esther eventually broke the silence. 'The world still doesn't feel anything like "normal" yet, at least not to me, nothing like it felt before the war.'

'I don't see how it can feel normal while we've still got food shortages and so many bombsites that haven't been cleared,' Wendy said

'And too many people who will never be coming back,' Esther added.

Wendy sat silently for some time after that, thinking about the fickleness of fate.

Wendy found she had precious little time to spend in the staffroom though she welcomed whatever contact she did have and often made a point of engaging the other teachers in a discussion. She felt it gave her invaluable insights into the Bessie Street children who were, as Mr Jackson had once pointed out, 'quite different' from the children who were lucky enough to live on the coast.

'I was concerned after our last discussion that you might have been put off by our children not always responding as you'd liked or even expected.' It was Mrs Newlands, one of the longer-serving teachers in the school who had taken the trouble to talk to Wendy directly and there was a look of genuine concern on her well-lined face.

Wendy recalled their previous conversation and wasn't sure how best to respond.

'You're in an unfortunate position in one respect, teaching the older children,' Mrs Newlands was saying, 'because some of those who were good pupils in their early years often seem to lose interest by the time they're in the older classes.'

'Of course there are always going to be some jokers in the class who, from day one, have never been able to take school seriously.' Mr Jackson joined in the conversation with a wry smile. 'I don't think you need to feel too badly if they're not always full of enthusiasm, Miss Collins, if that's what you were saying, because, predictably, they are usually the kids from the poorest homes.'

'The trouble is that often they're too hungry to care and too tired to be able to stay awake.' Richard hung up his coat and came over to join them.

'I must agree,' Mrs Newlands said. 'Reading, writing, basic arithmetic, a bottle of milk and a free school dinner is what they're all about, and they don't reckon on needing much else. They've absolutely no incentive to learn anything other than mischief-making,' she finished and rolled her eyes.

'Whichever way it is, however, I can assure you that it's nothing personal,' Mr Jackson said. 'I used to think it must be my boring teaching,' he added, and as a titter of laughter rippled through the group, Wendy noticed Richard did not join in.

'I meant it seriously,' Richard insisted and he sounded slightly irritated. 'Some of those kids are deprived in more ways than one. They probably don't get enough food or sleep on a regular basis and they come to school looking red-eyed and exhausted before they even start the day.'

'Oh gosh, isn't that true?' Wendy said immediately. 'I'm thinking of the Rushworth twins in my class.' There was a murmur of general consensus.

'Indeed, my dear, I think we can all agree with that,' Mrs Newlands said. 'I think at some point we've all been disturbed by having one or other of the Rushworths in our class. They are well-known in these parts as there's at least one member of the family in every year group in the school right now. It sounds like a really desperate home situation.'

'That's my point, it's the kids that suffer,' Richard said.

Wendy was shocked to hear a change in the timbre of his voice and she looked up, astonished to see that his eyes were glistening. She was aware that the others had turned to look at him too and he quickly turned away. No one spoke for a second or two then Wendy said, 'You can't help feeling sorry for them. I wish I was able to do something to help them somehow.'

'I think the best thing we can do for some of these children is to make sure that they at least get the nourishment they need to keep them awake during school hours,' Richard said.

'But not all the children in my class are as desperate as that,' Wendy said, 'and yet there's quite a number who have no real interest in the work we're doing in class, no matter how hard I try to make it more exciting. And they certainly won't ever be able to see the relevance of sitting the eleven-plus exam in their final year.'

'That's a shame, but by the time they come into your class,' Mrs Newlands said, 'even those who were keen on taking the exam at first have often been talked out of it by their parents who either can't afford the uniform or don't want to see their children rise above them, and so the children manage to convince themselves that they never really wanted to go to grammar school anyway. It's hardly a surprise when they don't do half as well as we'd hoped.'

'The trouble is that we, as teachers, think it's our fault, but it isn't,' Mr Jackson said. He took a final deep draw on the cigarette butt that was burning down between his fingers and then ground it out in the ashtray on the table. 'And it's not really their fault either. Because by then it will have been hammered into them that they must take the fastest route through secondary school so that they can get out there and earn money as soon as possible.'

Mrs Newlands nodded. 'Sadly, it's true,' she agreed. 'A lot of boys are earning a few bob even as young as eleven years old. And as far as the girls are concerned, they see no further than having babies and getting married, usually in that order, as soon as they're done with school. Unfortunately, at that age the kids are too young to understand what it will mean to leave school without a basic education.'

Wendy sighed at the grim picture that was being painted. 'I know that so many of these children have a difficult home-life, and I do try to be realistic in my expectations, but it still seems sad.'

'You won't be able win them all, no matter how hard you try,' Richard said, and Wendy was surprised when he turned to her and smiled, aware that for once Denise was not about to interfere. 'I've got a small gang of boys in my class who love to muck about,' Richard went on, 'and they do their best to distract the rest of the class.'

'Ah! The disruptors, I call them,' Mr Jackson said. 'Determined to spoil things for everyone else and always trying their best to justify their behaviour.'

Wendy nodded in agreement; she had already had to face those kinds of challenges. 'I'm glad to hear it's not just me,' she said with relief and she made an exaggerated movement of swiping her brow. 'Certainly, in my class they ask a load of unnecessary questions in an effort to distract me, and they give me a lot of lip when I ignore them. But I do know from past experience that it's not just the older year groups; it wasn't necessarily any different with the younger ones.'

Wendy was aware that Denise now seemed ready to join in, though from the look on her face she was far more likely to contradict and start an argument, than to agree.

'Perhaps you're lacking natural authority, unlike some of us.' Denise said pointedly with a sniff in Wendy's direction.

'I suppose kids will be kids at the end of the day,' Richard said, ignoring her, 'and there's only so far you can push them.'

'And there's only so far they should be able to push you,' Mr Jackson said, lighting another cigarette as he riffled through his folders, and everyone laughed.

When Wendy got home that evening Esther was sitting at the table with an unopened envelope in front of her. 'I told you I never liked getting letters, didn't I? Well, here's another one I'd rather not have received,' Esther said, a resigned look on her face.

Wendy was puzzled and glanced across at her friend. 'But it's addressed to your mother, not to you,' she said.

'Do you think that makes it any better?' Esther's tone was sarcastic.

'I presume you know who it's from, then?'

'Of course I do.' Esther sighed. 'My beloved brother.'

Wendy gasped. 'He's not coming home soon, is he? I thought you said . . .'

'Not as far as I know.' Esther began turning the envelope over in her hands as if looking for clues. 'He must want to soften Mum up for something when he does get out. That's all he ever wants out of any of us – money.'

'I presume you're going to show her the letter?' Wendy said tentatively.

Esther shrugged. 'I can hardly keep it from her. He'd soon be on to me if she doesn't reply fast enough.'

Wendy hesitated before she asked cautiously, 'Would you like me to take it up to her?' She was surprised when Esther's eyes lit up.

'Would you? That would be great. Then at least I don't have to see her face when she reads it. There are some days when I can't bring myself to mention his name.' Esther gave a half-smile. 'Mum likes you, you know.'

Wendy raised her eyebrows. 'You can hardly say that, she's only known me a few weeks.'

'That doesn't matter, she's a great reader of character, is my mam. She can be quick to form judgements and she doesn't often change her mind. But she's not often wrong, except when it comes to Tom, then she's totally blind. Fortunately for us both, she took a shine to you soon as she met you.'

'I'm flattered,' Wendy said.

'I didn't want to tell you but she wasn't happy at first when I told her I'd given Ada's bed away, but then she was quick to let me know that she thought you were all right.'

Esther blushed and that made Wendy smile. 'Nice to know,' she said, and she stared down at the spidery handwriting. 'If she's awake I could take it up now, then we can relax and enjoy our tea afterwards.'

'She was ten minutes ago when I took her a drink,' Esther said.

'Coward!' Wendy said with a broad grin as Esther tossed her the letter.

Wendy made sure the thud of her shoes on the wooden stairs warned Alice that someone was on their way up and when she knocked on the bedroom door there was no hesitation in Alice's reply.

'I'm not asleep love,' Alice called out, though her voice sounded sleepy. 'I've been waiting . . . Oh!' She stopped in surprise, as though not sure how to react.

'It's not Esther, Mrs Hayes, it's me, Wendy. I do hope you don't mind,' Wendy said.

'No, not at all love.' Alice lolled back against the cushions and touched her hand to her forehead as Wendy stepped inside the stuffy room. 'It's nice to see a pretty face. Esther can be a right gringe sometimes, which doesn't help as she's plain enough to start with.'

Wendy ignored the barb. 'She's getting the tea, but a letter's come for you so I said I'd pop up with it.'

'A letter? Let me see.' Alice suddenly scrambled to sit upright and practically snatched the envelope out of Wendy's hand. She stared down at the address and held it close to her chest for a moment. 'I suppose Esther's told you who it's from?'

Wendy nodded.

'Who knows, maybe he'll be coming home soon if he's been behaving himself.' Alice waved the letter like a banner. 'He was always such a good boy; I never did understand how he managed to get into so much trouble.'

Wendy didn't say anything, remembering how both Ada and Esther had always seen their brother in a different light, and she knew he was unlikely to come to Coronation Street even if he was freed from jail.

'It wasn't his fault,' Alice said. 'He was just unfortunate enough to have got mixed up with the wrong crowd and they put him up to it. They were more like a gang, really. They did some shocking things and he just went along with them. I was only thankful his dad wasn't around to see what happened to him. It would have broken his heart.' Alice sighed heavily then she picked up the letter and inspected it from all angles as if she could read it through the envelope. 'Anyone could have told him they were just hooligans and he should avoid them like the plague. I tried and Ada tried, but he was having none of it. He knew better. I'm sure you must know how it is, you're a teacher, aren't you?'

Wendy nodded.

'So you'll understand how easy it is for a young, impressionable lad to go off the rails.' There was a pleading tone in her voice, but Wendy thought it best not to respond.

'He went to Bessie Street, you know,' Alice said, her face suddenly lifting. 'How are you finding it there?'

'Fine. It's a good school,' Wendy was surprised by the question. 'Though to tell the truth I doubt its changed much since he was there,' she said and she gave a little a laugh.

'Still no new classrooms?' Alice said. 'Wait till I write and tell our Ada.' She let the letter fall onto the bed cover as if it had suddenly become too heavy to hold, a sad, wistful look crossing her face. She sniffed and, pulling a small cotton handkerchief out from under the stack of pillows behind her, dabbed affectedly at the end of her nose. Then, with an abrupt movement, she slipped the long nail on her pinkie finger under the sealed corner of the envelope and slit open the flap along the top.

'I'll leave you in peace then and go and see if Esther wants any help.'

Wendy was surprised by Alice's swift reaction. 'No! Don't leave me on my own,' she cried out. 'That's what Esther does, when she wants to be cruel. She teases me with something then disappears before I can even say anything, but I can see you're not like that. You will pop in again to see me, won't you?' Alice's voice dropped to a whisper. 'Esther hates it when he writes to me, you know. I don't even bother to show her what he's written because she's always got something nasty to say. I think she's jealous and the truth is that she doesn't like me giving him money. But how can I not help him out when he's in trouble? My own son!'

She began waving the envelope about once more and pointing it in the direction of Wendy's face. 'I've told her before, it's easy for her to bad-mouth her brother as a scrounger when she's got a roof over her head and a cushy life to go with it. What would she have done if she'd had to rely on finding a husband in order to keep body and soul together? A plain Jane like her, that's what I'd like to know. Men haven't exactly been queuing outside the door.

Our Ada was lucky; Esther would never have found a husband so quick, though sometimes I'm not sure she realizes how well off she is, and that she's far better off living here with me.'

Chapter 7

'I suppose kids like Kenneth Barlow must be every teacher's dream,' Wendy said, the next time the staff were gathered for their regular dinnertime chat. She wanted to sound out her colleagues about the boy she considered to be her star pupil and she was not surprised to see everyone's eyes light up.

When she had first seen his name in her class register, Wendy had been delighted, remembering her meeting with Ida and Frank Barlow briefly at the Rovers Return when she was newly arrived in Weatherfield. She wondered what his parents had made of the fact that she was now Kenneth's teacher and how they would feel if she offered extra sessions for Kenneth, as Ada Hayes had once done.

'I'm sure we all think well of Kenneth Barlow,' Philip Jackson said. 'Let's face it, bright kids stand out in a school like this and there's certainly no doubting he's very bright. I've followed his progress with interest ever since he was a nipper in my first class.'

'He's always shone head and shoulders above the rest and been a great role model for the other children in the class,' Mrs Newlands said. 'He loved reading from day one and I seem to recall he cottoned on to it really quickly. If he ever went missing you could guarantee that he'd be sitting in a corner somewhere, leafing through one of the library books.'

'Fortunately I don't think he's changed much,' Wendy said. 'He's the only one in my class who thinks to ask the meaning of a word he doesn't know, and he'll even use a dictionary himself.'

All the teachers of the younger classes who had once taught Kenneth nodded in agreement.

'If memory serves me rightly, I rather fancy his parents are aware of how good he is,' Mrs Newlands said, 'and his mother in particular was very encouraging, eager to push him to do well.'

'That's true,' Mr Jackson said, 'his mother has always attended parents' evenings regularly.'

Wendy smiled at that, not wanting to express her fear that someone like his friend Lionel Brown could all too easily lead him astray.

'As far as I remember,' Mr Jackson continued, 'Ada Hayes, his previous teacher, used to tutor him outside of school hours. She felt he was one of those kids who really did benefit from extra help and she was determined to keep him on his toes. I believe he was very disappointed when she left the country, so play your cards right, Miss Collins, and the Barlows could be interested in you taking over her classes.'

'That's a good idea,' Wendy said, not wanting to admit that the thought was behind her original introduction of the subject. 'I might even look into that,' she said and she made a mental note to contact Ida to see if that might be worth considering.

Mr Jackson rose as the bell marked the end of dinnertime and passed a sheaf of papers across the table. 'It's a reading age test you might want to try with some of the brighter ones in your class,' he said.

Richard showed an interest as she pushed the papers into her briefcase and she was about to show them to him until she suddenly became aware of Denise Unwin in her peripheral vision. Richard looked as if he was about to say something to Wendy when Denise made an ostentatious show of whispering something in his ear. Richard frowned and shook his head as Denise engaged him in a private-looking conversation. Wendy clicked the clasp of her briefcase into place as Richard glanced up and smiled and Wendy could see from Denise's face that she was displeased. Wendy wanted to laugh and make some kind of stinging remark but she didn't think now was the time to engage Richard in any kind of a conversation and she knew for certain that he wouldn't be asking to accompany her home today. That would best be left for another time.

Esther was clearing away the dishes from the table after they had finished their tea when Wendy asked, apropos of nothing, 'If you had three wishes what would you like to do that you haven't been able to do since the war began?' She made a deliberate effort to keep her voice light.

Esther looked taken by surprise. 'I'm not sure,' she said. 'I'd have to give it some thought. But what makes you ask? Have you got something in mind?'

'Yes,' Wendy said, 'I've been thinking lately that I would love to go to the seaside; to have a nice little holiday, even if it was only for a few days.'

'I get it. What you really mean is that you'd like to go back to Blackpool,' Esther said and to Wendy's relief she gave a little laugh.

'Yes, I suppose I would.' Wendy joined in the laughter. 'Though I hadn't realized that's where I'd been thinking about.'

'Why can't you go? There's nothing to stop you, is there, if you really fancy it?' Esther sounded suddenly serious and she sat down next to Wendy.

'I'm afraid there is.' Wendy sighed and she began counting off on her fingers. 'Number one,' she said, 'How would I get there? Number two where would I stay? I couldn't afford a hotel; number three, I wouldn't really want to go on my own but it's bad timing because, number four, it's the middle of term, not a good time for anyone to be dashing off for an extra few days holiday.' She laughed. 'Shall I go on? I'm sure I could think of loads more reasons not to go right now.' She paused, aware that Esther was staring at her and she wondered how long she could manage to avoid mentioning the two most painful reasons for not going back.

'You know, come to think of it, that sounds like a great idea and I also wouldn't mind a—' Esther began, but she didn't get any further for there was a knock at the front door and she got up to answer it.

Wendy heard a little squeal, followed by subdued voices in the tiny hallway and then there was a loud laugh that she recognized immediately, so it was no surprise when Elsie Tanner followed Esther into the living room. What did surprise Wendy was how pleased she felt seeing Elsie again, for she was not the sort of woman Wendy could ever have imagined counting as one of her friends. But now that she thought about it, she hadn't seen their neighbour for several days and she had actually missed her.

There was something about the way she breezed into the house that was like a breath of fresh air and Wendy found it uplifting. Right now Elsie seemed to add the spark that was needed to lighten the gloomy mood that had somehow descended on the Hayes household.

'I was telling Esther that I've come to offer my services,' Elsie said when brief hugs had been exchanged. 'I'd be happy to sit with Alice for a couple of hours, so that you two could get out for a bit together for a change. I thought maybe you'd fancy getting off to the pictures.' She flopped down onto the sofa and spread her arms along the cushion tops as though she was ready to be implanted for the evening. 'Grab me while you can, ladies.' She giggled. 'Such offers don't come your way every day of the week.'

Wendy had moved to sit at the table and she perked up straight in her chair, suddenly alert, at the mention of the word 'pictures'. 'What's on?' she asked, though she could see from the way Esther's face lit up that it almost didn't matter; she looked ready to fly out of the house, regardless of what film was showing. Wendy had to admit that she too was ready to take up Elsie's kind offer immediately, when only a few moments ago she had been convinced that she was really too tired to do anything other than stay home, glued to the chair.

'*The Third Man* is on at the Roxy,' Elsie said without hesitation. 'I don't know if it interests you? Or if you've even heard of it? But it really is a great film with Orson Welles and Joseph Cotton and the wonderful Trevor Howard, who I absolutely adore. He's so good-looking.' Elsie closed her eyes and looked as if she was about to swoon.

'We have heard of it,' Esther said, 'because it's a film we've both been talking about wanting to see as soon as it was out locally. Of course the problem was that we didn't know how we would manage to both be out of the house at the same time, but if you're really offering . . .' Esther said.

'I didn't know it had been released yet,' Wendy said eagerly, delighted that Esther had not squashed the idea. 'So, likewise, if you're offering, it sounds like a wonderful idea to me!' She grabbed hold of Esther's arm and turned to face her with a huge smile, but Esther seemed to abruptly change her mind and she sank back onto the sofa and said, 'If it's such a good film, Elsie, why don't you and Wendy go and I'll go another time.'

Unusually for Elsie, her cheeks filled with natural colour. 'Actually,' she said, 'I've already been. That's how I know it's so good. I went to see it last night.'

For some reason that made Esther laugh. 'And if I was to ask you "who with?" am I likely to get a proper answer? Or are you going to tell me to mind my own business?'

Elsie looked surprisingly coy, though she did join in Esther's laughter. 'All I'll say is that he's new to Weatherfield.'

Elsie got up and smoothed her skirt over her generous hips. Then she went to stand in front of the mirror above the mantelpiece and flicked the edges of her abundant red hair as if there was a man in the room that she was trying to impress.

'His name's George,' Elsie said, and Wendy noticed that as she said this her eyes suddenly had an added sparkle.

'And . . . ?' Esther said encouragingly.

'And he's a salesman working for a large cosmetics company. With lots of free samples,' she added as she pulled a brand-new lipstick from the pocket of her skirt and smiled into the mirror while she generously applied it to her already bright lips. 'He lives in Derbyshire and he's only recently been appointed to this patch. He's going to rent a room in Weatherfield whenever he's in this neck of the woods.' She winked before she turned away from the mirror. 'This week was his first trip up here and he's been sampling the local alehouses.' Now she grinned. 'It wasn't surprising that he ended up at the Rovers a few nights ago, and guess what? He bought me a drink.' Now her face lit up with a flirtatious smile. 'Tit for tat, I suggested we go to the cinema last night – and he bought tickets for the back row!' She turned to face

Wendy and winked again before she smiled. 'We went to the first house and ended up back at the Rovers for a drink afterwards. Not a word of a lie.'

Wendy cast an admiring glance in Elsie's direction, thinking that she really was quite a character, but with the type of personality that people couldn't help being drawn to. She didn't know any details about Elsie's family apart from her two young children, but she did know that she had not had an easy life, and that her marriage had ended in a rather nasty separation from a husband who'd spent most of the war years away in the navy. If all the stories Wendy had heard about Elsie were true, she couldn't help but admire how the redhead refused to be knocked down and always seemed to come bouncing back.

'Did you take him there just to set tongues wagging, Elsie Tanner?' Esther's teasing broke into Wendy's thoughts.

'Oh, go on! You know me better than that,' Elsie said, laughing.

'Yes, exactly! And that's why I'm asking,' Esther said with a mischievous grin. 'I suppose that means that Ena Sharples has already had a chance to cast her beady eye over your beau?'

'If by that you mean George, then she has indeed,' Elsie conceded.

'And what did she have to say on the subject?'

'Strangely, nothing much, though you're right, she

kept eyeing him up and down like she fancied him herself.' Elsie cackled at that.

'How long is he here for, this George? Will you be seeing him again?' Esther asked.

'What you really mean is, will you get a chance to meet him?' Elsie said, 'and the answer is I dunno, I can't be sure, but you never know your luck. He seems to think he's gonna be in Weatherfield for a while. In the meantime, go and get ready and get yourself off to the cinema now before I change my mind; Wendy's waiting for you already, aren't you, love?'

'I must admit it is a film I would like to see,' Esther said still sounding uncertain. 'I think Orson Welles is a great actor.'

'Then stop talking about it, say thanks to Elsie, and go and fetch your coat,' Wendy said.

Esther held her hands up and took a deep breath as she suddenly said, 'Thank you very much, Elsie, I'll happily go to the pictures tonight if you promise to take Wendy with you to the Rovers again soon.'

Wendy looked up sharply, about to protest, but Esther went on, 'I know that she's working extremely hard at the moment and I feel responsible about her being stuck indoors here with only me for company every night. She thinks she has to stay in just because I'm trapped in the house, though she doesn't have to do that at all, and I worry that she isn't getting out enough.'

'That's no problem,' Elsie said.

'Excuse me!' Wendy managed to say at last. 'You're talking about me as if I wasn't here.' Esther looked embarrassed, so Wendy hastened to add, 'I really appreciate your concern, Esther, but honestly, you don't have to feel responsible for me.' She put her hand on Esther's arm.

'I know that, Wendy,' Esther said, closing her fingers over Wendy's, 'but you need a chance to meet more people and Elsie's the one who knows where they're all hiding.'

'Happy to drag you along to the Rovers any time,' Elsie said with a broad grin. 'So long as you realize that George is already spoken for.'

'I don't think you have to worry there, Elsie. It wasn't George I had in mind,' Esther said with a wink.

'Oh?' Wendy looked surprised. 'What does that mean? What scheme are you cooking up then, in that head of yours?' Wendy asked.

'I'm not cooking up anything,' Esther said innocently, 'but there's no harm in helping things along a bit sometimes, is there? Creating opportunities, that's all I'm saying.'

Wendy stared at her in astonishment. 'And what opportunities are those, may I ask?'

'Eh! Hopefully you'll find out for yourself one of these days,' Esther said.

* * *

Wendy was glad Esther had agreed to go to the cinema for they both really enjoyed the film.

'It was every bit as good as I'd hoped,' Esther said. 'Don't you agree?'

Wendy nodded enthusiastically. 'The ending was a bit dark – quite literally, what with all that rain on the Viennese cobbles, but I suppose it was inevitable. I'm really pleased we went, thanks to Elsie. It has been nice getting out for a change, the two of us together.'

'And you've got another treat to come. I'm sure Elsie will keep her word and go with you to the Rovers again one night soon. That is, if you regard an evening at the Rovers Return as a treat.' She suddenly looked apologetic. 'I'm sorry . . . I didn't check with you before I asked her, I just assumed you wouldn't say no.'

'No I wouldn't and it was a very kind thought, Esther. I'm sure an evening with Elsie will be great fun,' Wendy said, knowing that after being confined indoors for so long as the two of them had been, a trip to the local pub with Elsie actually seemed like an inviting prospect. And when Elsie stopped by a few nights later, ready to fulfil her promise, Wendy was delighted to find that she wasn't the only one who was in for a treat, because Bessie Tatlock, Albert's wife from number 1 Coronation Street, was standing behind Elsie on the front doorstep.

'Come on you two, look lively!' Elsie said. 'Tonight's to be the big night,' and she bustled her way into the hallway. 'See who I've picked up on my travels,' she said and she turned as if to introduce Bessie. 'You'd best get shifting yourselves,' Elsie said, 'because Bessie here insisted on coming with me when she heard where I was going, so now the three of us can go out together while she stops to sit in with Alice.'

'Oh, but . . .' Esther hesitated and frowned but Bessie responded immediately. 'You've no need to worry, Esther, love, I'm quite happy to stay in with your ma, while you two have a night out with Elsie.'

Esther looked dumbfounded. 'Oh, but . . .' she began again. 'You can't . . .'

'Oh, but I can, and I'll brook no arguments, lass,' Bessie said. She stepped forward confidently, although Wendy could hardly hold back the laughter as Bessie tried to stride over the threshold alongside Elsie only to find that she had to take a step back as they couldn't both fit into the doorway side by side. 'All you need to do is to straighten the seams in your stockings and add a dab of lipstick to your lips and cheeks,' Bessie said when she finally managed to move into the tiny vestibule.

'Bessie, you really don't have to . . .' Esther said again.

'I know that,' Bessie said, 'but in my book you both work hard and you should be able to enjoy a night out together every now and then. I've brought some sewing with me so I'll be kept busy. Now be off with you to get ready before I change my mind,' and she made a shooing motion with her arms.

'But that will be twice in one week . . .' Esther had one last try and this time Bessie merely laughed. 'I won't tell if you won't,' she said. 'Make the most of it for it might never happen again.'

Chapter 8

As they walked through the main bar to the counter in the Rovers Return, Wendy recognized several familiar faces and she was aware of a warm feeling as she responded to their welcoming gestures and greetings.

Esther insisted on buying the first round of drinks while Wendy followed Elsie to sit at a table with Ida Barlow. At the next table Ena Sharples and her cronies, Minnie and Martha, were nursing what was left in their bottles of milk stout, while nearby a group of men were clustered about the dartboard, obviously in the middle of a game.

'Hey, George!' Frank Barlow called to a good-looking young man in a fancy waistcoat who was rescuing his darts from the wooden board. Wendy hadn't seen him before, or the redheaded boy who was standing beside him though they both seemed to be well integrated into the group that was playing. 'Hurry up and get your darts out, George,' Frank admonished the waistcoated man. 'No time for day dreaming, it's young Arthur's turn to go,' he said, 'and we're all waiting.' He tapped the man he'd called Arthur on the shoulder and as the other man removed his darts from the board and turned to stare at the women who had just arrived, Wendy recognized George from Elsie's description.

'It's no good, Frank, we won't get much more sense out of him tonight. I think we've lost him already now that his fancy woman has arrived.' It was Albert Tatlock who spoke and he threw his hands up in surrender as he said that.

'That's no fancy woman,' Frank said, staring across at the bar counter, 'that's Elsie Tanner.' He gave a bellow that sounded like a cowboy's hoot and whatever was said next was drowned out by the men's raucous laughter.

Eventually Wendy heard Albert say, 'Well, if we don't want to lose George tonight, maybe Elsie had best come over here and play with us,' and Wendy stared at him, eyebrows raised, as she couldn't tell if he was being serious or not.

'Over my dead body!' There was no doubting the seriousness of Frank's explosive response.

'That's exactly what it will be if her aim is off,' the man called George quipped. 'I don't think you want her to get riled up or you never know where the darts might land.'

Wendy looked over at the speaker who winked and smiled directly at Elsie.

Elsie raised her large gin and tonic to him and took a sip before she sidled over to where the men had paused and were gathered around the dartboard. Albert looked at Elsie a little nervously, as if unsure whether to continue, while she stood provocatively, with her hands on her hips as she confronted Frank.

'What are you saying, Frank Barlow?' She taunted him. 'Did I hear you right? Do you fellas think we women don't know how to play darts? Is that it?'

'Well, do you?' Frank guffawed. 'Bloody women, you can't leave us alone to have a decent game in peace.' He turned to George. 'Have you noticed how they always want to butt in to everyone else's business when they should really be at home looking after the house and taking care of the kiddies, not leaving them with a sitter when it suits them?' He took a step towards Elsie when she ignored him until it looked as if he was almost shouting into her face. 'Get back to doing what you do best, your tittle tattle and your gossip,' he said, 'and leave the serious stuff to us men.'

'Yer what?' Elsie said cupping her hand behind her ear as if she hadn't heard him right. 'You mean you want me to show you what I can do? With or without the darts?' and without a moment's hesitation, in one quick movement she hitched up one side of her skirt and flashed enough leg to make most of the men ogle and blush as she tilted her hip in their direction.

The predictable lewd comments that followed made Elsie and the rest of the women who were within earshot roar with laughter, but she stood her ground and didn't move.

It was Albert Tatlock who eventually said, 'Now, come on, gents, we're wasting good playing time here, are we having another game or not?'

'Don't mind me,' Elsie said with a dismissive wave of her arm. 'If I want to play I can get my own game going. I wouldn't dream of interfering with yours. We women are perfectly capable of providing our own entertainment without having to rely on you lot.' As she spoke she winked back at George who had been listening intently, a smile playing on his lips. Frank picked up his darts from the table in front of him and, turning his back on Elsie, indicated to Arthur that he should get ready to play.

Elsie shrugged. 'When we really want a game of darts we'll organize our own, thank you very much,' she said and she twisted her wrist inwards then flicked her fingers outward, several inches away from her body showing off from different angles the varnished sheen that covered her brightly painted fingernails. 'I don't know about the other girls,' she said, 'but I'm not ready to play just at the moment. I don't want to chip my nail varnish.' And with a toss of her head and a loud laugh she turned and sashayed back to her table.

'Well done! That's telling them,' Ida giggled. 'I could see my Frank was getting more and more livid. But it serves him right.'

'He should know better than to mess with me, eh, Ida?' Elsie said.

'You're dead right, Elsie,' Ida said. 'Glad to see George was on your side, you've got him well-trained already.'

'Well, ladies,' Elsie turned to Esther and Wendy who were looking on astonished as they sipped their lager and lime. 'I told you tonight would be a treat,' she said, 'and I didn't exaggerate, did I?' She giggled. 'Though it's turned out to be an even better one than I'd predicted.' And at that they all burst out laughing. 'And in case you hadn't guessed, my young champion over there in the rather fine waistcoat is young George Allen who I was telling you about. He's cute, isn't he? And I'm delighted to say that even he's beginning to get the hang of Rovers' politics.'

'If that's George, then who's the other one, the one with the red hair?' Wendy asked. She had noticed the way Esther was looking at him and wondered if she knew him. 'I thought he looked like he might be a salesman?'

'Not if his fingernails are anything to go by, he isn't,' Ena Sharples chipped in from the next table. 'I'd have said more like he was a gardener, but as that's hardly likely in Weatherfield, more like than not he's a mechanic or some such.

'He must be that new bloke who's just moved into those digs across from the Mission.' Martha Longhurst joined the conversation.

'And what would you know about a bloke as has moved into digs near the Mission?' Ena queried.

'My Percy told me that they've been advertising a room in the *Gazette*, that's what I know. And that him as has taken it has come to work as a mechanic at the new garage. You know, the one that's opened down by The Field,' Martha said.

'That's right. I've heard that too. I believe his name's Arthur Wilde,' Minnie said, and she clasped her hands in her lap with a smile of satisfaction.

'Come to think of it,' Ida said, 'I've seen him in here before. He's very quiet but he always likes to join in their game of darts. Frank says he seems like a nice enough bloke, though I've never actually spoken to him myself.'

'If you ask me, I think he's a bit backward in coming forward as far as women are concerned; if you get my meaning,' Ena Sharples said. 'He looks like he wouldn't say boo to a goose.'

'You mean he's shy? That's not a problem; we can soon help him get over that, can't we girls?' Elsie said with a grin and she rubbed the palms of her hands together. 'Is it a problem for you, Wendy?' she asked and she made to stand up as if she was about to go and accost him. 'Want to be introduced?'

Wendy felt a moment of panic and turned to stare at her in alarm, until she realized Elsie was teasing. Then she took a deep breath and laughed as she shook her head. 'Not for me, thanks. I'm fine,' she said, and she meant it, though she wished she could stop her cheeks from flaming.

'Funny, I could have sworn you fancied him,' Elsie insisted. 'I'm sure he'd scrub up well, if that's what you're worried about,' she joked. 'Nothing a bit of Swarfega on his hands won't cure. I bet they'll look like new. I'll tell him then, shall I? He might even go and do it now.'

'Don't you dare do anything of the kind!' Wendy started out of her chair, desperately hoping that her protests were enough to hold Elsie back and she was relieved when Elsie sat down again. But even as she spoke she noticed that Esther's eyes had sparked with interest as soon as they'd started discussing the redheaded young man.

'Oh well, if I can't introduce you to him maybe

we can drag him in this direction and can interest him in an altogether different game of darts.' Elsie's smile was conspiratorial as she pulled her chair closer to the table and encouraged the others to do the same. 'You know what I was saying before about forming our own darts team? Well, maybe we should think of actually doing it, and getting some of the men to join us instead of the other way round.' Elsie looked around the table at the surprised faces. They were all listening intently.

'I thought you were kidding,' Ida said.

'Well, maybe I was then, but maybe it's time to think again,' Elsie said pointedly looking over to where the men had resumed their game and seemed to be having a good time. 'You know, it might put the wind up them if they think they've got some new opposition in the pub. They've had it all their own way till now, but maybe we should think of getting a team together for a regular game so that we can think of challenging them. There must be a women's league we could apply to play in to get ourselves up to standard.'

'That would mean making a commitment and practising,' Ena Sharples said, not disguising the doubt in her voice.

'I don't mind doing that,' Ida said immediately. 'It would be a great excuse for popping out of a night. "I've got to practise for the dart's team",' she said, putting on a childlike voice that made them all laugh.

'That would be just the ticket.' Ida clapped her hands in delight and gave a quick glance over her shoulder to where the men's game seemed to have picked up pace.

'OK, then! Let's do it.' Suddenly, Elsie stood up and raised her glass. 'And we can start by making a toast. To the Rovers' ladies team,' she cried and the other women echoed immediately, 'To the Rovers' ladies.'

There was a momentary halt in the conversation while the women sank their toast and the men stopped and stared. Then Minnie Caldwell's strained tones broke the silence.

'But I don't know anything about playing darts and neither does my good friend here, isn't that right, Martha?' she cried plaintively and she pulled her chair away from the table, a fearful look on her face as she glanced from one to the other of her friends for support.

'You don't have to actually play on the team, you daft ha'p'orth. They'll need supporters as well as players, so you can still toast them and help to cheer them on.' Ena Sharples made an impatient gesture and Wendy thought she was about to hit Minnie on the head with her beer mat.

Elsie turned towards the men, her glass still in the

air and she caught Frank Barlow's eye. 'Have fun, gents, while you can,' she said. 'We'll let you know as soon as we're ready to challenge you to a game and won't you look sick when we win?'

'You can't seriously think that could ever happen?' Albert Tatlock sounded shocked.

'I'll not have my wife even *thinking* she can better me,' Frank Barlow retorted, 'so don't you go filling her head with fantasies that can never happen, Elsie Tanner. I shan't waste my time taking up a so-called challenge against any women,' he finished, scornfully.

'Why not? Are you worried we might put you to shame?' Ida called back. 'I'm afraid I'm with Elsie on this one.'

Frank frowned while Elsie cheered. 'That's good, thanks, Ida,' she said. 'You'll be first on the list to play. But you don't need to panic yet,' she called across to Frank, 'you can wait until we're actually ready to throw down the gauntlet before you start eating your words. For now you can wait and see,' she laughed, and she wagged her finger in Frank's direction.

Wendy had listened, fascinated by the exchanges and amazed that feelings could run so high over something that, in the end, was only a game. 'You've really got them going, Elsie,' she said. 'It was worth coming out tonight if only for this,' and she laughed as she rubbed her hands together in delight.

'Glad you're enjoying it,' Elsie said. Then she turned

to Ida. 'What I really came for tonight was to give our two friends here an evening off from looking after Alice,' she explained and Ida nodded approvingly.

'Seems like you're getting more than you bargained for,' she said to Wendy.

'But of course it doesn't have to stop there,' Elsie said. 'Can either of you actually play?'

Esther looked surprised. 'I don't know as I've ever tried,' she said. 'But I'd be willing to give it a go.'

'Unfortunately, I don't think I'd be much use in front of a dartboard,' Wendy said quickly. 'Me and games don't seem to go together and I'm not sure I'd trust myself with a potentially lethal weapon like a dart.'

'Actually,' Elsie suddenly leaned across and whispered to Wendy, 'although I hate to say it, it's Ena Sharples we really need if we are ever going to put a team together.'

'What's that you said, Elsie Tanner?' Ena said sharply, clutching her handbag to her chest. 'Did I hear my name being taken in vain?'

'Not in vain, I hope, Mrs Sharples,' Elsie said, 'but a birdie told me that not only do you know how to play darts but that you're good at it.'

'And what if I am?' Ena stared at Elsie directly without blinking.

Elsie grinned. 'Then you might suddenly find you've become very popular round here, that's all I was saying.'

'I don't need to be popular with the likes of you,' Ena retorted, and she got up and went over to the bar to get some fresh drinks. 'You know,' she said as she turned back to face Elsie, 'women's darts is hardly anything new in this neck of the woods. Women have been playing all over Weatherfield, particularly before the war, so don't you go off bragging as if you've invented the game.'

Elsie gave a little smile of triumph that she had hit a nerve. 'It is true then?' Elsie said. 'You do play?'

Ena suddenly looked embarrassed realizing she'd been trapped.

'I *did* play,' she corrected. 'When my Alfred was alive we used to drink at that pub down by the viaduct and we both played – on separate teams, of course.'

'I bet you had a lot of fun, though?' Elsie said. 'So maybe you could be persuaded to play again?'

Ena shrugged as though not wishing to concede that she'd enjoyed it.

'Well, all I'm suggesting is that we have a bit of fun.' Elsie defended her position. 'Even you couldn't begrudge us that, Mrs Sharples? I think it's long overdue. We've all been moaning lately that life's still tough even though the war's been over for years, but I don't see anyone doing owt about it.'

'Elsie's right,' Ida said. 'I'm all for us having a go at something different.'

Ena picked up the fresh bottles of milk stout the barmaid had placed on the countertop and she handed one each to Martha and Minnie when they joined her at the bar. Then she carefully counted out her contribution to their kitty from the small purse in her handbag and added it to the pile of coppers her two friends had already placed next to their dead glasses.

Elsie raised her glass once more, its contents now well-reduced, and this time she pointed the remains of the gin in Ena's direction. 'I'm ready to drink to a new adventure,' she said, 'and here's to us all having some fun.'

'Regardless of what my husband might think, I believe we really can turn this into something that'll be good for all of us, so thanks, Elsie,' Ida Barlow added and this time all the women raised their glasses and toasted Elsie.

'Well done,' Wendy said, and patted Elsie on the back. 'It sounds like something that can really pull all the neighbourhood together.'

'At least one half of the residents, anyway, even if it means pitching them against the other half,' Esther added with a laugh.

'It really sounds quite exciting,' Wendy said. 'When do you think you'll start?'

'Good question,' Elsie said, and Wendy noticed that her words were beginning to glide together slightly. 'There's one or two others I need to try and persuade to join us, like Bessie Tatlock for one, and maybe we can get hold of someone who could teach the finer points of the game to those of us who don't really understand what we're doing but didn't want to say so,' she said with a giggle, 'and then we'll be in business.'

There was the sound of much throat clearing over Elsie's shoulder and a woman's voice suddenly said, 'I hate to burst your balloon with a mere practicality.'

Wendy looked up to see who had had the temerity to break into their conversation and she was surprised to find it was the landlady, Annie Walker.

'If I may be so bold, I'd like to know where you think this team is going to play?' Annie said. She seemed to be addressing her question to Elsie, although she didn't look at her. 'I'm asking because I'm afraid I can't see the men giving way easily in order to let you take a turn on what they clearly consider to be *their* dartboard,' she said with a supercilious look.

Elsie glared at her, her mouth slightly ajar. She looked as if she was still composing her response when a man's voice from behind her spoke, and he was definitely addressing Annie.

'That's not a problem, love,' he said, before Elsie had a chance to say anything. 'The women can have their own board. I could put one up in the Snug for them.' Jack Walker had come back into the bar through the thick curtain that divided off the landlord's living quarters. He was standing with his feet firmly planted on the ground, his arms akimbo as if challenging his wife to disagree with him. Annie stopped drying the pint glass she had removed from the bowl of soapy water and threw the tea towel over her shoulder as she stared at him.

'Really, Jack!' she said. 'Is that all we are aspiring to provide by way of entertainment? I thought the Rovers had far greater ambitions than that. I understood there were several other things under consideration with the brewery. What will they think if that's all we can muster for our suggestions list?'

Wendy was surprised to hear the landlady using such sharp words to her husband in front of customers and she was shocked by the strength of feeling that seemed to lie behind them.

'There's nowt wrong with darts as entertainment, is there, missus?' a man's voice suddenly chipped in, 'providing you can keep the men and women well separated.'

Wendy looked up to see Albert Tatlock approaching the bar with an empty pint pot in each hand.

'I'm sure Newton and Ridley won't look down their noses at us if we decide to expand the number of dartboards,' Jack Walker said with a chuckle.

'I don't reckon they will,' Albert said, lowering his voice when he saw Frank Barlow coming up behind him. 'I'll have you know darts is actually considered by some to be a very respectable game for ladies, though I know not everyone agrees.'

'A game for ladies? What makes you say that, Mr Tatlock?' Annie Walker challenged him, making no attempt to soften her tone.

'Perhaps you didn't know that Queen Elizabeth had a go at playing before the war?' Albert said. 'And I say that if King George thought it were good enough for her, then it should be good enough for anyone.'

'I don't imagine she was playing against the King though,' Annie said loftily.

'And none of the women here at the Rovers would be daft enough as to challenge their own menfolk either. That wouldn't do at all now, would it, Albert? Though I gather she's a bit of a player, your Bessie.' Frank Barlow's laughter resounded around the room as he came to join his friend at the bar while they waited for Jack to fix the tap on a new barrel. He elbowed Albert in the ribs in a jocular way as he spoke.

'Oh aye! Stick to your own is what I say.' Albert drew in his breath. And went on, 'And never get involved in any husband versus wife nonsense, either your own or other people's.' He waved his arms in the air as though fending off the idea. 'I know I wouldn't dare, especially when my wife's not here to speak up for herself.'

'Where is Bessie, by the way?' Ida looked around the room as if expecting her neighbour to suddenly appear. 'I'd like to hear what she has to say.'

'So would I, as she's been a keen player in her time,' Ena Sharples said. 'I'm sure she'd have had something sensible to say on the subject.'

'She's gone to sit with Alice Hayes tonight, as it happens,' Albert said, 'as Elsie well knows, but if she's a mind to make up the numbers on any women's team, then nothing I'd say would stop her.' He lowered his voice as he added, 'Between you and me I value my marriage too much to try.'

Wendy felt a sharp tap on her leg underneath the table as he said this and she looked up to see Elsie trying to contain her laughter. Wendy chuckled too, for she was having difficulty picturing the gentle-natured Bessie getting the better of sharp-tongued Albert Tatlock.

The two men collected a round of fresh pints and took them back to where George and Arthur were waiting for them to continue their game.

'Bloody women. They're never satisfied,' Frank grumbled as he set the glasses down on the small table. 'But they may just have bitten off a bit too much this time, trying to copy everything their menfolk are doing. I reckon it's time they were put back in their place and I for one will be happy to remind them of where that is.' He took a huge slurp then put down his drink before picking up a dart, chuntering under his breath the whole time and looking more and more angry as he narrowed his eyes and took aim, firing off the dart with unusual force.

Albert sighed. 'We'd all be a helluva lot happier if they could just let us get on with our lives while they get on with theirs.'

'But we can't let them get away with encroaching onto our territory,' Frank said crossly as he lined up his next throw. 'Crikey, it's almost as bad as during the bloody war when they started taking over our jobs.'

'I'll tell you summat for nowt,' Albert said. 'I don't want to be in the line of fire if my Bessie signs up to any women's team.' He stared over to the table where most of the women were gathered and he began to laugh as he said it, light-heartedly at first, then he almost choked as it transposed into a spluttering cough.

Frank looked up, surprised to hear his friend talk in that way, and he had a sudden vision of his own wife and the rows they'd been having of late, with her demanding more freedom and greater independence like she'd had while he'd been away. Mostly he'd paid no heed and had done his best to ignore her, but now he wondered if maybe he was missing something? Was the world changing all about him as Ida kept insisting it was, and leaving him behind?

Frank scratched his fingers across the newly sprouting stubble on his chin. 'Do you seriously think we should let them go ahead with such nonsense?' he said, suddenly looking thoughtful. 'Next thing, Ida for one will be using it as an excuse to be out every night instead of stopping at home. I keep telling her, she should be spending her time making the place nice for us all and looking after the kids. That's her job.' He shook his head. 'I say they should be leaving men's business to the men and women's business to the women otherwise the world will get into one impossible tangled mess, even worse than it is now. Imagine that,' he said, 'and it will be all their fault.'

Frank hadn't realized he'd raised his voice loud enough for Ida to hear him so he was surprised when he heard Elsie say, 'Don't look so shocked, Ida, it isn't anything we haven't heard before.'

'And it's not just Frank Barlow as thinks that,' Ena Sharples added, 'I bet if you took a poll right now there's loads of fellas in this pub who'd agree with him.'

'Not me,' a male voice said. 'I must say I'm with you ladies on this one,' and George Allen winked at

Elsie and put both of his hands up in the air in a gesture of surrender. 'I like a woman with a bit of spirit and enough of a streak of independence to throw down the odd challenge or two,' he said and he shared a flirtatious glance with Elsie. Then he narrowed his eyes and nodded his head in her direction. 'She can challenge me to a game of darts any day of the week,' he said. 'I'd rather enjoy teaching her the proper stance and how to hold her arm nice and steady while she takes aim.' He made a rather clumsy, drunken grab for Elsie that looked more like he was groping her, as he shouted, 'Give it all you've got, babe!'

'Gerroff! Or I'll give you all I've got.' She grabbed a fistful of his shirt as she batted him away and did not look very pleased.

'No harm meant!' George sobered up quickly and lifted his arms in self-defence. 'Fancy another gin then, Elsie?' he said to take the sting out of the moment and he swivelled his gaze to include Wendy and Esther in the offer at the same time. When they both politely refused, he smiled and turned to Ida with a hint of amusement in his eyes. 'And what can I get you? It's Mrs Barlow, isn't it?'

'At this moment, the way my husband is behaving, I'm ashamed to admit that it is,' Ida said, as she glared in Frank's direction. 'And you're not much better, grabbing at poor Elsie like that – but I'll not say no to another port and lemon, thanks very much.'

'The problem is that some of these men don't seem to be able to move beyond the war,' Elsie said as George gave his order to Annie Walker. 'They don't want to know that things have changed. They seem determined to hang on to the old ways and "the good old days". They want to keep things exactly the same as they were before the war.' She shook her head. 'But life's not like that. Things have moved on.'

'I agree,' Ida said. 'As far as I'm concerned, there's no going back; and I'm not sure that I want to. The old days weren't necessarily all good. '

'I'm with you there, gal,' Elsie said. 'How about you two?' She turned to Wendy and Esther who had been following the discussion with interest.

'Hear, hear! is what I say,' Esther agreed. 'It can no longer be assumed that women should be automatically tied to the house and kids. Lots of them have to go out to work these days and that's not always a bad thing.'

'My goodness, but we've chosen a great time to come here tonight,' Wendy said. 'It's been fascinating. The banter in the staffroom at school is tame compared to this. And of course, no one there is dying to get back to the so-called "good old days". That would probably take us right back to Victorian times as far as education is concerned – and I don't know of anyone who wants to go there.'

'No, the war has certainly changed a lot of things

for the better,' Elsie said, her words now definitely slurring. 'There is really only one way for us to go now and that's forward. To the future!' Elsie stood up, slightly uncertainly, and raised her glass. She was unsteady on her feet but she looked very pleased with herself as she clinked her glass against Wendy's and Esther's. She grinned at Annie Walker and didn't seem to notice that the landlady was standing by the washing-up bowl, grim-faced, with her arms firmly folded across her chest, not grinning back.

'Well!' Annie said when Elsie finally sat down again, 'I can only hope my Jack values his wife as much as Mr Tatlock seems to value his, for I'm with Mr Barlow on this. I don't agree with all this "women must be allowed to do everything that men can do", nonsense. I'm perfectly happy caring for the house and providing a loving home for my husband and children. As far as I'm concerned, if the woman's role in the home is in danger of dying then more's the pity for I have no desire to be treated like an honorary man.'

Her comments were greeted with complete silence; even those who might have wished to agree with her not daring to say a word.

'The need to take over men's roles was all very well when times were really hard during the war,' Annie continued, 'but surely we should be over that by now?' And she lifted her head and glared about her once more with a supercilious air. 'I can tell you that I, for one, shan't be participating in what I consider to be men's games, either. Women playing darts here indeed – the very idea!' She avoided looking in Ena Sharples' direction and shuddered as if she found the notion utterly distasteful. 'Personally, I don't see why any woman would want to play darts, any more than she'd want to play . . . football. Neither of which have any appeal for me!' She shot a sharp glance in the direction of her husband who was now standing behind her at the bar, a congenial smile on his face.

'That's all right, love, because nobody *has* to play. Nobody *has* to do anything they don't want to,' Jack said pointedly, 'but I can see no harm in us providing an opportunity for them as wants to play.' Jack's smile broadened as he looked over to Elsie. 'All I have to do is to get a new dartboard in place in the Snug and mark out an oche for you so that you're not throwing further than you need to. Oh yes, and I'll find you some new darts. Then you can get your team together and play in peace without having to bother the men.'

'That sounds good to me, thank you, Jack,' Elsie called across to him while she studiously avoided making eye contact with Annie.

'No trouble,' he said, 'I'll have it all set up for you by the weekend.'

Chapter 9

The bar continued to buzz for the rest of the evening with the pros and cons of allowing the women to encroach into what several still referred to as the men's exclusive territory. There were strong feelings on both sides and the bickering and name-calling only worsened throughout the evening. By the time Annie Walker rang the bell to signal last orders it was clear that no matter what happened regarding the future of darts in the Rovers Return, the two teams and their supporters would have to be kept well apart.

'Well, that was certainly a lively evening,' George said with a sardonic smile as he and Elsie emerged arm in arm at closing time, joining Wendy and Esther as they began to stroll up Coronation Street. There was a lingering warmth to the end of the day that still passed for summer. 'You didn't realize what you were starting, Elsie, did you?'

'Oh, I don't know,' she said with a mischievous grin, 'it doesn't do any harm to set the cat among the pigeons from time to time though I certainly didn't think opinions would be so divided.' Elsie giggled. 'Goodness knows how many couples will be rowing at home tonight because of me!'

'I'm sure the Barlows are, for one,' Wendy said. 'Poor Ida. I was hoping to talk to her about something completely different tonight but I never got a look in. Her husband's like a ferret. Once he's got hold of something he won't let go, will he? I felt quite sorry for her.'

'Oh, they'll be all right after they've ranted a bit,' Elsie assured her. 'They've been here before and Ida's stronger than she looks. I think she can give as good as she gets.'

'But tempers were running high by the end of the evening,' Wendy said.

'That's true, higher than I've seen in a while,' Elsie admitted, 'which was a shame, really, as it was never my intention to upset anybody. I thought we were just going for a quiet drink and at best to have a bit of fun.'

'I presume that included seeing me,' George said, with a grin. 'Go on, you can't deny that.'

'I wasn't even sure you were in town,' Elsie protested coquettishly.

'Well, it was a good job that I was there, as things turned out,' George said, 'because at least I was available to defend you. Annie Walker can be quite formidable when she gets down to it. That husband of hers must be a saint.'

'Even Ena Sharples seemed tame by comparison, tonight,' Esther said with a chuckle. 'Did she sign up for the team in the end?'

'Indeed she did! Her and Ida Barlow were the first on the list.' Elsie looked delighted as she pulled a piece of crumpled paper torn from an exercise book from her pocket; it had been filled with signatures.

'That's pretty good going to get so many names at the first time of asking,' Wendy said.

'You can almost guarantee that in future no night at the Rovers will ever be dull again,' Esther said and Elsie laughed.

'Well, I really enjoyed tonight, so thanks,' Wendy said as they stopped outside number 5.

'And so did I,' Esther said. 'We'll both do our best to come as often as possible, we don't want to let you down.'

'And I'm sure you won't want to let young Arthur down either,' Elsie said with a chuckle. Esther looked startled and she turned abruptly and glared. 'Whatever do you mean, Elsie?' she asked, but Elsie merely laughed enigmatically.

'I'm sure you won't let anyone down, and I'd hate you both to miss the fun,' she said, 'though I can't guarantee there'll be fireworks like this every time.'

Now Wendy laughed. 'Whichever way, believe me, it'll be more fun than marking homework,' she said, and she and Esther watched as Elsie linked George's arm and they continued on their way up Coronation Street.

The girls waved goodbye and let themselves in their own front door leaving Elsie and George to stride on to number 11. As they entered the kitchen they weren't surprised to find Bessie had fallen asleep on an easy chair. She shot up guiltily when the front door caught the through draught and banged shut and despite her ample figure she somehow lithely jumped to her feet, though she stood still for a few moments seemingly disorientated.

But she soon recovered and was quick to reassure them. 'I looked in on Alice several times during the course of the evening,' she said, 'and we had a little chat. The last time I went to see if she needed anything she was fast asleep, all natural-like and peaceful, so there's no need to worry.'

'I'm sure she's fine and I don't blame you at all. If anything, it's our fault for being so late.' Esther was contrite. 'I'm sorry to have kept you up like this. We intended to leave long before last orders, didn't we, Wendy? But somehow . . .' She patted Bessie on the back. 'Thanks for staying on,' she said, 'but there was a lot of excitement in the Rovers tonight,' and she proceeded to summarize the events of the evening.

'I'm almost sorry I missed it,' Bessie said, 'but at least I managed to get quite a bit of sewing done before my eyes started closing. Business has been booming since Ida and me started to make up some of those lovely new clothes patterns. It seems everyone wants something different. Did I tell you we've got hold of some lovely fresh fabrics that look great made into longer-length skirts?' I could run up something like that really quickly if either of you fancy something special.'

'I might indeed fancy something new,' Esther said, 'I'll let you know.'

'And I've found some up-to-the-minute patterns for tops, or dresses if you prefer. You really should come and have a look at what we've got.'

'I'll bear it in mind, thanks,' Esther said.

'And I will too, as soon as I've got a minute,' Wendy said, 'because I really could do with something different to wear for a change.'

The two girls saw Bessie to the front door and the older woman put her hand on Esther's arm as they stood together in the narrow hallway. 'It goes without saying if you need any more help with your mum . . .' she started to say.

'Then I'll definitely ask you again. Thanks so much for tonight. It really puts my mind at rest when I'm out, knowing Mum is in good hands with someone I can trust. Though you'll probably prefer to go and have a game of darts of an evening once the new team is up and running. I believe you're a bit of a player.'

Bessie suddenly looked coy. 'It's true, I did play quite a bit,' she said a faraway look coming into her eyes. 'I used to quite enjoy it and my Albert . . .' But at that moment there was a loud bang and the front door shook. Bessie grabbed her coat from off the bannister and reached out to slide back the lock on the front door. 'That'll be him now, worrying why I'm not home yet, now that the pub's closed,' she whispered. 'I just hope he hasn't woken Alice. Men, honestly! I'm sure he must have seen you were still at the Rovers so couldn't he guess why I was late?'

'Oh yes, he saw us at the Rovers all right.' Wendy managed to stifle a giggle. 'No doubt he can't wait to tell you his version of the evening's events.'

As Wendy had predicted, when the women's darts team finally came to fruition there were several households in Coronation Street where opinion was divided and families such as the Barlows were at serious loggerheads as underlying tensions increased. As far as the darts were concerned, it was mostly the same old arguments, Frank unhappy that the women were making a bid to take over the men's territory at the Rovers as he saw it, and his own wife trying to redefine her role at home.

'It's just an excuse for you to be out every night what with your practice sessions and your meetings,' Frank ranted. 'You're never here, woman!'

Ida stood her ground; she felt he was exaggerating the importance of the new darts team to her and was ready to argue with Frank over every objection he raised. She was determined to enjoy the growing independence that she felt membership of the new team gave her, but he always found something new to complain about.

'When was the last time me or the boys came back to some home baking, eh?' he tried, but Ida laughed when he said that.

'Is that really what you're missing?' she chided. 'My, but you are badly done to.'

'When was the last time you stayed in with the boys to look after them?' was his latest complaint, but Ida batted that one away too.

'The boys don't need looking after, they're growing up, or maybe you hadn't noticed!' she shouted back at him. 'Kenneth certainly doesn't need me watching over him every minute, and he's old enough and sensible enough to watch out for David every once in a while.'

'Once in a while? When were you last at home?' Frank threw scorn on her words but the arguments did nothing more than go around in circles because Ida was convinced that Frank's real concern was nothing to do with the boys. What Frank really hated was the fact that she was capable of earning her own money through her and Bessie's little sewing enterprise and he resented the degree of independence that that had given her. She had to admit it was true that, since they had started the business, she didn't always put her husband's needs before her own and she went out far more frequently, which at first had been fun, particularly when she had started playing darts. But eventually this had led to more small fights and these had quickly made way for bigger ones until these days she came home every evening to a grumpy, miserable husband, to a Frank she was beginning not to recognize.

She had always said that she would not give up the opportunities that her new life offered her, but now the constant bickering that it led to at home was grinding her down and she was no longer sure that the newfound freedom that she had once treasured and believed in was worth losing her husband over. The more they argued, the less certain she became.

Frank had always been quick-tempered but he had

never been one to sulk or bear grudges for any length of time. Now, however, there were increasingly long silences and periods when he was shorter and snappier than usual and she was finding it difficult to bear.

There was only one thing that Ida still felt was really worth fighting for: the boys' future, and that was something she would not give up on. She was concerned about Kenneth, in particular. He must not be forced down the same closed-off career route as his father, Ida thought, and she would fight tooth and nail to ensure that he was given all the opportunities a good education could offer; but she knew she would have to act quickly if she was going to have her way.

Chapter 10

Wendy felt that it had taken no time at all for her to settle into a routine with the children, and when she looked at their work, especially the art that now adorned the walls of the classroom, she hoped they were as pleased as she was with the evidence of what they had achieved. She had soon got used to working in the limited space of the overcrowded classroom and the children didn't seem to notice that the desks were pushed so closely together there was hardly room for a child, let alone an adult, to walk between them.

They were halfway through the first day of another week and the bell had already rung to mark dinner-time. As Wendy watched, she marvelled at the children's energy levels when they spilled out of their various classrooms. Those children who were earmarked for the first sitting of school dinners were already forming a reasonably orderly line in the corridor outside the hall-cum-gym that also served as a dining room. The meals were delivered daily and even though most of the children complained about the quality, they couldn't wait to get into the room to start eating before the food became even more unappetizing and cold. Those who had to wait for the second sitting raced each other to get outside into the school yard so that they could be among the first to raid the large box of skipping ropes and balls that were available for them to use.

Wendy turned and stood for a moment by the open window that looked out onto the playground. She gazed out at the scene framed by the leaded panes and she could hear the squeals of laughter with the occasional cry of anguish that seeped into the jolly atmosphere. It might be the beginning of autumn, she thought, but there was plenty of strength left in the yellow blob of sun that was still high in the clear blue sky. It had been shining for most of the morning, heating the glass and beyond, as the day clung to its remaining warmth. Everyone was making the most of what was being called the Indian summer and she watched the busy scene for a few moments as the children ran about, unencumbered still in their lightweight clothes. Some of the boys were clambering up the grassy banks that led to the spiked railings, scrambling to see who could get to the top first, and they were followed by a trail of girls, not caring that the dust soiled their pretty cotton frocks and even clung to their underwear each time they slipped and had to start the climb from the bottom again.

A small group of boys were mindlessly scuffing their shoes as they bounced a heavy football on their insteps, trying to pass it from one to the other without letting it touch the ground; others were playing tag, determined not to cry when they fell too hard on the uneven concrete, screaming joyously each time they were released, ready to race up and down the yard again trying their best to avoid re-capture. Some of the younger girls were diving in and out of rotating skipping ropes that were anchored by two older girls, one at each end. They were all chanting rhythmic couplets in sing-song voices, supplying the missing names as the rope was rotated to a steady chant. 'A house to let, apply within, when I move out Mrs so and so moves in,' linking the names of supposed boyfriends/girlfriends as the watchers gasped.

The tableau could have been cut out of any children's book, Wendy thought, particularly one of those illustrating Enid Blyton's stories. She smiled at the thought of the image that was now frozen in her mind. It was days like this that she realized how much she enjoyed being at Bessie Street and working with the young Weatherfield children.

She turned back into the room and, as she pulled the window shut, was immediately aware of the stillness. It was different from the usual hustle and bustle of her busy classroom and in complete contrast to the bedlam that was going on outside. She took a deep breath. She needed to make the most of it; any breaks in the school day were not only precious but were usually short-lived.

She began laying out on each desk the freshly printed sheets of comprehension exercises she had duplicated on the Roneo machine in preparation for the session that was to take up the first part of the afternoon. They were still damp and smelled, not unpleasantly, of the white spirit of the copying fluid. She stopped when she got to the desk marked Kenneth Barlow and glanced over the first few questions on the paper in her hand before laying it on his desk and smiling. Here was one boy who would have no difficulty answering the questions that related to the readings; one boy who she was convinced would have no difficulty passing the eleven-plus exams; a boy to whom she hoped she might be able to lend a helping hand.

Wendy had intended to approach Kenneth's

parents to offer her services for some out-of-school tutoring but she had not yet found an appropriate moment to broach the subject with them. She was pondering the topic now, however, when she was brought back into the present by a loud knock on the door. The next thing she saw was Richard Faulkner's face as he peered into the room. Wendy paused in her task, the remaining question papers still in her hand.

'Sorry to interrupt but I've come to invite you to join us down in the staffroom,' Richard said.

Wendy blinked rapidly as she looked up. 'What? Now? But dinner is nearly over.'

He nodded. 'I know, but I wondered if I could persuade you to come and join us for the last little bit.'

'Is it for anything special?' Wendy looked at him questioningly and was surprised to see his cheeks flush.

'Actually, it's my birthday,' he said.

'Oh, goodness, happy birthday!' Wendy said 'Poor you having to celebrate by working. It's so much nicer to have a birthday at the weekend.'

Richard laughed. 'I agree, but I couldn't quite manage to arrange that this year.'

'That's a shame,' Wendy said, 'though it's still not too late. You could put the rest of the day on hold and finish the celebrations at the weekend.'

Richard grinned. 'I could – though to be honest,

if it had been up to me I wouldn't have said anything about it to anyone. I hate making a fuss of such things but the secretary collared me when I was leaving last night. Apparently, she checks in the files because it's become a bit of a tradition for birthday people to bring in something for the rest of the staff to share. Once she told me that, I did feel sort of obliged to do something, and dinnertime seemed as good a time as any. I didn't want to appear a cheap-skate.' Wendy couldn't help smiling.

'I managed to find a small cake and I'm just about to share it, so please say you'll come and help me get through the necessaries.'

'At least I'm not too late to wish you many happy returns,' Wendy said, 'and to congratulate you on managing to find something we can share.'

'Believe it or not, I found it on my way in this morning in the window of the bakers. I even found a tiny holder and a candle at the newsagents. Rather silly, really, but it's better than people lighting up fags. Maybe we can persuade them not to do that for half an hour.'

'Now wouldn't that be nice?' Wendy said.

'So, will you come?'

She could feel the colour rushing to her cheeks, but she was unable to think of an excuse not to go. 'Yes, of course. Thank you,' she said instead. 'That will be nice. It will be the first cake I've eaten in quite a while.'

'It's not a proper birthday cake,' Richard said by way of a warning, 'but I'm sure there'll be enough for everyone to have at least a little bit.'

'Well, if there isn't enough to go round, I'll still come and watch you blow out your candle,' Wendy said.

The rest of the staff had already arrived by the time Wendy got there, and those on dinner duty apologized in advance that they would not be able to stay long. Wendy was surprised that even Mr Lorian put in an appearance, briefly muttering a few words of congratulations before he bowed out again. She was not surprised, however, to see Denise Unwin at the front of the queue once the candle had been blown out and the cake had been cut into small squares for everyone to help themselves.

'Thanks for coming, Wendy,' Richard said when she had taken a piece and had turned to leave. He stepped up close to her and practically whispered, 'Do you know, I think I'm going to take up your suggestion and put the rest of my birthday on hold until the weekend. Then I can celebrate in my own way and do my favourite thing.'

'Oh? And what's that?' Wendy couldn't resist asking.

'I can go for a long walk on the moors; I might even take a picnic if—'

Before he could finish, another voice said, 'Never mind waiting until the weekend, what about going for a drink tonight?'

Wendy looked up in surprise and even Richard looked startled as he glanced round at Denise. 'Nothing like celebrating while the iron's hot,' she said, her eyes engaging with Richard's. 'Why don't you come too?' she said, a bit reluctantly, glancing briefly at Wendy. 'I'm sure Richard wouldn't mind. We could make quite a party of it.'

Wendy took a deep breath, taking the moment that gave her to frame her response and she said quickly, 'I'm afraid I've already got arrangements for tonight, but have a lovely evening.' She thought Richard looked disappointed when Denise stepped up closer to discuss where and what time they might meet, but as she walked away, she didn't feel the need to explain that it was her turn to stay in with Alice while Esther had a night off.

'You're doing pretty well, considering you told me the first time we came in here together that you weren't a great one for going to pubs,' Elsie said as Wendy joined her in the Rovers Return a few nights later. 'And yet here we are again.' Elsie put down two tall straight glasses that looked as though they were filled with water. 'I got my usual, of course,' she said, placing one of the glasses on her beer mat, 'and I got one for you too.' She pushed the other glass towards Wendy. 'Get that down you; you can't go on drinking lager and lime for the rest of your life.' Elsie chuckled. 'Leastways, not when you're with me. Carry on like that and you'll ruin my reputation!'

Wendy could see Elsie was partly in earnest and she looked about her guiltily before sampling the gin and tonic. But no one seemed to find it strange that she was in the Rovers for the second time that week, and certainly no one was interested in what she was drinking.

'Esther and I have come to an arrangement that we take it in turns to stay home with Alice while the other one goes out,' Wendy said. 'That way we don't always need to be bothering you or Bessie and we both get a chance to go out.'

'That makes a lot of sense and it will do you both good to get out of the house more – and not only to go to work. But I don't mind doing the occasional turn if you ever want to go out together. It's not much fun going out on your own.' Elsie screwed up her face with disdain. 'It's much better to have company, I always say.'

'That's true,' Wendy agreed.

'We'll have to see what we can do about fixing you up,' Elsie said. She spoke in a jocular manner but Wendy felt her stomach tighten.

'At least I'm beginning to get to know people here,' Wendy said, 'and I do appreciate you taking the trouble to come out and meet me like this.'

'It's no bother for me. I love going out, any day of the week. In fact, this week it's you who's doing me the favour as George is back home in Derbyshire. But don't forget you're still a newcomer round here and the neighbours are being nice to you so it won't do any harm for them to know that you've got me right behind you.'

'That's true.' Wendy matched Elsie's smile.

'When you're a comparative stranger to a place, I always think it's easier to go into battle with someone at your side who knows the territory,' Elsie said.

Wendy laughed. 'I wasn't aware that I was going into battle,' she said.

'In this neighbourhood, you can never be sure,' Elsie said. 'Things can change on a sixpence.' She sounded serious, though her eyes were laughing. 'And that's where I come in. There'll always be someone looking to trip you up and I can certainly show you the lie of the land and stop you disappearing down a great gaping rabbit hole.'

Wendy chuckled as she pictured herself suddenly disappearing underground like the white rabbit in *Alice in Wonderland*. She had to admit that so far no one had tried to trip her up, but Elsie had been kindness itself since she'd moved into Coronation Street and Wendy smiled her thanks.

'I was a stranger here once myself and I well remember there were some folk who were not very nice to me,' Elsie said. 'I shall name no names, but I shan't forget either, even now that I'm part of the furniture.' That made Wendy laugh again. 'On the other hand,' Elsie said, 'there were some as were really kind. They helped me a lot, especially when things got tough with my new husband. Of course, I was still very young then and I didn't really know which way was up.' She put her hand on Wendy's arm and Wendy grinned, thinking she could take an educated guess as to who had helped Elsie and who hadn't.

'The only thing I will say is that I hope you've got no skeletons in any of your cupboards,' Elsie said with a giggle, 'because folk round here have an uncanny way of rooting them out. And the more you try to hide them, the more likely they are to find them.'

Wendy glanced at Elsie quickly, wondering if she was hinting at anything, and she felt the blood rush to her cheeks as she laughed nervously. It had taken her long enough to uncover the details of Andrew's betrayal herself, but how long would it take a determined someone to unearth such skeletons, she wondered. She was aware of Elsie's questioning look when she didn't respond immediately but she continued to sip her drink thoughtfully, not wanting to jump in too quickly and say something that she might later regret.

'You've got to admit that it beats lager,' Elsie said

eventually, pointing to Wendy's glass before taking a long sip of her own drink.

Wendy nodded.

'All I have to do now is to turn you into a half-reasonable darts player so you can join the team. Then you'll become a regular at the Rovers and it will be like you've lived your entire life on Coronation Street,' Elsie said with a grin.

'I fancy that's going to be too great a task, even for you to manage,' Wendy said. 'As far as darts go, I think you're on a safer bet encouraging Esther. She's much better than me, and she really enjoys it.'

'Hmm.' Elsie thought for a moment. 'She does seem to have a natural talent, I must say. And talking of darts, look who's just coming over. Isn't that the young ginger who was playing darts with Frank and Albert the other day? Seems like he's heading this way.'

Wendy looked up to see the young redhead, Arthur, heading towards them, his cheeks flaming almost as red as his hair by the time he reached their table.

'Hi, I-I'm Ar-Arthur Wilde,' he stammered, 'a-and—'

'Don't worry, we know who you are, we met the other week if you remember,' Elsie cut in, not unkindly, though Wendy felt sorry for him as his neck and forehead joined in his embarrassed flush. He was gripping his pint of ale so hard that Wendy's gaze was drawn to his hands. Not only were his knuckles white, but his fingers and even his nails looked freshly scrubbed.

'What can we do for you, Arthur?' Elsie asked, and as the young man's blue-green eyes seemed to light up, Wendy thought of Elsie's words earlier about welcoming strangers.

'I-I . . . was wondering if your friend will be in later?' he said.

'Now which friend would that be?' Elsie teased him. 'As you may have noticed, we're quite popular around these parts.'

'I-I'm sorry. I-I don't know her name,' he said seriously, 'but you were sitting together last time when I saw you and I think you left together at closing time.' His shoulders drooped and he dropped his gaze. 'We weren't actually introduced . . . b-but . . .' He looked up at Wendy then, with an almost pleading expression.

'I think you must mean Esther,' Wendy responded quickly. She couldn't bear to see him suffering.

'That's it.' He looked relieved. 'S-someone called her Esther, I remember now.'

'Esther Hayes,' Wendy said, 'though I'm afraid she's not here and she won't be coming in tonight.' He looked so crestfallen as she said it that she added, 'But I can tell her you were asking after her if you like? She'll probably be in later in the week.'

'Oh n-no! It doesn't matter,' he said quickly. 'She

probably won't even remember me. I-I'm sure I'll see her in here again some time.'

'I'm sure you will, now the ladies' darts team is really getting going.' Elsie lowered her voice. 'You'll have to watch her because she's really going to be good.' And she gave him a wink before he turned away, a surprised look on his face.

'Well, you young ladies are certainly in demand today,' Annie Walker said when Wendy went to the bar to take her turn and replenish their drinks after Arthur had gone back to the dartboard. 'Is Esther all right?'

'She's fine, thanks, but what makes you say we're in demand?' Wendy looked puzzled. 'Who else has been asking about her?'

'Not her, *you*. Didn't anyone tell you?' Annie said. 'Someone was looking for you earlier, not long after we opened as a matter of fact.'

Wendy shook her head. 'No one said anything to me.'

'A nice, presentable young gentleman. Well-dressed and cultured-looking, with his hair neatly styled. I don't remember seeing him in here before,' Annie said in what Elsie referred to as her irritatingly condescending voice. 'He said he worked with you,' she added as an afterthought. 'In fact, here he is now.' And she gave a beaming smile as

Richard walked in, his face lighting up when he saw Wendy.

Ida and Frank had had their biggest argument to date earlier that evening and when Ida had announced that she was off for a game of darts Frank had actually forbidden her to leave the house. Ida stood looking at him, speechless, her jaw dropping open. But both boys were out playing so she had no qualms about challenging him at the top of her voice.

'Since when do you tell me what to do and when I can come and go?' she shouted.

'Since I made you my wife twelve miserable years ago!' was Frank's retort. 'You ignore me at your peril, woman.'

Now she laughed. 'Are you *threatening* me?' She stopped short of squaring up to him – she knew she was too short to be credible.

'No! I'm not threatening. I'm *telling* you,' he said, the decibels still increasing. 'I won't have my own wife defy me!'

Ida's mind was racing as she suddenly realized that she wasn't sure where to take this next, though she felt so angry that she knew she couldn't just let it go.

'It's not right that you leave the boys on their own as much so that you can go off for a game of darts.

I've told you before. It's not as if it's for real, for a proper tournament or anything, yet they have to play out whether they want to or not.'

Now Ida laughed. 'No they don't, cos they've got a key. They can go in whenever they like. And you tell me what boys you know that don't want to play out in the street all the hours of daylight?'

'Sure, they might like it, but they don't want to be forced into it because their mother's too busy gadding about to be at home for them.' Frank folded his arms firmly across his chest in the manner of 'so there!'

'What nonsense you talk, man,' Ida said. 'How does my playing darts make one bit of difference to them?'

'It makes a difference because you're never there for them!' Frank yelled.

'Oh, and you are? If you're that worried then you should stay home with them every night. P'raps you'd like to keep them locked up an' all?'

'I don't have to be with them all the time, cos it's not my job.' Frank took a step closer to her, and when he spoke again, Ida could feel the warmth of his breath. 'Just because you earn a few bob you seem to think it gives you the right to do just what you want with it like . . . like . . .' He was struggling to find the words. 'Like flashing it around the pub every night,' he finished lamely.

'Well, doesn't it give me that right?' Ida was about to turn her back but thought better of it.

'No!' he exploded. 'By rights, woman, that money belongs to me. Count yourself lucky that I let you keep it.'

He seemed to be grasping at straws and Ida gave a rasping laugh, her voice full of scorn as she said, 'I'd like to see you try taking it,' and she realized she was breathing hard.

Frank's jaw was clenched tight shut and she could see a muscle working involuntarily in his cheek, but that only made her more determined than ever. These arguments could not go on; sooner or later they would be bound to escalate if they weren't resolved, so before anything happened, she must make sure she had safeguarded Kenneth's future. It was not that Frank had ever been a violent man, though in this mood she didn't know what he might be capable of, but he had always been stubborn and if he really dug his heels in it might be too late before she was able to shift him when it came to making the final decision about Kenneth. She must do what she had promised herself she'd do some time ago. She would go to the Rovers as she'd originally intended but she wouldn't get tied up with the darts – she would see if she could have a chat with Wendy Collins.

* * *

Ida saw Wendy as soon as she arrived at the Rovers and she planned her opening gambit as she made her way across to the table where the teacher was in conversation with Elsie. But before she had a chance to attract Wendy's attention, she saw the tall, good-looking man she recognized as Mr Faulkner, David's class teacher. He was striding across from the bar and he seemed to be heading in Wendy's direction. Ida quickly ordered a port and lemon which she then took to the Snug where she ended up playing darts after all; it seemed tonight was not the night to engage in conversations about her son.

Richard brought his pint of bitter and the two gin and tonics that he'd insisted on paying for to their table and at Elsie's invitation he sat down opposite Wendy. She was surprised to find that she wasn't as fearful of being in his company as she had once been, having worked with him for several weeks now, but after making the introductions she nevertheless felt distinctly uncomfortable. It was as though she was under scrutiny from both sides of the table, with Elsie sitting upright, grinning broadly on one side and Richard balancing precariously on a red velvet stool at the other; and he seemed to be glancing at her covertly from time to time.

'Thank you very much, but really, Richard, you should have let me pay for the drinks,' Wendy said as he set the glasses down on the beer mats, 'to wish you a belated happy birthday.'

'It's your birthday? Well, that always calls for a celebration.' Elsie looked delighted.

'It was a few days ago,' Richard said.

'Well, I'll certainly drink to that. Many happy returns,' Elsie said and they all chinked glasses.

'It's embarrassing, all these celebrations,' Richard said. 'I don't usually bother about birthdays, but this year I was forced into it.' He made Elsie laugh as he related the story about the cake he'd been urged to buy for the staff at school and the solitary candle.

'Oh, I think birthdays can be fun,' Elsie said. 'No one needs to know what number it is, but you should always do something to celebrate. Something that *you* can enjoy at least. Have you any family locally?'

Richard shook his head. 'All my family live down south. But I am thinking of doing something I enjoy at the weekend.'

Wendy looked up.

'I intend going walking on the moors, maybe taking a picnic,' he said. 'And I was wondering if you might like to join me, Wendy?'

'Brilliant idea!' Elsie said before Wendy could respond. She sounded as enthusiastic as if she was the one who'd been invited.

Wendy was taken aback by the unexpectedness of the invitation and felt flustered. She wanted to ask him what had happened to Denise? Or had he already asked her and she would turn up as an unpleasant surprise? Wendy held her breath, stalling while she desperately tried to think of an excuse.

'When exactly *were* you planning it?' she said at last.

'I was thinking about Saturday and I reckon we would be out for most of the day,' he said. 'Might that be possible?' His eyes were bright as he looked at her expectantly.

Wendy froze momentarily. 'I usually help my house-mate look after her mother at the weekends . . .' she began, thinking that she had promised Alice she would spend a bit of time with her, but before she could say more Elsie jumped in.

'Don't let that stop you,' she said. 'I'm sure me or Bessie could help out if necessary.'

Wendy could feel the heat in her face and knew her cheeks must have rippled through a variety of colours ranging from pink to scarlet by now. She glared at Elsie then tried to look away, hoping she could discourage her from engaging further with Richard, but Elsie seemed determined to force them together and wouldn't let the matter drop.

'Have you got a car, Richard?' Elsie persisted.

'No, I'm afraid not. Not yet, anyway, though it's certainly on my list of things to own one day. I've already tried my hand at driving and that was great fun,' he added with a grin. 'But it doesn't matter for now because there are several fairly regular buses that would take us right up to the moors and let us off close by some of the best walking trails.'

'Well, there you are then. It sounds as if there should be no problems,' Elsie said and she turned to Wendy. 'You can leave Esther and her mother to me without feeling any guilt. All you have to hope is that the weather holds.'

Elsie crossed the fingers on both hands as she sat back with a satisfied smile and Wendy stared at her, bewildered by the speed with which Elsie had settled the matter while Wendy was still trying to work out how she could refuse Richard's invitation without causing offence. And when Richard spoke again, he also seemed to be of the opinion that the problem had now been solved.

'If you remind me of your address, Wendy, I could come and pick you up on Saturday morning,' he said. 'Not too early! Shall we say ten o'clock?'

Wendy opened her mouth to speak but before she could say anything Elsie said with a chuckle, 'That should give you plenty of time to make up a bag of sandwiches,' and she worked her eyebrows up and down with an occasional glance at Richard as though she were sending him a private message.

Wendy sat staring, unsure what had just happened, but there didn't seem to be much left to say after that.

Richard prepared to leave, only staying long enough to finish the last of his pint. Then he excused himself, saying that that he had work to finish at home.

'I rather rashly threatened the children with an arithmetic test in the morning when they didn't behave,' he explained, 'but the threat has rather backfired on me because I haven't finished setting it yet.'

'I promise not to tell,' Elsie chuckled, 'and I'm sure you won't either, eh, Wendy?'

Wendy looked up to see Richard smiling down at her as he slipped his arms into his coat and adjusted his hat.

'It was lovely meeting you, Richard.' Elsie thrust her hand out, 'and I hope you enjoy the rest of your birthday, even if you do have to wait till the weekend.'

'Nice to meet you, Elsie.' He shook her outstretched hand and then turned to Wendy. 'No doubt see you tomorrow,' he said, 'after the test,' he added with a grin. 'And I shall look forward to Saturday.'

Chapter 11

'Well, that was an interesting evening one way or another.' Elsie stood up as soon as Richard had gone. 'And talking of a walk, I think that's precisely what we should think of doing now, before we grow roots.' She downed the remains of her glass and stood it next to Wendy's already empty one. 'I think you've had enough gin for one night, don't you? Seeing as it's your first; and it won't do me any harm not to have another.' She made a burping sound and giggled as she put her hand to cover her mouth. 'We don't want to get squiffy now, do we? Can't have teacher rolling home drunk.'

She held out her hand as if to steady Wendy when she stood up but that only resulted in both of them having to catch each other in order to stand up straight.

'Why don't we take a stroll up to my place?' Elsie said. 'It's time I checked on the kids anyway. They're usually very good when I tell them I'm going out and they put themselves to bed. They're quite capable of looking after themselves, even at their age, so I don't see any harm in it, do you? But I don't like leaving them too long on their own, especially at night. That's why I always ask George to come and have a last drink at my place.' She gave a girlish giggle. 'If we go now, we can have a cuppa at home to sober up,' she said with an enigmatic smile, 'and I think there are one or two things we might want to discuss.'

Both of Elsie's children were upstairs in the bedroom when Elsie slammed the front door shut, but from the sounds of their shrieks and laughter they were a long way away from sleep.

'I'm home!' Elsie shrieked. 'Linda! Dennis! It's high time you two were in bed!' Elsie yelled up the stairs. 'And in case you're thinking of answering back, I've got a visitor with me, so no misbehaving.'

Wendy heard a giggle and a girl hissing 'Sshh!' Then a young boy was guffawing, the sound gradually becoming stifled as if he had stuffed something into his mouth. Finally, two young faces with puffed-out cheeks appeared over the top of the bannister and all went quiet for a moment as they both stuck out their tongues. Elsie groaned and the faces disappeared but this was followed by an outbreak of giggles and whisperings of 'It's Miss, it's Miss, I told you it would be Miss!' 'Is she drunk?' and Elsie had to run up the stairs with the threat of punishment before complete silence finally reigned.

Wendy was not surprised to find that Elsie had left the children on their own for the evening for she knew it was quite normal for some parents to leave their children alone for a few hours. At school she had heard of some children who were left to fend for themselves most of the time; particularly those whose parents were working in factories and heavy industry who were out toiling from dawn until dusk, and who then invariably spent their meagre earnings in the pub especially on a Friday night.

Things had certainly improved for folk since the war, and no one wanted to go back to the poverty and hardship that most working-class communities had known. However, Wendy had seen nothing that even hinted at that kind of neglect of any of the children on Coronation Street. They were all well looked after, and the whole street kept an eye out for them.

'Tea or coffee? What can I get you?' Elsie asked when she came back downstairs. 'I've got the luxury of having both on offer tonight.'

'That's very impressive,' Wendy said.

'George has his uses.' Elsie smirked. 'And I don't make too many enquiries where little extras are concerned.'

While a large pot of tea was brewing, Elsie swiped a tea towel over the oilcloth that covered the rough wood of the kitchen table, sending crumbs skittering across the floor, and as they both sat down she produced not only the final inch in a pint bottle of milk but a large bowl filled with sugar cubes as well.

'What did you make of that cute young man with the amazing red hair who was asking after Esther?' Elsie asked.

'You could hardly miss him, though I think he looks more like a boy, really,' Wendy said.

'What was his name again?'

'Arthur Wilde,' Wendy said. 'And did you notice that he didn't have any dirty oil under his fingernails tonight?'

'He seems really sweet on Esther, don't you think?' Elsie said.

'Yes, I agree,' Wendy responded, 'though I don't think she realizes she's got an admirer.'

'What does she think to him? Does she fancy him?'

'She hasn't really said, but I did notice there seemed to be something between them if the way she looked at him the last time we were in the Rovers together was anything to go by.'

'You must tell her he was asking after her,' Elsie said.

'Of course I will.'

'And while we're on the subject of fellas, what about you and that Richard?' Elsie said. 'You're a dark horse, aren't you?'

Wendy's brow furrowed. 'What do you mean?'

'I mean exactly that. What's going on between you two?'

Wendy stiffened. 'Don't be so daft! There's nothing going on.' She sounded indignant and that made Elsie laugh out loud.

'My point exactly!' Elsie said. 'Because I'm thinking maybe there should be.'

'Elsie! Really!' Wendy looked shocked.

'Put it this way,' Elsie said, 'from the look on his face he certainly would like there to be.'

Wendy could feel the heat in her cheeks giving her away once more. 'And how would you know that?'

Elsie tapped the side of her nose. 'I just know these things. And if you want my opinion, I think he's lovely. Too bad I'm spoken for. But I can tell you summat for nothing, he doesn't half fancy you.'

Wendy stared at her, not knowing what to say.

'Honestly, Wendy, anyone can see that he's keen on you,' Elsie persisted. 'And for the life of me I can't imagine why you seem to be trying so hard to keep him at a distance.'

Wendy could feel her chest tightening and would have liked to put a stop to the conversation, but she could see that now she had started, Elsie was not about to give up.

'You should have seen your face when he mentioned a picnic,' Elsie said with a laugh. 'Yet what was so terrible about that? That's what I'd like to know.'

Wendy picked up her cup of tea and concentrated on sipping it steadily as it was too hot to swallow a large mouthful at a time. Eventually she looked up. 'If you must know, he's not available even if I was interested,' she said. 'There's someone at school, another new teacher. New to Bessie Street as well as being new to teaching. She's called Denise and she's made it very plain from day one that she's interested in him. In fact, I was wondering why she wasn't with him tonight. Would you believe *she* asked *him* to go out for a drink on the day of his birthday? The bald nerve of the woman!'

'What if she did?' Elsie said dismissively. 'So long as she wasn't in evidence tonight. To me he looked like he was up for grabs, and you should have been in there, staking your claim.'

Wendy shrugged. 'I don't see how I could have done that. Not when I know for a fact that they've been stepping out together. Anyway, I don't want to get involved, not with him or anyone else.' Wendy wasn't sure she believed what she was saying, feeling a hot prickle on the back of her neck at the thought of Richard and Denise giggling together in a pub over his birthday drink.

Elsie made an aggravated gesture as if pulling her hair out. 'Do you always give up that easily?' she challenged.

'Give up? But I'm not after him.' Wendy said, deciding that she really did mean it.

'No, you're obviously not,' Elsie agreed with a sigh. 'But the point is, maybe you should be.'

Now Wendy shot Elsie an astonished glance.

'There's no point in being coy,' Elsie scolded. 'It would be obvious to a blind stranger that he's got his eye on you, so why can't you play along, flirt a bit, have a bit of fun? You might find you like him more than you think.'

Wendy looked at her in amazement but Elsie hadn't finished. 'You turned your nose up when I suggested trying to find someone for you, and here you've got someone on a plate in front of you and what do you do? You practically freeze him out. You didn't give the poor lad a chance. If I hadn't butted in you wouldn't even be seeing him on Saturday.'

'Maybe I didn't *want* to see him on Saturday!' Wendy suddenly snapped back, though she regretted the words immediately when she saw the look of dismay on Elsie's face.

'Well, pardon me for breathing,' Elsie said.

Without warning, Wendy burst into tears, crying so hard that she began to sob.

Elsie jumped up. 'Hey up, lass.' She immediately stretched her arms across Wendy's shoulders and gave her a squeeze. 'Come on, chuck, there's no need for that. Me and my big mouth! I'm sorry. I didn't mean to say anything to upset you.'

Elsie topped up Wendy's teacup and, without asking, dropped two sugar lumps into it before adding a touch of milk and sliding it across the table. She poured a second cup for herself and put her hand gently on Wendy's arm before sitting down again.

'Now,' she said, 'are you going to tell me what all this is really about? It's not just about this Denise woman, or whatever her name is, now is it?'

Wendy fumbled for a handkerchief in her skirt pocket and, avoiding the lavender-coloured W that had been neatly embroidered in one corner, blew her nose. 'No,' she said, her voice strained, 'it's got nothing to do with her really.'

'Want to tell me what it is about? Why did you look so horrified when Richard talked about a picnic? What made you freeze up like that? I thought he seemed rather nice. Is there something about him I should know?' She fired her questions in rapid succession.

'No, nothing; it isn't even about *him*,' Wendy said.

'Then who is it about? You can tell me. You know what they say about a problem shared and all that.'

They sat in silence for several minutes, then, 'It's about a man called Andrew,' Wendy began eventually. 'A man I thought I loved and who I thought loved me. A man I was once engaged to when I lived in Blackpool.'

Tears continued to trickle down Wendy's cheeks as she spoke and she made no attempt to stop them; nor did Elsie try to intervene.

'I met him at a dance at the Tower Ballroom one summer and we fell in love almost at first sight. Honestly, it was just like you see at the pictures. It was so romantic; *he* was so romantic and good-looking too. He had the most gorgeous blue eyes. Barbara Cartland would have called them navy, and I can't begin to describe his smile. Anyway, we started stepping out and he told me he hadn't gone to war because he was in a reserved occupation, though I was never clear quite what that was. I was just grateful because it meant we had a lot of extra time together. I couldn't believe it when he asked me to marry him. It wasn't long after we met, but I said yes right away, that's how sure I was of him.'

'And you were on your own, you had no family left by then, if I remember rightly, so it makes sense,' Elsie said softly. 'Why would you refuse?'

Wendy's breathing became very shallow as she struggled to control her voice but between sobs she managed to say, 'Not only that, but I truly loved him.' She paused as she was having difficulty breathing. 'The problems started after he'd proposed,' Wendy began again. 'After several months had gone by, I tried to pin him down about planning the actual wedding and every time I tried to get him to even *think* about the future. he always found some excuse not to. And, of course, there was no one I could discuss things with. I didn't want to admit to friends that I was having problems and they assumed we were waiting till the war ended to tie the knot. I felt too ashamed to even consider why Andrew might be stalling, but every time I tried to broach the subject with him he cut me off, telling me to be patient and not to nag. So I didn't nag because I didn't want to scare him away. I told him I loved him and he kept insisting how much he adored me and I thought that would be enough.'

Wendy began to rub the wedding band finger on her left hand. 'He was always buying me bits of jewellery and things, "to prove his love", he said. He even bought me a huge engagement ring. Now I know that that was to shut me up but then I really believed it was because he loved me.' She wiped her eyes with her handkerchief. 'Honestly, Elsie, I reckon we could have gone on like that forever.'

'But thankfully you didn't,' Elsie all but whispered.

Wendy shook her head. 'I received a note,' she said, her fingers tracing the outline of the embroidered motif on her handkerchief.

'Who from?' Elsie asked leaning in towards the table. 'What was in it?'

'To this day I don't know who sent it,' Wendy said, then she paused.

'I'm sorry, I didn't mean to press you. You don't have to go on if you don't want to,' Elsie said softly. 'I can see how difficult it is.'

Wendy looked at her and gave a grim smile. 'I've come this far so I may as well finish,' she said, 'because I can remember the words on that piece of paper as if it arrived yesterday.'

'Why? What did it say?' Elsie asked, and she put her hand once more on Wendy's arm.

Wendy looked up. 'It said that I should ask Andrew about his wife and children.'

Elsie gasped. 'Oh, my goodness! What did you do?'

'At first I thought it was a hoax. Some of my friends liked playing practical jokes, you see.'

'But it wasn't that?'

'I refused to believe it. I was convinced there was nothing in it, so I did what the writer suggested: I confronted Andrew.'

'Did he confess?'

'Not at first. He tried to bluster and deny everything, to pretend that such a family didn't exist. But I could tell from the expression on his face that that wasn't the truth. It took a while for him to change his tune, but eventually he sort of "confessed". He said that they did exist but he hadn't thought it necessary to tell me because they weren't important to him as he was getting a divorce. Then he tried to tell me his wife was ill and that he had no kind of life with her anyway, but it was obvious that he was making up one story after another. Then I did begin to believe what was on the note and I realized it was the kids I felt most sorry for.'

'Oh, they were real too?'

'So it turned out, sadly for them. To be caught up in a web of someone else's lies like that is horrendous.' Wendy shook her head. 'You really are a victim, and you can't affect anything. Anyway, eventually I came to my senses and I walked away. I made it quite plain that I wanted nothing more to do with him.'

'And he accepted that?'

'He kept bugging me at first. It took him a while to believe that I meant it, but eventually he stormed off and left me alone.'

'That was brave to cut him off like that,' Elsie said. 'That must have been a very difficult thing to do, particularly as you had no family for support.'

'It was. You can imagine, I was heartbroken.' Wendy nodded. 'My friends did their best to keep me going but, as far as he was concerned, I felt utterly betrayed and very alone.' Her eyes were filling once more at the memory and she couldn't prevent the catch in her voice. She heard Elsie heave a great sigh.

'I know what that's like, to be betrayed like that,' Elsie said. 'I like to think I'm strong enough not to care any more if it were to happen again, but I know that it can take a while to get over it.'

Wendy looked at her friend and she could see the pain in her eyes.

'I heard that he left Blackpool,' Wendy continued eventually, 'and where he went I've no idea – I'm just pleased to say that I've never set eyes on him since. But I couldn't bear to stay in Blackpool any longer and I vowed that I'd never trust another man again as long as I lived.' Wendy swallowed hard, fighting to hold back her distress but she couldn't prevent one more heaving sob and she was forced to let the tears flow freely again.

'Men can be surprisingly good at making things up,' Elsie said. 'They know how to manipulate us and press all the right buttons. I'm sorry you had to find out about him the hard way, Wendy, but not all of the buggers are like that, you know. One day you'll find someone who doesn't cheat and lie, I know you will. And then you're going to have to take the plunge and open up. At some point you'll have to take a chance and trust him, unless you want to be on your own forever?'

'But h-how do you stop loving them even when you know they are liars? And how do you know who to trust?' Wendy's voice, even to her own ears, sounded more like a wail.

'You don't.' Elsie gave a sardonic smile. 'All you have to go on is your gut feeling. I suppose I learned pretty early on in our marriage that I could never trust Arnold, but I couldn't afford to just toss him away. At some point you have to stop asking too many questions of any fella, because you might not like the answers you get.'

'But if I'd have asked Andrew more questions I'd have known a lot earlier that he had a wife and kids and I could have saved myself a lot of heartache.'

'Not necessarily; not if he really didn't want you to know.' Elsie stretched out her hand and patted Wendy's arm. 'You know something, Wendy?' she said. 'You and I aren't so very different after all.'

Wendy gave her a watery smile 'I never said we were.'

'I know you didn't,' Elsie said, 'but there are plenty of folk around here that do – and not always politely. I know that in some things we *are* poles apart, I don't kid myself about that.' She gave a rueful laugh. 'But when it comes to choosing men, then maybe we're not so different after all.'

Wendy dried her eyes and was trying to smile and that made Elsie smile too. 'One thing I do know is that you're too young to lock yourself away like a hermit. You deserve, at the very least, to have some fun while you can. Don't you think you could learn to trust a man like Richard?'

Wendy put her face in her hands for a moment, then she shook her head. 'I don't know how any more. He's probably better off with Denise.' She picked up her cup, as if only just realizing it was there, and made a face as she gulped the cold, sweet tea. 'What about you and George?' she asked Elsie. 'Do you trust him?'

Elsie shrugged. 'Let's just say we have a lot of fun together – and when push comes to shove, I don't ask too many questions.'

Wendy took Elsie's words to heart and decided that she would try to act on her advice when she met up with Richard on the Saturday, determined that she would do her best to be more trusting and open. She knew she would have to banish all thoughts of Andrew if she was to relax and have fun – and that, she knew, would be the hardest thing of all.

She was up early on Saturday morning, having taken ages to get to sleep the night before. She did her best not to disturb Esther as she carefully chose a skirt and a top from her limited wardrobe and some sturdy shoes that she hoped would be appropriate for walking on the moors. There was some bread in the breadbin that she had bought specially for the picnic and she spread a thin film of margarine over several slices. She was hunting for a paper bag for the sandwiches when she thought she heard a gentle tapping on the front door and it wasn't until she opened it that she felt the blast of the wind and realized how hard it was raining. On the doorstep she was confronted by a bedraggled-looking Richard hugging a knapsack to his chest, trying desperately to keep it dry.

'You'd better come in quickly,' she said, ushering him into the hallway so that she could close the door, and he ventured no further before stripping off his heavy walking shoes without waiting to be asked and stood them on the doormat while he pattered into the kitchen behind Wendy in his stockinged feet.

'I had no idea it was raining,' Wendy said. 'I didn't draw back the curtains as I didn't want to wake Esther.'

'I'm afraid it's been like this all morning,' Richard said. 'I've been up for quite a while, trying to decide whether to come here or not because we hadn't made any contingency plans. Then I thought I should come anyway, in case it cleared up and we decided we'd still like to go.'

'From the look of your coat and the rivers that are dripping off the end of your cap I would say that there's been no let-up at all,' Wendy said.

Richard apologized and removed his flat cap. 'I think you're right, and no, I won't sit down, thanks, not until I know what we're doing,' he said when Wendy indicated a chair. 'I don't want to soak the upholstery.'

Wendy went to the window and pulled back the curtain but she could barely see through the glass which was streaming with rain. 'This is not a passing shower,' she said. 'This looks set for the day.'

'I'm afraid that's what I was thinking as I walked here,' Richard agreed. 'As you can see, I'm drenched already.' He shook his head. 'I know we won't melt and I'm not usually soft about these things, but I must admit I'm thoroughly wet through and feeling extremely uncomfortable already – and we haven't officially started the day yet.'

Richard held up his knapsack which had changed colour from khaki to a muddy brown and pretended to squeeze it out. 'I can't bear to think about the state of my sandwiches. The fish paste has probably become reconstituted and was last seen swimming down to the weir.' He gave a rueful laugh.

'It's such a shame; I was looking forward to seeing what the moors look like,' Wendy said.

'I don't think you'd be able to see much on a day like this, even if it wasn't raining so hard,' Richard said 'Most of the hill tops will be buried deep in low cloud and mist.'

Wendy nodded agreement. 'Sadly, I think we'll have to give up then and go another time.'

'Shame! I was looking forward to finally celebrating my birthday.' He shrugged. 'But we really can't go in this, it's even worse than when I set off. And I don't want to sit down either because I'll only make a mess of your furniture, quite apart from leaving the room feeling damp and chilly,' he said, 'So I'm afraid we'll have to do what the Americans say and take a rain check.'

'I've always wondered what that meant,' Wendy said, 'a rain check.'

'It means that if we'd had actual tickets for this event then we would be given a replacement voucher to be used on another day – when it isn't raining,' he added with a grin.

Wendy lifted her eyebrows. 'That seems sensible. As you say, we can't possibly go out in this.' She checked at the window again. 'So, yes please, I'm prepared to take a rain check.' She was surprised how disappointed she felt. She had worked hard gearing herself up to enjoy the outing and she now found herself upset that it would have to be postponed.

Richard stepped back into the hallway to force his feet that were clad in damp socks into his boot-like shoes. With some difficulty he retied the laces. 'I think the best thing we can do today is to curl up on the sofa with a blanket and a good book,' he said.

Wendy nodded. 'That sounds like a good idea to me. Oh, I'm sorry! I haven't even offered you a cup of tea.'

'Don't worry. I think it best if I go straight home right now before I spread the wet any further. I'll see you on Monday – and let's hope it might have stopped raining by then.' He fastened his coat and pulled his cap well down onto his forehead then stopped only long enough to give Wendy a brief wave. She waved back, feeling a little flutter in her tummy as he disappeared into the misty gloom.

Chapter 12

Esther was delighted that she and Wendy had been able to settle into a routine, taking it in turns to stay home with Alice, because the careful preplanning now meant that they could both go out more frequently in the evenings than they had done at first. Esther really appreciated Wendy's generosity and felt so much happier now that she was able to share the day-to-day burden of her mother with her new friend, and the two of them became much closer than they had been before. Not only that, but her mother seemed happier too. Alice liked Wendy and appreciated when she spent time reading to her in her room. Alice had also ventured downstairs for an hour or two on several occasions when

Wendy was home, something Esther had not been able to persuade her to do. Esther's mind, however, was also concentrating on other things as she had begun to look forward to her nights out in a way that she hadn't been able to contemplate for a long time. She mostly went to the Rovers 'to improve her darts skills, and to practise with the newly formed team' was what she told her mother, but she admitted to Wendy that it was no longer a coincidence that a certain redheaded young man called Arthur happened to be there without fail on whatever night she was scheduled to appear.

What's more, recently he had taken to calling at the house early in the evening on what he called an 'Esther Night' so that they could walk to the pub together, and he would hang back after the official Rovers' closing time so that he could walk home with her again.

The more she saw him, the more Esther couldn't avoid feeling a certain frisson of delight, though she hoped she hadn't made it too obvious how much she was enjoying his attentions. She felt a natural diffidence when she was asked about her new boyfriend but she refused to rise to comments from people like Elsie, who seemed to enjoy teasing the pair whenever she saw them together, getting a rise out of firing off jocular comments that made Arthur blush to the roots of his ginger hair.

'I won't be pushed into something before I'm ready,' she told Wendy, 'just because others think that, at my age, I should be rushing to get married as soon as a boy so much as looks at me. I don't have to explain to the world about Jack.'

'Quite right too. It's nobody else's business and it's good for you to spend time getting to know him,' Wendy said approvingly when they were enjoying a late-night cup of tea before bed. 'You must do what's right for you, but I take it you do like him, don't you?'

Esther looked up sharply but then her head nodded from side to side to indicate the uncertainty that lingered in her mind.

'You know, I don't mind if you want to invite him in for a cup of tea after he's walked you home,' Wendy said. 'I'll disappear if you prefer – I'm usually ready for bed at that hour anyway.'

For a moment Wendy thought Esther looked apprehensive. 'Thanks, that's a kind thought,' Esther said quickly, 'but you don't need to disappear on my account. In fact, I'd like you to meet him properly outside of the Rovers and have a chance to get to know him.' Now Esther laughed awkwardly. 'He's very nice, and he's easy to talk to, not at all pushy . . . In fact, I've been thinking of trying to introduce him to my mother when he comes early in the evening. The only thing is, it's taking me a while to get used to the idea of stepping out with a young man again, never mind having to appear in public. You know how it is . . .' She spread her palms.

'I certainly do know,' Wendy said. 'After one bad experience, no matter what form it takes or what the reason was behind it, you can't help but be cautious.'

'Something like that,' Esther said. 'Fortunately, I think he likes me,' she said, trying to look nonchalant.

'I have no doubt about that!' Wendy chuckled, but Esther didn't respond.

'He's very encouraging about my darts prowess,' she said eventually. 'He thinks I've got hidden talents.' She giggled. 'He's even praised what he calls my mean competitive streak and said how much he'd love me to be on the men's team.'

Wendy gasped. 'Oh, my goodness! Could you imagine Frank Barlow's face if you tried that? I think you'd better stick to improving your game and start playing in tournaments with the women. That might be the best way to show them what you're made of.'

'What's amazing is that although him and me are so different and we have such different jobs, we do find lots to talk about.' Esther changed the subject and looked away. 'I found out the other day that we enjoy the same kind of films. Isn't that marvellous? In fact, he's asked me to go to the flicks with him next week instead of the Rovers.'

'I hope you said yes?' Wendy asked and she smiled when Esther nodded.

'Of course! We're going to see *Edward, My Son*, the Spencer Tracy film with Deborah Kerr that's showing locally.'

It was a great disappointment to Esther and the rest of the darts players when Elsie announced that their application to join the women's league had been turned down, with no reason given, and there were general murmurings of annoyance and frustration. What was even more disappointing, however, was the alarming rate that the teasing from so many of the men began again and it picked up momentum as the news spread through the Rovers. Despite all their hard work to gain some respect and support, it was upsetting that it seemed to take no time at all before the misogynistic barbs and comments began to filter through to the Snug once more, and the women felt as if they had to start their battles all over again.

Frank Barlow, in particular, lost no time in making his feelings known and, as usual, he took it out on his wife.

'I told you, you should never have started with all this nonsense.' Frank had a look of triumph on his face as he wagged his finger at her. 'It serves you right for meddling in things you know nothing about, thinking you could beat us at our own game.' He gave a derisive snort.

Ida was standing next to Elsie at the bar when Frank started his tirade, and for a moment she didn't react, but as his wagging finger came closer and he thrust his face in front of hers, her hands stiffened by her side. It was all she could do not to throw her drink over him as she turned away, scowling in disgust. She was determined to show him that he couldn't have his own way all the time but she was not prepared to get embroiled in a public argument so she clenched her teeth and said nothing until Frank had gone back to the group of men who were standing by the dartboard.

'Why does he always think he can say whatever he wants and get away with it?' she said to Elsie through clenched teeth as they returned to the Snug. 'He never cares about my feelings. Or how any of the rest of us might feel.' She pointed towards the others who were sitting at their tables in the Snug, wondering what all the shouting had been about, but she didn't expect a response. 'He'll pay for this, shouting at me in front of my own friends like I was a naughty child. I'll show him he can't have his own way all the time!' she said with a sudden determination as she clenched and unclenched her fists.

'Are you all right?' Esther asked as Ida sat down again. Ida stared blankly at her for a few moments then her eyes lit up. 'I'm absolutely fine, thank you very much,' she said, 'and all the better for seeing you.'

Esther frowned. 'Oh? And why's that?'

'Because seeing you here means that Wendy must be at home and right now she's the one I most want to see! Nothing personal, no offense,' she added quickly, realizing what she had said, and she touched Esther's arm.

'None taken,' Esther said, not sure if she should laugh to indicate no hard feelings. But before she could say more, Ida grabbed her cardigan from the back of her chair and left the Rovers. She ran most of the way up to number 5, as time was of the essence. She knew that if she could act quickly and decisively she should be able to complete her business with Wendy while Frank was still at the pub.

Ida was surprised by the warmth of Wendy's welcome when she opened the door and immediately invited her in.

'I hope you don't think I'm being cheeky, calling on you at home like this?' Ida said.

'Where else could you call on me and hope to find me available at this hour?' Wendy gave a good-natured laugh. 'Come on in. I was just going to put the kettle on and you can join me. I've been marking English compositions all evening so I'm more than ready for some adult company now.'

'Ta, I won't say no to a cup of tea,' Ida said. 'I've been on port and lemon at the Rovers most of the evening and that doesn't really do much to quench your thirst.'

'A good turnout tonight?' Wendy asked.

'There was almost a full house in the Snug at least, except for your good self, of course, because I know you and Esther have to take it in turns.' She looked around the room and Wendy could see that she had noted Alice's walking stick and the hot water bottle in its jazzy hand-knitted cover that was waiting to be filled.

'Alice actually ventured downstairs for an hour earlier this evening,' Wendy said when she saw Ida's gaze stop to take in the extra cushions that had been piled onto one corner of the couch. 'She likes to take the opportunity every now and then but she needs to be fully propped up on such occasions, or she's in danger of toppling over. Her balance isn't great any more so we can't risk her having a fall, but she did look as if she was enjoying herself, even if she doesn't actually say so.'

'Honestly, what you do for Alice is only one stop short of sainthood.' Ida shook her head in amazement. 'And she's not even your mother. I only hope she appreciates it. I know Esther does; she's been a changed woman since you arrived.'

Wendy gave a rueful smile. 'I do it as much for

Esther as for Alice and I know she appreciates it, even though I don't think Alice is ever likely to tell us something quite so positive. But at least taking it in turns has meant that Esther's had a chance to become quite the star of the darts team,' Wendy said.

'Hmm. Unfortunately that doesn't mean very much at the moment – the team's had a bit of a setback tonight, I'm afraid,' Ida said, and she outlined the events of the evening, omitting any details about the confrontation between her and Frank. 'I'm sure Esther will fill you in on the details,' she said instead. She watched as Wendy poured the tea into cups and neither spoke for a few minutes until Ida said, 'But it wasn't the darts that I came to see you about, and that's why I was apologizing for being here. The fact is that I'm wanting to talk to you about a school-related matter and I thought tonight might be a good time. But if you want to tell me to get lost and to talk to you during school hours only, then I'll understand perfectly well and I'll disappear.'

'Don't worry, Ida, I'm not that precious about my time,' Wendy said with a laugh. 'Not if I can be of any help. And now I'm intrigued, so you can't leave things in the middle like that, you've got to tell me more. I've already poured the tea so sit down and tell me why you're really here.'

Ida looked so serious Wendy felt a flash of concern

about what it might be that had brought her to number 5.

Ida's brow furrowed and she took a deep breath. 'I know it might not be fair to ask you this, but I'll come straight to the point,' she began as she sat down at the table. 'I need to know what you think of our Kenneth.'

Wendy wanted to laugh. That was not what she had been expecting, but she managed to keep her face serious. 'What do I think of him? In what way do you mean?' she asked ingenuously, while she carefully considered what tone it would be best to take when talking to the mother of her star pupil.

'Well, when Kenneth was younger both Mr Lorian and Mr Jackson were always singing his praises and I must admit they got my hopes up thinking about his future. But you're his teacher now, so I want to know what you think about where he's up to and what he might hope for in the future.'

'Aha!' Wendy said. 'You mean with regard to the eleven-plus, I suppose, and the tests the children have been having recently? I should have guessed.' Wendy looked thoughtful as she nodded and raised her eyebrows. 'Of course, it didn't escape my attention that Kenneth came top of the class in almost every subject.'

Ida put her hands up to cover her face and giggled

self-consciously. 'That was right, then? He wasn't kidding me?'

'Not at all,' Wendy said, 'why would you think that? He doesn't generally fib about such things, does he?'

Ida shook her head. 'No, of course not, but honestly, I do wonder sometimes where he gets his brains from. It certainly isn't from me and I wouldn't have thought it was from his dad's side of the family either, though you never can tell.'

'No, you can't, and that's why I always like to think of children as individuals in their own right,' Wendy said. 'Kids are themselves, not copies of someone else and that's why they don't necessarily follow in anyone else's footsteps. I mean, if you take Kenneth, it doesn't really matter where his brains come from. Whichever way you look at it the fact is that he is very bright.'

'So, you do agree?' Ida leaned forward, an excited expression on her face now.

'Of course,' Wendy said. 'There's no getting away from it.'

'It's not just me being an over-proud mum?'

'Not at all,' Wendy chuckled. 'He's the top of my class and there aren't too many others, even in any of the leavers' classes who can beat his marks.'

'It's really good to hear you say that . . .' Ida paused, then, 'But the problem is . . .' she lowered her voice as if to share a confidence although there was no one in the house apart from Alice in bed upstairs '. . . the problem is that my Frank is dead against Kenneth going to grammar school. He's even against him sitting the eleven-plus exam.'

'Really?' Wendy said and she was genuinely surprised. Most of the parents she'd come across, apart from those from the poorest of families, enjoyed the kudos if their child did well in the county-wide examinations and were usually thrilled to hear they'd gained a place at the grammar school. The only reason they wouldn't be allowed to attend was if the family felt they couldn't afford the uniform.

Ida nodded. 'I'm afraid so. He says he doesn't see the point. Unfortunately, Frank's made up his mind the lad's to go nowhere but the local secondary school and he's worried that if Kenneth sits the exam and passes it might put ideas into his head, so he's threatening not to let him take it.'

Ida sounded angry as she admitted this, becoming agitated as she began to tie and untie knots in her handkerchief. 'He seems to have no more ambition for Kenneth than for him to be recruited by the post office when he leaves school, like he was. I ask you! And the worst of it is that Frank would be happy for him to stay at the GPO for the rest of his working life – like father, like son.'

Wendy thought about this. She could see some parents being happy with such an outcome for their child, but not for Kenneth.

'I'm not sure what he's afraid of,' Wendy said eventually, 'I wonder if he realizes that everyone in the leavers' classes next year will be sitting the exams as a matter of course, so he may as well let Kenneth have a crack at them, there's nothing to lose.'

'Except all the arguments that would follow if he did well!' Ida sighed then she pocketed her handkerchief and sat forward, extending her hands across the table in despair. 'I've tried to tell him that but he won't listen. Would you believe he still talks about "not letting our son rise above his station"? As if we were servants in some grand house with unrealistic ambitions of advancement. I don't know what age he's come out of, because he seems to think that if Kenneth starts mixing with any of the toffs, as he calls them, at the grammar school, then he'll not only become a snob, thinking that he's better than the rest of his family, but that he'll be teased and bullied by the rougher kids in the neighbourhood who might see him as "getting above himself". Well, you know what some of the kids can be like round here. And if you don't, I'm sure you can guess.' Ida slumped back again in her chair and Wendy was aware as she stared at her that Ida's eyes were glistening and her face was beginning to crumple.

'I take it from the way you're talking that you want Kenneth to aim higher than the GPO?' Wendy said. She wanted to be quite clear what Ida was asking for.

Ida dropped her head in her hands and the tears began to seep through her fingers as she whispered, 'Most definitely I do. What mother wouldn't?' She hesitated, then said firmly, 'I want him to go to the grammar school. I'm not worried about bullies. If he does go, he'll not let anyone push him around and neither will I. He'll find a way to stick up for himself, I'm not worried about that.' She looked up at Wendy, her voice still tearful, her eyes pleading as she retrieved her handkerchief and dabbed at them once more. 'The only thing I need to know is whether or not you think he's capable of passing the exams; and if the answer's yes, then I'm prepared to do whatever's necessary to help him to make sure that he does.' Ida stared steadily at Wendy now. 'I don't want him to have to settle for the secondary school or one of them technical schools, no matter what Frank says. They're not a patch on the grammar.'

'I see.' Wendy nodded. 'Well, in my opinion he should certainly be capable of passing for the grammar school though you must understand they are county-wide exams. He'll be up against children from schools across the county, involving different children from all kinds of different backgrounds so I can't guarantee—'

'That's all right.' Ida rushed in. 'I'm not asking you to. But, having said that, I need to know whether or not you'd be willing to help him? Would you be willing to give him some extra tutoring that would then give him an even better chance?'

Wendy was pleased – and when she looked up and met Ida's determined gaze, she realized that not only had Ida's tears dried up, but that her voice was sounding strong again.

'I want to make sure that my son gets every possible chance to pass those exams with flying colours,' Ida said. 'And I'm prepared to pay the going rate, whatever it comes to. I'm not asking for favours.'

'Ida, there's no need for that! I thought we were—' Wendy began to protest, but Ida waved her hand away, not waiting to hear whatever it was Wendy had to say.

'You know that during the war I started my own little sewing business with Bessie Tatlock?' Ida said in a rush before Wendy could finish, and Wendy nodded. 'Well, I've a bit put by and now we've started making up our new patterns and stuff for many of the local ladies I'll be happy to put that money towards our Kenneth's education – and David's too, of course, when he's old enough,' she added quickly. 'I don't see what's wrong with giving them a helping hand if they want to try to better themselves, do you?'

Wendy fully sympathized with Ida but she didn't respond immediately. She would be happy to help, wasn't that what she had been nerving up to ask Ida herself? And she would have no objections to working with Kenneth, but what she was not willing to do was to take sides and become embroiled in someone else's family feud. From what Ida had indicated she was in danger of doing just that and she certainly wouldn't be happy at the thought of coming between Ida and Frank. She tried to take a moment to think before responding but, having got so far, Ida was not giving her the time or the space.

'To tell you the truth,' Ida said sharply, 'I'm fed up with the whole wretched business. Frank has been impossible to live with lately, so much so that I can't talk to him.'

'And you're saying it's all to do with Kenneth's exams next year?' Wendy asked tentatively. She was not at all comfortable with the direction the conversation seemed to be taking, but she didn't know what else to say.

'Not as such,' Ida replied. 'There's a bit more to it than that . . .' She paused. 'In fact, it's been brewing ever since he came back from the war.'

'Do you want to talk about it?' Before the words were out of her mouth Wendy realized that Ida had already begun.

'The thing Frank hates the most is the idea that I can earn my own money and that I don't have to rely on him for every last penny. And if I show so much as *that much* independence . . .' she held the tip of her first finger and thumb close together until they were practically touching, 'it drives him mad. He's got it into his head that I'm just out to show him up, though that's not true. But he can't bear the thought that me or the boys could in any way better him. He knows best and he's always got to be top dog. I've always given in to him before because it made for a quiet life, but I will not let him mess about with the boys' future! If he's going to be so pig-headed about it, then I will do whatever it takes to show him that he's not going to have his own way on this one.'

Ida sat up straight and puffed out her chest as she finished her little speech, as if she was taking up a bragging stance, but then suddenly she sagged onto the table like a ball deflating and her face clouded over. When she tried to speak her voice sounded tearful again, but she swallowed hard and balled her fingers into tight fists once more. She took a deep breath. 'I'm telling you, if he continues to carry on with all this nonsense regarding our Kenneth, then I swear to God that I will show him up – in public. I will use my own money to help either of my boys and I don't care who knows it. I won't let him treat me as if I have no say in anything.' She sighed. 'Don't get me wrong, Frank's always been a good provider,' she said and there was sadness in her voice. 'He's never been out of work and we've never gone short; but he needs to feel that we rely solely on him for everything and that's no longer true.'

Ida looked down at her hands that were in her lap now, as if she was noticing for the first time the chipped nail varnish; she seemed to be unaware that she was making it worse, cracking the polish off her thumbs with the closely cut nail of her first finger. 'The problem is,' Ida continued, 'Frank hates when I get involved in something that he doesn't agree with.' Something suddenly caught in her throat and the sound that came out was halfway between a schoolgirl giggle and a sob.

'Like playing darts, you mean?' Wendy tried to make her own voice sound light as she filled the awkward moment.

'Exactly that,' Ida said, with a grateful smile. 'That's what's set him off on his latest anti-Ida campaign. He would never be able to live it down if I ever beat him. You should have seen the way he behaved tonight when the news spread about us not being accepted by the league! He was like a child, he was so happy, and he made me really cross. He took so much pleasure calling us names that he was downright rude to Elsie and there was no need for it. Elsie might be a bit of a character but she's not a bad person and she didn't deserve it. Thankfully, being Elsie, she didn't seem to take it too personally. But it made me determined that he's not going to have things all his own way in future and I reckon that me contributing towards our Kenneth's education is as good a place as any to start.'

'Do you really think you can win?' Wendy ventured to ask.

Ida spread her hands and pulled a 'don't know' kind of face. 'I'm sure he'll try digging his heels in to show me who's boss, but now that I've made my mind up that Kenneth will take those exams come what may, he'll not find it so easy.' Ida set her face with a strongly determined look. 'You've assured me that Kenneth has the potential, so now I'll do everything I can to make sure that he passes when the time comes.'

'And what will you tell Frank?' Wendy asked.

'I shall tell Frank that either he carries on paying for the extra tutoring or I will. But I won't let him wriggle out of making the choice.'

There was silence for a moment. Ida was frowning, deep in thought, Wendy was worrying about what she might be letting herself in for if she agreed to take Kenneth on. Finally, Wendy held her hands up.

'Ida, I'll be honest with you: I want to help you but what I don't want to do is to come between you and Frank.'

'No, of course you don't,' Ida conceded glumly even before Wendy had finished speaking. 'But would you be prepared to say yes if I told you I'd managed to persuade Frank to go along with it?'

Wendy wondered how reliable such an agreement was likely to be.

'Before I answer that,' she said eventually, 'there's one other question that you must answer for me, that I should really have asked at the beginning.'

Ida drew her brows together questioningly.

'How sure are you that Kenneth will agree to tutoring?' Wendy said. 'Here we are, talking as if it's all been agreed, but do we know for certain that, even if you do manage to persuade Frank, Kenneth would be willing to give up his leisure time to do all the extra homework that will entail?'

Two pink spots appeared on Ida's cheeks. She seemed surprised by the question and she paused before replying. 'I've never actually asked him,' she admitted. An uncertain smile played on her lips until at last she said, rather flippantly, 'But once he knows that it's you who would be doing the tutoring, I feel sure he'll do whatever you ask.'

Now it was time for Wendy to blush and she had to look away.

'It's true that if he thinks he's likely to pass anyway,' Ida added more seriously, 'there is the danger that he might not consider that he needs help, and my main worry would be that he won't put much effort in if he thinks his dad won't let him go the grammar school anyway.' Now Ida sounded anxious. 'I reckon that if I tell him *I'm* going to have to pay for the extra sessions, then that would be an incentive; he'll know that I'm serious and that his father is too and he might begin to believe that, if he works hard enough, not only will he have a good chance of getting into the grammar, but that he will be allowed to go.'

Wendy considered this. She was still hesitant to commit herself but eventually she said, 'I really would love to help. Kenneth is one of my best pupils and he deserves a chance as you say, but you must understand that I won't agree to anything if Frank really is dead set against it. And I won't go behind his back. I don't think that would be fair on anyone. So I'll be relying on you to tell me the truth.'

Ida pursed her lips and looked ready to argue, but eventually she capitulated. 'OK, that's fair enough,' she said with a laugh that sounded almost like a cough. 'You've got to live in this street too. But if it was all arranged and accepted . . . ?' She let the sentence hang.

'Then I would agree to it,' Wendy said. 'So long as Kenneth is agreeable as well,' she added with a smile.'

Ida grinned now and folded her arms resolutely as she sat back in the chair while Wendy went to fetch her large appointments diary that she carried to and from school each day. It was on the sewing table behind her and she carefully flicked through the pages that outlined her complete timetable and special appointments for the rest of the school term. 'It certainly looks as if I could see him for an hour after school, once a week,' Wendy said, 'And I would set him some extra homework to be completed in between the sessions.' Wendy looked at Ida then and she could see her neighbour was beaming. 'But I meant what I said about Frank, so it's over to you now, Ida,' she said.

'Don't you worry, I'll win him round,' Ida said. 'I won't give up now I've come this far. You can leave the rest to me.'

Chapter 13

Elsie refused to get downhearted, dismissing what she referred to as the darts team's little setback and doing her best to keep up a cheerful front when they all had a drink together in the bar before they met for their next practise session. She took a sip from the large gin and tonic George had presented her with when she first sat down. The tables had been pushed together so that they could accommodate the whole team and Elsie pulled her chair in closer to make room for them all.

'We need to put the disappointment behind us,' she said. 'It mustn't stop us still enjoying playing and we can always apply again. In the meantime, I think we should plan a special treat for ourselves by way of compensation. Not getting into the league doesn't have to stop us doing something else instead to cheer ourselves up.'

Wendy rolled her eyes at the predictable, crude comments and derisive laughter that emanated from some of the misogynists on the other side of the room but, she was pleased to see George put down his glass and come over to pat Elsie on the back. 'That's my girl, that's the spirit!' he said, the sudden movement making her cough. 'Have you got something in mind?'

'I have, as a matter of fact,' Elsie said with a smile. 'I've been thinking recently that it was high time Coronation Street went back to Blackpool for a day trip.' Elsie noted the looks on people's faces and sat back, gratified by their reactions.

'Blackpool!' Ida Barlow exhaled noisily and smiled. 'Now that's somewhere I haven't been in years.'

'Blackpool?' Even Wendy was jolted by the suggestion and she frowned, thinking about what that might mean.

'It's a bit late in the season, isn't it?' someone grumbled. 'It's far too cold to be going to the seaside at this time of year.'

'Of course, it's too cold for buckets and spades on the beach,' Elsie joked, 'and I'm not suggesting anyone has to take a dip. Though I'd like to see Albert in his knitted swimmers!' She waggled her eyebrows suggestively, as everyone laughed, 'But what we are in perfect time for is going to see the illuminations – and this is the first time they've been lit since before the war in 1938. Didn't you read in the papers about them being switched on again?'

'Gosh, yes, of course, I did. Oh, what a good idea!' Bessie Tatlock beamed at Elsie. 'I've not been there for so long; not since the war began, at any rate. And we used to go regularly to see the lights in the old days.'

'Went every year,' Elsie said. 'Never missed. I'm glad you remember those days too, Bessie. There was nothing like it for a smashing day out and we had some good times.'

'The illuminations! It's so long since I've seen them,' Ida said, surprised. 'Well, since anyone's seen them because they stayed off all during the war, didn't they? I didn't know they were back on again.'

'They are indeed,' Elsie said.

'Elsie's right.' Albert Tatlock surprisingly spoke up. 'And I saw an advertisement for coach trips in the *Gazette* only the other day; make up your own party and hire a charabanc, it said, I meant to tell you, Bessie. Apparently, since Anna Neagle switched them on folk have been flocking.'

'When will they be on till?' Ida asked.

Albert spread his hands and shrugged. 'Dunno exactly, but until November, I think.'

'Our daughter Beattie was evacuated to Blackpool during the war, wasn't she, Albert?' Bessie added. 'She loved it there.'

'That's not strictly true,' Albert said pedantically. 'According to her the family she lived with were in St Annes on the south side, not Blackpool itself, and she gets quite sniffy about the difference.'

'I wonder if she'd like to come with us?' Bessie said paying him no heed. She was speaking as if the trip had already been organized and everything was settled.

'I doubt she'd want to be associated with us or have anything to do with Coronation Street in that way,' Albert muttered and he buried his nose in his pint of beer.

'Maybe not.' Bessie sighed. 'Though the air is wonderfully clean and healthy all along the Fylde shoreline.'

'It would be lovely just to get out of Weatherfield and breathe in some of the ozone from anywhere along that coast,' Ida agreed. 'You can smell the freshness of it as soon as you step out onto the promenade.'

'And there's not only the wonderful air to breathe and the illuminations to see,' Elsie added, 'there's lots of other things to do. For anyone here who doesn't happen to have been there before, there's the piers and the funfairs and the Tower, not to mention the Pleasure Beach. I reckon it's the closest place to Weatherfield where you can really have some fun.'

'And what kind of fun's that?'

Wendy had been listening with interest while Elsie was trying to sell the notion of a seaside trip and she jumped when Ena Sharples' voice boomed unexpectedly behind her.

'What mischief are you cooking up now, Elsie Tanner? Ena demanded. 'You can't stop yourself butting in and organizing other folks' lives, can you?'

At the sound of her voice Elsie rolled her eyes before turning her attention in Ena's direction. 'And what's wrong with trying to bring some fun back into people's lives? Unfortunately, it's the kind of fun you never seem happy for others to have,' Elsie retorted.

Ena drew in such a deep breath that it seemed as though she grew several inches taller; she almost matched Elsie who had gained at least three inches in height in her faux snakeskin high-heeled shoes. 'I'll have you know I never begrudge anyone a good time, and don't you go saying otherwise,' Ena snapped. 'So long as they know how to behave themselves.'

'Shock me, then,' Elsie challenged. 'Tell me you'd be in favour of us organizing a trip to see the Blackpool illuminations.'

Ena glared at her. 'Actually, I'd have thought a trip to the seaside would be in everyone's interests right now. It's been a long time since we've been able to do anything like that. And from the colour of your face, Elsie Tanner, I'd say a chance to take advantage of a bit of sun and the fresh sea breezes certainly won't come amiss!'

'Thanks for your concern, Mrs Sharples,' Elsie said with a sneer. 'I'll bear that in mind.'

'There is something else you might want to think about before you finally decide,' a thin, reedy voice piped up and Wendy looked up to see Minnie Caldwell standing beside Ena at the bar.

'Oh?' Elsie said. 'Such as what, Mrs Caldwell?'

Minnie cleared her throat. 'I was reading in the *Gazette* about this poor man called Tom Lingard and it's made me think twice about ever wanting to go to Blackpool.'

'And who's he when he's at home?' Elsie's brow wrinkled.

'Apparently, he lived in Coronation Street before the war. Number 13, wouldn't you know,' Minnie said. 'Anyways, he went to Blackpool for a weekend, booked into a boarding house and then suddenly went missing.'

'Go on with you!' Ena snorted. 'Fancy repeating such nonsense.'

But Wendy couldn't help shuddering.

'You can mock, but nobody saw him again,' Minnie said, then she lowered her voice, 'until one morning they found his body washed up with the tide under Central Pier.' A strangely satisfied smile played on her lips. 'The police thought he'd been murdered, but no one knows for sure.' Minnie clasped hold of her handbag protectively and puckered her lips as she stared defiantly at Ena. 'That's it,' she said. 'That's the end of the story.'

'And that's all it is,' Ena scoffed, 'a story. You must be soft in the head if you think folk round here are going to take a blind bit of notice of a tale like that. Unless maybe it happened last week?'

'No, it didn't,' Minnie said stoutly. 'It happened quite some time ago,' she admitted, dabbing at her nose with a fine lawn handkerchief.

'Like when?' Ena challenged.

Minnie hesitated. 'It was sometime in the twenties, I think.'

At that Ena hooted with laughter and turned away.

'It doesn't seem to have put off too many people in the past from going to Blackpool, Mrs Caldwell,' Elsie said her voice suddenly gentle, 'and I don't think you should let it put you off now.' She stifled a giggle. 'I think it happened long enough ago for us not to have to worry about murderers being on the loose, don't you? It certainly won't stop me from going, and I doubt it will stop anyone else.'

'Forgive me if I change the subject,' Ena said, her back still to Minnie, 'but if we're going to take this Blackpool business any further then I think we still need some practical details.' All eyes quickly swivelled away from Minnie to focus on Ena. 'If you don't mind my asking,' she said, 'there's the little matter of 'how much?' still to be filled in. How much is a little jaunt to the seaside going to cost?'

Elsie had lived in Weatherfield long enough to know that that was really the question everyone was dying to ask and she wished she'd thought to get all the information together before shooting off her mouth with her suggestion, but she managed to parry Ena's sarcasm.

'I wanted to know if there might be enough takers to make up a coachload before I went to the chara company to get all the details,' she said, trying not to sound defensive, and she asked for a show of hands from all those who thought they might like to go. As she had hoped, there was a great deal of enthusiasm for the trip and she was delighted with the response. 'That's great,' Elsie said. 'I'll pick up some leaflets and will let you know the details as soon as possible.'

A few nights later the large crowd that had clustered around Elsie to get one of the charabanc leaflets broke up, and as they slowly dispersed to the tables and banquettes to digest the details, Wendy was surprised to see Richard Faulkner come into the bar. She had seen him several times in the school corridors since the morning of the abandoned birthday picnic but they had shared no more than a brief nod and a smile and she had not seen him outside of school hours since then. She wondered if he was trying to avoid her and she tried to look away now to save him any further embarrassment but she wasn't quick enough and she stiffened when she saw that he was heading in her direction. Since the story of the unsuccessful picnic had been bandied about the staffroom, Denise Unwin's behaviour towards Richard had become even more possessive and, as Richard had made no direct move to contact Wendy again socially, she'd felt it would be best to keep out of his way. There were whispers that wherever he went, Denise was sure to be not far behind, and so Wendy instinctively looked to see if Denise was with him now, but as far as she could tell he seemed to be on his own. However, her resolve for openness between them was long forgotten and she wondered if they would actually have anything to say.

'I think I'm coming in on the tail end of something that sounded very interesting,' Richard said with a smile, indicating the crowd by the bar. 'Am I right that they're planning a trip to your old neck of the woods?'

'Something like that,' Wendy said awkwardly. 'It was Elsie Tanner's idea. But I'm not sure whether I would want to go, even if they do manage to get it organized.'

Richard raised his eyebrows. 'Too close to home?' he said, but Wendy didn't respond.

'Your glass is empty,' he said and plucked it from her hand. 'Why don't you let me get you a new one and you can tell me all about it? That is, unless you fancy something stronger perhaps?'

'Not at all; in fact, I was ready to go home.'

'Oh, please, don't rush off. I've been trying to track you down so that we could have a chat and I'm delighted that I've finally managed it. It's really good to see you, Wendy – and we have a date to rearrange.'

Wendy wavered for the vital second beyond which she knew it would be rude to refuse.

'Another lager? With lime?' he said indicating the empty glass.

'No, I . . .' she wavered.

'Oh, go on,' he urged and she knew she was trapped.

'I'll just have a quick half then,' she said resisting the urge to run away. 'Thank you.' She forced a smile as she went to sit at the empty table he had indicated while he fought his way through to the counter.

Wendy sat back and listened to the chatter in the room as she waited for him to return, wondering if she'd done the right thing. The talk was mostly about Blackpool and whether or not they could afford to go on the trip. Wendy closed her eyes, absorbing the banter. It seemed everyone had their own nostalgic memories of the popular seaside resort as they reminisced about previous visits, though to Wendy's mind not all of them were accurate. As far as she was concerned, recollections of endless sun-drenched days before the war were wishful fantasies that were not based in reality. When she had been growing up there had been just as many rain-filled days with storm clouds and battering winds. Of course, she accepted that her memories had been somewhat tainted by the traumatic events that had taken over her life and she felt sad that she was no longer able to think of her hometown in the warm, expansive way she once had.

The last time she had been there, even though the blackout had long since been lifted, many of the amenities were still closed. Hotels and boarding houses were no longer full and the whole town was suffering from the constraints of stringent rationing. Life generally had been tough for everyone once the war came, and hers had been compounded by personal tragedies . . . Wendy squeezed her eyes even more tightly shut for a few seconds to hold back the threatened avalanche of tears. If they did organize a trip, would she really want to go?

The chatter seemed to be getting louder and when she opened her eyes again, she looked across to the next table where Elsie was now sitting with George.

They were in animated discussion and Elsie suddenly burst into loud laughter at something George said. Ida and Frank Barlow were sitting with them, but they both remained straight-faced and serious-looking, not joining in the banter and Wendy wondered if Ida might have tackled Frank on the issue of her tutoring Kenneth. Elsie waved at Wendy and beckoned that she should come and sit with them, but she held up her hands and shook her head to say no. She smiled and, lifting her eyebrows slightly, glanced towards Richard, indicating that he would be coming back soon to fill the empty seat. Elsie followed her gaze and then grinned her approval. When she gave her the thumbs-up sign, Wendy suddenly understood why she had such mixed feelings about going back to Blackpool. She was beginning to feel one step removed from her home town as there was no one left there from the people who had once been her life. It was these people here, from Coronation Street, who were her friends now. They were the ones she should be thinking about, not dwelling on the life she'd once had.

Wendy glanced across to the next table once more in time to see Albert and Bessie Tatlock sitting down to join the others and they were quickly immersed in what looked like a spirited conversation. Wendy felt the warmth of a blush creeping up her neck as she watched the group together and she had to look away. She felt vulnerable sitting on her own like this and was regretting saying that she would stay for another drink. She wished Richard would hurry up – the sooner he came back, the sooner she would be able to go home.

Wendy wasn't aware that she had been holding her head in her hands until she heard Richard say, 'Are you all right?' with genuine concern and she opened her eyes and quickly tried to shake herself free of all the painful memories that had suddenly piled in on her.

'I'm fine,' she said, consciously stretching her lips into what she hoped was a brief smile.

Richard put down the two tall glasses he was carrying and pushed one in Wendy's direction. Wendy tried her best to maintain the smile as he sat down.

'I thought you'd got lost,' she said, attempting a laugh to keep her voice light.

'Sorry it took me so long,' he said, 'but as you can see there's quite a queue at the bar.'

'Maybe I should have gone for them, I'm used to queues,' she said and she manged to jokingly waggle her elbows as if barging her way through a crowd. She was gratified when Richard laughed.

'But cheers anyway and thanks for the drink,' she said as she lifted her glass and clinked it against his.

'Cheers!' he responded before taking a good long

mouthful. 'I was brought up in the sedate and quiet countryside, where sheep and cows far outnumbered people so any queues, even with our ration books during the war, were always calm and orderly affairs,' he said. 'I can imagine it was quite different living somewhere more boisterous.'

'Yes, it was, nothing orderly about Blackpool,' Wendy said.

'It must have been great growing up at the seaside, being able to take a dip whenever you fancied; racing down to the beach every night after school.'

Now Wendy genuinely laughed, remembering again what good company he was. 'As if!' she said. 'Wishful thinking!' And she was suddenly transported back to the endless days of high winds and lashing rain when they were warned away from the beach as the crashing waves spilled over onto the promenade and it wasn't safe to swim. She shook her head. 'Sadly, this is England you're talking about,' she said ruefully. 'For me the sea was never warm enough to enjoy a regular swim.'

'Really? Then the sales promoters have a lot to answer for,' Richard said with a smile.

'In any case, we usually had too much homework set by our wicked slave-master teachers,' Wendy added, 'so we weren't much different from the Bessie Street kids.' This time they both laughed.

'Tell me more about this trip they were planning

before I arrived,' Richard said. 'Are they really thinking about going to Blackpool?'

'That's the general idea,' Wendy said, 'and it's the natural choice. Where else would you want to go from here if you were looking for somewhere to cheer yourself up?'

'I hadn't thought about it like that,' Richard said.

'Apparently it was a Coronation Street tradition before the war to hire a coach to go to see the illuminations. This time it was Elsie Tanner's idea. She remembers all the earlier trips and she thought it would cheer us all up.'

'And did everyone agree?'

'I'm sure most of those who remember the original excursions will want to go, but Elsie has only just distributed the leaflets confirming the details, like costs, so nothing has been decided yet.'

'I suppose it will feel strange for you to go back there as a visitor,' Richard said after a brief pause. 'Will it be bearable, do you think, or does it hold too many memories?'

Wendy could feel his eyes on her face and she suddenly felt her throat tighten as she tried to reply but she knew she couldn't trust herself to speak without her voice quavering. 'I don't know,' she ventured finally, staring off into space. 'It would be painful, that's why I'm not even sure I want to go.'

Richard didn't say anything further but she was

aware that he was still scrutinizing her face and she had to look away.

'It's been some time since . . . since my life changed,' she felt strong enough to say at last. 'And I'm slowly getting used to my new life now,' she added haltingly, but she was grateful that he let the matter rest.

'Is the trip going to be restricted to Coronation Street residents, or can anyone go?' Richard said, his eyes shining with kindness, that almost brought a tear to her eye.

'As far as I know that hasn't been discussed yet.' She composed herself enough to answer. It will probably depend on how much it costs. I imagine we'll need to guarantee a certain number to the chara company and agree to a minimum flat-rate charge.'

'I'd have thought folk would be really eager to go on any outing after having been virtually cooped up for so long,' Richard said.

'I'm sure that's true, but there are bound to be some who won't be able to afford to go.'

'Of course,' Richard agreed, 'though I suppose people could pay off the money weekly in instalments rather than having to fork it out all in one go.'

'That's true,' Wendy said. 'At my last school they used to run a Christmas Club like that.'

'I must admit I'd be interested in going to see the illuminations if the trip's open to all,' Richard said.

'Is there anything else to see if they decide to make a day of it?'

'Oh yes, lots. Blackpool's full of fun and the beach itself is lovely if the weather's nice.' Wendy sat up her voice suddenly animated. 'There's the Pleasure Beach with all the rides, the big dipper and the big wheel and things like that. There are the piers with the slot-machine arcades; there's the Winter Gardens and shows at the end of the piers and, of course, the famous Tower, which is a bit like the Eiffel Tower, and there are some amazing views from the top.' Wendy was surprised to hear the old enthusiasm gradually creep into her voice.

'Can you go up the Tower?'

'We always did, so I would presume you still can,' Wendy said.

'I've never seen the illuminations – well, I've never even been to Blackpool! – but I've heard about them, of course. Blackpool's lights are famous, even where I come from.

'They really are worth seeing,' Wendy said. When they first started I believe that there weren't many of them and they didn't stretch very far down the promenade. But when they opened them up again after being shut down during the Great War they added to them, and they kept adding to them so that people kept coming back because there was always something new to see. I think it would be special to see them again after so many years of darkness.'

'What would be really special would be if we could organize a grand trip and take all the kids from school,' Richard said. 'I'd love to see their faces; that would be a real treat, wouldn't it?' His face suddenly looked so eager Wendy wanted to laugh but instead she heaved a great sigh.

'Funnily enough the caretaker suggested the children should be taken to the seaside on the first day of school,' she said. 'But all I can say is that while it might be a treat for the kids, I'm not so sure that the teachers and escorts would enjoy it much.'

'I wonder how many kids in the school have ever been to Blackpool, let alone seen the lights?' Richard said.

'The families where the fathers are in work may well have gone on a trip or two during the summer but I bet the majority of Bessie Street kids have never been out of Weatherfield, never mind to the seaside,' Wendy said.

Richard nodded. 'I doubt kids like the Rushworths have been anywhere,' he said, 'or that they ever will go to a place like Blackpool, and the sad thing is that families like that are the ones that would benefit the most.'

'Yes, it's a shame the way the world works sometimes, isn't it?' Wendy agreed.

Richard chuckled. 'I bet a trip to the seaside wouldn't be a new experience for the Barlows' boys,' he said. 'They always seem to have those little bits of extras.'

Wendy looked at him sharply and then looked across to where the Frank and Ida were finally enjoying a joke with Elsie and George but, fortunately, they didn't seem to hear. And when she pointed them out in a whisper to Richard, he put his hand to his mouth in horror because he hadn't known who they were.

'It's a good job I didn't say anything untoward,' he whispered back. 'Thanks for telling me – I shall have to be more careful in future. I didn't realize this was their watering hole.'

'It's where most of the residents of Coronation Street drink,' Wendy said, and she couldn't help wondering what Richard would say if he knew that the Barlows' 'little bits of extras' he had referred to just might include individual, personalized tutoring from Wendy Collins.

Chapter 14

'Well, ladies!' Elsie said as she sailed into the kitchen at number 5 ahead of Wendy and sat down at the table where Esther was still sitting, 'I've just been to the Rovers and I thought I'd bring you an update of the illuminations situation. Hot off the press!' Then she hesitated.

'I hope I'm not interrupting anything,' she said, looking from Esther to an anxious-looking Wendy who glanced despairingly at a stack of children's exercise books piled on the floor beside the couch. Elsie didn't wait for an answer but proceeded to produce a large sheet of paper bearing what looked like a list of names from her handbag. 'Well, it's all settled. The trip will be going ahead. It seems I was right; we've all been starved of having any fun and no one's been anywhere like Blackpool or any seaside for that matter since well before the war – ever since petrol was first rationed and we all had to hide behind our blackout blinds. I think folk are so happy to be offered the chance to get away for a few hours we could have offered them a trip to Timbuktu, but I think more of them have actual happy memories of Blackpool and its famous illuminations.'

Esther clapped her hands. Then she stopped, a rueful look on her face. 'I don't know what I'm getting so excited about because I shan't even be going.'

'Why ever not?' Elsie asked.

'Because we can't both be out at the same time as you know and I think Wendy should have priority on this one. After all, it's her home town.' Esther made a face that suggested that there was no further discussion to be had on that subject as far as she was concerned.

'We were just talking about that as a matter of fact,' Wendy said, 'in between me trying to get through that load of compositions.' She glanced down at the mound of books and was about to expand but Elsie carried on talking without pausing again.

'Hmm,' she said, 'we'll have to have a think about that one. There must be some way we can get around it because everything else is sorted.' Elsie rubbed her hands together and beamed, then she whipped off what looked like a new silky scarf and twirled it above her head. 'We're off to Blackpool on a chara,' she sang out. 'It will be just like the old days when we used to have a coach trip out there every year. I did check the prices of the trains but filling a charabanc is much cheaper and a lot more fun because we'd all be together and we can have a sing-song. So we've hired a charabanc for the last Saturday in October.'

'You mean you've booked it already?' Esther asked.

'We had to.' Elsie looked particularly pleased with herself. 'They were almost fully booked. But I used my womanly wiles to persuade them to lay on an extra chara specially for us, as regular old customers.' She fluttered her eyelashes and pursed her lips, before continuing. 'Fortunately they remembered the Coronation Street trips from before and would you believe I only had to bat these eyelashes at him and he agreed to hold the booking for us until we could put together the down payment?'

'Gosh, that was lucky,' Esther said, and she looked at Elsie admiringly

'There was no luck about it. Purely charm,' Elsie said patting her hair and putting on a coquettish air as if she was a film star. 'We thought folk would like to make a full day of it and we'll aim to arrive about dinnertime. It's only a couple of hours drive so it won't mean leaving too early, but we'll be coming back late at night so we'll need to be prepared to arrive home in the early hours.'

'That's a really long day,' Wendy said. 'It makes me feel tired already, just thinking about it.'

Elsie laughed. 'It's meant to be enjoyable! We need to make the most it; make sure we get our money's worth.'

'As it's a Saturday, you won't have school the next morning so it won't matter what time you get home,' Esther said to Wendy.

'Exactly,' Elsie said with a wink in Wendy's direction. 'No excuses, you'll have plenty of time to really let your hair down.'

'I take it people were happy about the cost, then?' Esther said.

Elsie nodded. 'To be honest,' she said, 'all the coach companies charge pretty much the same for a chara, though naturally the cost of the rest of the day will be up to each individual. Them as wants could take their own sandwiches and a thermos and them as can afford it can splash out at a café or a pub or something, if they'd rather. Whatever takes their fancy. We're bound to stop for drinks and things – though trust Albert Tatlock, he suggested we take our own crate of beer!'

'I imagine everyone will want to do different things when they get there,' Wendy said.

'Well, they'll have the whole day to do it in,' Elsie

said. 'Most likely we'll all go our separate ways once we get there, and we'll arrange to pick up the coach later in time to go home.'

That made Esther laugh. 'You've got them going home already and they've not even gone yet! That was quick work, Elsie.'

'Have you any idea how many people want to go?' Wendy asked.

Elsie waved the piece of paper in her hand. 'These are the names of those who couldn't wait to sign up immediately and I'm sure there'll be lots more when word gets around.'

'Can anyone in the neighbourhood go?' Wendy wanted to know, remembering Richard's interest.

Elsie shrugged. 'Why not? The more the merrier, I say, on a first-come first-served basis. We'll have to make sure we get enough money to cover the deposit as quickly as we can, but so long as there's room why would we want to turn anyone away?'

'I'm sure *you* wouldn't. I presume George will want to go,' Esther said. 'What did he have to say when you told him the cost?'

The colour on Elsie's cheeks deepened. 'George wasn't actually there tonight,' she said. 'He had to go back to Derbyshire to pick up some samples.' She giggled. 'So watch out for me in some explosive new lipstick next week. Something to match this.' And she flicked up the silky scarf from about her neck.

'I thought that was new.' Wendy said. 'It's very eye-catching.'

'A present from George. Real silk,' Elsie boasted. 'I wore it because I thought he was coming tonight so I'll have to wear it again next week. But what about you? Are you going to ask that nice young man you were with in the Rovers the other night?'

Wendy blushed.

'Is he the one you work with?' Esther asked.

Wendy nodded. 'Richard, yes, and funnily enough he was asking me about the trip. He's never been to Blackpool.'

'Well then, you definitely want to hang on to him. Put him down on the list and you can give him a personal tour of all the sights. It would be good to know my matchmaking skills won't be required.' Elsie cackled. 'And what about your fella, Esther? What's his name? Won't he want to go?'

'Arthur. And he's not my fella, you know.' Esther looked away.

'He may as well be, because anyone can see that he's well-smitten.'

Elsie giggled and Esther looked down into her lap as she said, 'He might well want to go, but it will have to be without me.'

'Oh, but we can't be having that.' Elsie frowned.

'Exactly!' Wendy said. 'That's what I was trying to tell her before you arrived, but she won't have it.

She keeps saying I should go, and you know how stubborn she can be.'

'Not to worry, there's time yet,' Elsie said, and she gave Wendy a wink. 'We're bound to sort summat out.'

'And what about kids? Can they come?'

Elsie gave a loud guffaw when Esther said that. 'Who in their right mind would want to take their kids on a Street outing like that if they want to enjoy themselves?' she said. 'I know I wouldn't fancy my two tagging along, not if I'm with George.'

Esther looked surprised. 'That's up to you, of course, but there are some as might not mind.'

'I suppose we could let a few kids on,' Elsie conceded. 'But according to the leaflet kids are half price,' she said, 'so we'd have to watch that there aren't too many of them or we won't be able to cover the cost.'

'At least with a chara they don't need to take up a whole seat. You can always squeeze an extra child or two onto one of the back-row benches, if necessary,' Wendy said. 'I know we always used to do that on school trips when we took whole classes away on an outing.'

'I don't think we'll come to blows about it,' Elsie said heartily.

'You might not, but I bet Mrs Sharples would have something to say,' Wendy said. 'I presume she's not tried to put a stop to it so far?'

'For once you don't have to worry about Mrs Sharples,' Elsie said. 'She's already agreed to everything. In fact, she insisted on coming with me to make the booking. And when we got back she lost no time in putting together a team who are going to do all the organizing. I didn't argue as that lets me off the hook. Talking of which . . .' As she spoke, she pulled out a foolscap ledger from her large handbag that looked more like a shopping bag and offered it to Wendy. 'She wants you to have this.'

Wendy looked at it, puzzled. 'What's that for?' she asked.

Elsie cleared her throat, then arranged her face into a serious expression. 'The organizing team – or should I say, Mrs Sharples – asked me to ask you if you'd be willing to be in charge of the finances,' she said, putting on a posh voice. 'In other words, they want you to collect the money. Once you've got the deposit together the final amount doesn't have to be paid in until the week before we go so you'd need to collect the rest in instalments like we talked about.'

'But why me?' Wendy was puzzled.

'Well, she's not going to trust me, now is she?' Elsie said with a grin.

'Why not you, Wendy? That's more like the question I'd ask.' Esther sounded indignant. 'You're the perfect person, if you think about it. I mean, if you can't trust a school teacher with the kitty, who can you trust?'

Elsie giggled at that. 'My thoughts exactly. I thought you might like to be involved behind the scenes of a local event like this. Going cap in hand, door to door, is a great way to get to know the neighbours. That is, assuming that you're planning to go on the trip yourself?'

'And what if I decided not to go?' Wendy said, suddenly feeling awkward, for her mind wasn't completely made up.

'It doesn't really make any difference, I suppose, you could still help out by collecting the money,' Elsie said, though her forehead wrinkled. 'You aren't thinking about not going, surely?'

'No, she's going, if I have to put her on the coach myself,' Esther said emphatically before Wendy could reply. 'I've already told her she deserves an outing; she's hardly been out since she's been here and, as I said before, as far as I'm concerned we settled that it has to be Wendy who goes before you came.'

Elsie looked at Wendy, her head cocked to one side. 'So you'll do it, chuck?' she said, eyebrows raised. 'Thanks,' she added though Wendy hadn't said anything. 'I knew you wouldn't let us down,' and she pushed the ledger across the table.

Wendy was about to protest that although Blackpool was a place she had once loved she had not left in the happiest of circumstances and she wasn't sure that she could face going back. Did she really want to have to go now to the very places that she had been so desperate to avoid? But as she looked across at her friends' faces, she knew she couldn't let them down and she changed her mind one final time when she saw the set of Esther's jawline.

Chapter 15

Elsie had been right about one thing, Wendy thought as she waved to Ida who had seen her to the front door of Number 3, the last call of the day. Being responsible for the finances concerning the trip meant that she had certainly met a large number of local residents she hadn't encountered before, though she arranged it so that she always ended her trawl with a familiar face. By the end of her round each week she knew that the large purse she had designated for the kitty would be satisfyingly stuffed full of shillings, florins and half-crown coins as well as several ten-shilling and pound notes and that she would have placed another tick against most of the list of names in her ledger. She had emptied out the purse after the first week's collection when she had paid the chara company the initial deposit to secure the booking. Now, as she placed the heavily weighted purse in the large shopping bag that hung over her shoulder, she was aware that it was full once more. The remaining instalments were gradually accumulating, ready for the final payment of the hire charge that was due nearer the time.

As usual, Wendy was exhausted when she finally returned home, having done what she called her Blackpool Round straight after work, and she kicked her shoes off and sank into a chair. She still had hold of the ledger and she flicked through the pages, checking all the names to remind herself who hadn't yet paid their dues. She expected most of the people listed to be in the Rovers later that evening and she would bring the books up to date when she had gathered together all of the money.

Minnie Caldwell was the first name on the list of those who had paid. She seemed to have forgotten all about her fears regarding the poor deceased Tom Lingard and had signed up to go on the trip when she had seen her friends Ena and Martha sign, although she now had another concern.

'Are you sure there'll be enough petrol to get us there and back?' was her first question when Wendy began collecting and Wendy had no doubt that she would have to spend more time tonight reassuring Minnie once again before she would be able to persuade her to part with the next instalment.

Martha Longhurst had had a different question that first week Wendy was collecting. 'Would it be all right for my daughter Lily to come with me?' she had wanted to know. 'Only she doesn't live locally any more. She's working on a farm down south, you know, and has been since the end of the war,' Martha had added proudly. 'But she's coming home on a visit that weekend and I thought it would be a proper treat for her to join me. I'm certain she won't want to be left behind while I'm off having a good time.'

Arthur Wilde was the last name on the list and he was the first person Wendy met when she went up to the Rovers after tea. He offered to buy her a drink. 'I-I've been w-wanting to have a w-word with you,' he said, the deep blush on his cheeks and his slight stammer even more painful than usual. 'I know I've not yet paid anything towards B-Blackpool, but I've been thinking about it. I haven't said anything yet b-but the thing is . . .' He hesitated, then the words came out in a rush, 'I want to pay for Esther's ticket too.'

Wendy looked at him, surprised, as he pulled out his wallet from his back pocket and took out a ten-shilling note.

'But I thought you knew? Esther probably won't be able to go,' Wendy said. 'And I can't promise to be able to give you your money back if she doesn't. Not unless someone else fills the space.'

'Esther did tell me that you can't b-both be out of the house at the same time,' Arthur said, his voice subdued as he stared down at his shoes.

'I'd be happy for her to go,' Wendy said, 'but she keeps insisting that if only one of us goes then it must be me.'

Arthur looked up, a resolute smile on his lips. 'I'm prepared to b-buy her a ticket and hope for the b-best,' he said. 'I'm sure I'll be able to figure out something b-between now and then.' He put his finger to his lips. 'B-but for the moment let's keep that a secret b-between you and me and then it can b-be a surprise.'

Part Two

October 1949

Chapter 16

It wasn't until she got to school the next morning that Wendy realized that she still had the Blackpool kitty purse in her handbag, having forgotten to remove it the previous night. It was very heavy now and she didn't want to carry it about at school all day so she took it out of her bag, and put it in her desk, intending to lock it away. Before she could, there was a sudden noise outside the classroom and a loud scream and then much shouting which made her rush to the door and peer into the corridor to find two boys from her class brawling. A small crowd had gathered to watch them kicking and punching each other, and no one was trying to stop them.

Wendy acted instinctively and didn't hesitate to push the onlookers roughly to one side while she struggled to part the fighters. At first she was concerned that she was the only member of staff on the scene and she felt very vulnerable, but then she was relieved to see Richard sprinting down the corridor towards them, shouting, 'Stop this nonsense at once!'

Everyone looked up, shocked to hear his deep voice. They looked poised to run but they actually remained rooted to the spot and that was enough to give Wendy the time she needed to separate the two protagonists.

'I'll take this one,' Richard said, leaning into the group and grabbing the collar of the bigger of the two boys, 'if you think you can manage that one on your own?'

'Yes, I've got him, thanks,' Wendy said, holding on to the boy's arm tightly to prevent him squirming away.

'Have you any idea what was going on? Who started it?' Richard asked Wendy, frowning.

Wendy shook her head, though the boys lost no time in having their say which meant little more than them each trying to shout over the top of the other and inevitably blaming each other.

'Enough! Stop!' Richard said holding up his hand when several voices from the crowd began to join in the cacophony. 'I can see we'll get nowhere like this so we're going straight to Mr Lorian. You can tell *him* your story, though I warn you, it had better be the truth.' He glared at them as he added, 'We'll let him deal with you.' The boys tried to cower away when he said that but Richard was firmly in control as he led the way to the headmaster's office with Wendy following. Somehow the crowd magically disappeared.

By the time Wendy returned to her classroom after she and Richard had reported the incident and left the two chastened-looking boys to the mercy of the head, the first bell was ringing to signal that morning assembly was about to begin and she barely had time to gather her class and lead them into the hall.

When the two fighters were returned to Wendy's classroom later that morning by the headmaster, they looked suitably remorseful and contrite and Wendy almost felt sorry for them as they were forced to make a public apology to her and the rest of the class for the nuisance they had caused. However, she was genuinely distressed to see the redness on the backs of the boys' legs, stark physical evidence that they had each received several strokes of the cane, and she wondered whether what really amounted to nothing more than a boyish scrum was really worthy of such harsh punishment. She didn't believe in corporal punishment and wondered whether Richard had known that that would be the outcome when he had intervened.

Her thoughts were so bound up in the matter that she didn't notice at first when she went to retrieve her handbag at dinnertime that her desk was not actually locked; when she did, she realized it probably hadn't been locked at all that morning. For a moment she felt her stomach lurch in fear into a backward flip and then, carefully controlling her actions, she lifted the desk lid and propped it open as she slowly examined the items inside. But it was immediately apparent that the kitty purse was gone.

'*If you can't trust a school teacher to collect the money, who can you trust?*' Esther's flippant words came back to her; but Wendy had somehow managed to misplace that trust for she had failed to lock her desk and, as a consequence, the money had disappeared.

She wondered if she should report the matter to the headmaster, but she hesitated, having seen the cruel manner in which he dealt out his brand of so-called justice. And as she had no idea who had taken it, she didn't want to point the finger or throw suspicion in a way that might get someone into trouble inadvertently. Maybe whoever it was who had taken the money had acted in haste and might benefit from having a chance to rectify things. Perhaps she would be better off not reporting the incident but giving the thief an opportunity to reconsider their action and to return the purse without fear of recrimination.

As the last of the children ran out to play, Wendy locked the door behind them and sat down for a moment at her desk while she contemplated what she should do.

She would have to find a way of producing the money in time to make the full and final payment to the chara company, otherwise she would have to tell Elsie – and, worse still, Ena Sharples – though she was horrified at the thought that they might think that she had taken it. Who could blame her? Wasn't that what had happened to her on a previous occasion when she had been falsely accused?

That had been a long time ago when Wendy was a student in her final year at teachers' training college, but it was something she was never quite able to forget and the story now began to replay once more in her head. She had just cashed her grant cheque and was carrying a fairly large amount of cash with her in order to pay the rent for her residential accommodation. By accident, when she had left the college refectory after lunch, she left behind her bag with all the money in it. As soon as she realized she had rushed back to the dining hall but she was too late, for although the bag was still there, the money had already been removed.

When she innocently reported the matter to the principal, expecting some help and, even more importantly, sympathy, she was horrified to find herself under suspicion. The suggestion was that she had spent the money and then pretended that it had been stolen – and it seemed to Wendy that she had been pronounced guilty without any kind of proper investigation and it was up to her to prove her innocence. Fortunately, someone who had actually witnessed the theft being carried out by another student came forward to speak on Wendy's behalf and, when the police were called in to investigate, the matter was quickly cleared up. Although at first the accused student tried to deny it, almost all of the money was found in her possession. Wendy's name was completely cleared and apologies offered. Nevertheless, it had taken her a long time to get over the shock of the accusation and she had never forgotten how it had felt for her word to be doubted and she feared now that the same thing could happen again.

Unfortunately, her optimism that the money would magically reappear proved to be unfounded; the purse and its contents were well and truly gone and Wendy spent sleepless nights wondering how she could possibly replace it without anyone knowing it had gone missing. She knew that the longer she left it without reporting the incident, the more guilty she would appear, but she didn't know what else she could do.

Meanwhile she continued to collect the remainder

of the outstanding instalments while she puzzled over how to replace the missing amount in time to pay the final bill. A lot of people were looking forward to this trip and were relying on her in her financial role so she couldn't afford to let anyone down. And although she had been reluctant to admit it to herself, she had known from the start that there was really only one thing that she could do and that was to replace the money from her own savings.

The bank had advised her to put her request in writing and she stayed late at work one evening so that she could prepare the carefully worded letter that she had already planned in her head. She gave the date and time when she would be available to call in to collect the money in cash and, alone in the classroom, she sat at her desk and began to write in her neatest handwriting on the Vellum notepaper she had bought especially.

She had already decided that she could no longer bear the idea of going on the trip herself and all the time her mind was whirling as she tried to think of a plausible excuse to get out of it. After signing the letter she dipped her pen into the ink-well once more as she prepared to write the bank manager's name and address on an envelope. She didn't realize she was crying until she heard a familiar voice.

'Wendy? What on earth's the matter?' She looked

up to see Richard standing hesitantly at the classroom door.

She didn't respond immediately, reluctant to say anything about the money or the letter but, as the tears flowed faster, he stepped into the room and cautiously approached her desk. When she felt the touch of his arm across her shoulders she gave a shuddering sob and didn't even try to stem the flow of tears.

'Wendy, please tell me what's wrong,' Richard urged her. 'There must be something you can say, I'm worried,' and to her surprise relief flooded through her as she began to tell him the story. He didn't interrupt and when she finally lifted her lids to look up at him, she hoped she might see some sympathy or even empathy in his eyes. What she didn't expect was to see his face wreathed in a smile.

'I wish you'd said something sooner; I might have been able to spare you a lot of unnecessary anxiety,' he said, 'I think I may have found your purse, although the how and the where is another story.'

Wendy gasped and her hand flew to her mouth. 'Do you really think so? How can you be sure it's really mine?'

'I can't be one hundred per cent sure, not until you've seen it, but tell me more about what it looks like, the colour, shape, size, you know?' He continued to smile as she described it. 'First thing tomorrow you and I are going to see Mr Lorian,' he said when she'd finished.

'Oh, no!' Wendy was horrified. 'He's the last person I want to see.' Wendy was adamant. 'He'll think I stole it and am making it all up.'

'Now why on earth would he think that?' Richard laughed. 'From what you've described I think the purse I found has got to be yours.'

'When did you find it?' Wendy asked tentatively, hardly daring to hope.

'A few days ago,' Richard said, 'but I had no way of knowing who it belonged to so naturally I took it to the Head. I thought I'd better report it in case someone tried to claim it.'

'I can see why you did that, but what did Mr Lorian do with it?'

'He said he would look after it and at that point he put it into the safe in his office to await a claimant. But as far as I know, no one has come forward. You didn't have your name on it anywhere so we had no way of knowing who it belonged to. But why didn't you tell anyone you'd lost it, or had it stolen, or whatever?' Richard asked.

Wendy shrugged. 'That's also another story,' she said, though she didn't know whether to laugh or cry. 'But tell me something, did it still have some money in it?' Wendy asked hesitatingly.

'Yes, it did,' Richard said, 'rather a lot of money,' and

Wendy exhaled noisily. 'Mr Lorian and I counted it out together as it was an unusually large amount. More than your average teacher would carry about with them at school all day, which is why Mr Lorian put it in the safe and why we both expected someone to come for it. Now you tell me something if you don't mind my asking: why did you bring so much money to school?'

'That's the easy bit,' Wendy said, and she explained about being in charge of the kitty that she had then forgotten to leave at home.

'Do you know what?' Richard said suddenly, 'I think we should go and see if Mr Lorian is there in his office now. I know he often works late.' Then he grinned. 'But make sure you take your bag with you this time.'

Wendy was glad Richard had offered to go with her as she didn't feel strong enough to see the headmaster alone. Tears began to trickle when Mr Lorian brought the purse out of the safe and it took no time before she began to cry once more in earnest.

'I can assure you these are tears of joy,' she said with a self-deprecating grin. 'I can't believe I've got it back and with all the contents intact!'

'Well, I'm delighted you and your purse have been reunited – and all I can say is that it goes to show how honest Bessie Street pupils are, but please make sure you take better care of it from now on.'

* * *

'You must tell me where you found it,' Wendy said as she and Richard made their way back to the staffroom to grab a final cup of coffee before they went home.

'Well,' Richard said, 'it was brought to me by little Chrissie Jones. I don't know if you know her, but she's one of the younger ones in my class.' Wendy shook her head. 'Well, anyway, she said she'd found it in her desk and she had no idea how it got there.'

'And did you believe her?' Wendy said.

'I did,' Richard was quick to say. 'She seemed really shocked to find it. It was stuffed full and I don't believe she had any notion how much it contained but she handled it like it was literally a hot potato and she couldn't wait to pass it over to me.'

'But how had it come to be there?' Wendy was puzzled.

'I've no idea. I can only guess that someone must have taken it and planted it there for some reason, though I can't imagine what. Chrissie's far too timid to have taken it for a joke of some kind – and she certainly wouldn't have been able to lie about it afterwards. I think it's one of those little mysteries that we may never get to unravel.'

Another mystery that Wendy was unable to resolve was the change in Kenneth Barlow's behaviour when their additional tutorial sessions began the following week, and she couldn't describe the disappointment that she felt when she realized she had misread his interest. He suddenly became distant and detached; he never looked her directly in the eye and he constantly looked as if he was on the verge of saying something of ground-breaking importance, though he never did. He had always been such a willing and able student in school when he was in a class of thirty plus children that Wendy had been convinced that she would enjoy tutoring him one to one. He had agreed to the extra sessions readily enough, but he was proving to be so difficult to relate to and so unforthcoming that the sessions were not going as well as she had hoped.

'Is anything wrong, Kenneth?' she asked him several times, but he always looked down into his lap and responded with a subdued, 'No, Miss, everything's fine,' so that she felt she couldn't press him any further.

At school he had always seemed so keen to learn, so eager to absorb new knowledge and there was never any question about him completing his homework or preparing ahead when necessary. Now, even though he had agreed to the additional classes, he didn't seem to enjoy them. He couldn't wait for the hour to be over and often made excuses as to why he hadn't done the extra homework she set him that he had originally agreed would be a part of the package.

Wendy had never questioned how Ida had managed to persuade Frank Barlow not only to accept the offer of tutoring but to agree to pay for the sessions as well and so she'd consented to go to the Barlows' house once a week rather than disrupt Alice and Esther at number 5, and she made no fuss when Frank barely spoke to her. She was just thankful that Ida always had some welcoming words of greeting.

She was not surprised, however, to arrive one evening to find Frank waiting in the small hallway with his arms folded and a grim look on his face. Ida, having let her in, was hovering nearby, looking white-faced and subdued.

'Is anything wrong?' Wendy said, concerned that she had walked into the midst of a family row.

'Y-you'd best come in.' It was Ida who spoke and Wendy followed her into the kitchen and sat down where she indicated at the table where Kenneth was already seated.

Frank took over. 'Our Kenneth has something to tell you, haven't you?' He glared at his son who looked genuinely fearful.

'Have you lost some money recently, Miss?' Kenneth said after several seconds of awkward silence.

Wendy frowned. That was not what she had been expecting. 'Well, I did as a matter of fact, and thankfully I've found it again. But how did you know about that?'

A look of relief passed over the young boy's face and he breathed out noisily, not attempting to reply.

'Go on, tell her.' Frank said crossly, nudging Kenneth's shoulder.

'It was that day there was all that fighting in the corridor.'

'I remember,' Wendy said, wondering where this could be leading.

'Me and . . .' he hesitated. 'Me and . . . one of my mates had been thinking about playing a trick on my brother, David. He's in Mr Faulkner's class and we hadn't decided what and – and I don't know what made us do it, really . . .' Kenneth stopped and looked at his father, who scowled and made a 'carry on' gesture with his hand.

'Do what?' Wendy said, though she was beginning to think that she could guess.

'I-I noticed that you hadn't locked your desk . . . so we . . . we looked inside while you went to sort out the fighting and . . . and we saw your purse . . . It suddenly came to me that if we nicked it we could put it in our David's desk and he'd never know where it came from. It was only going to be a joke, really.'

'But you *stole* it,' Frank said angrily.

'We didn't *really* steal it! I always intended to own up if David got into trouble, even if Li . . . my mate didn't want to confess. The thing was that when I was carrying it along to Mr Faulkner's room I realized there was so much money in it that I changed my mind. But we were there by then and it was too late to put it back because the fight was over.'

Wendy felt the blood draining from her face even now as she recalled that stomach churning moment of horror and disbelief when she'd realized that the chara money had gone.

'So what did you do with it?' Wendy's voice was almost reduced to a whisper.

'We dumped it in David's desk then dashed out of the classroom and back to ours and sat down in our seats . . .' His voice trailed to a halt and Frank pushed his shoulder again. 'Get on with the rest of it, we haven't got all night.'

Wendy thought she saw Kenneth's eyes fill and she felt sorry for the boy, but she couldn't trust her voice, so she said nothing.

'I couldn't understand why David had never told anyone. But I couldn't ask him. Then I was worried that he might really get into trouble.' Kenneth's voice suddenly creaked and it was obvious he was having difficulty holding it together. 'Eventually I had to ask him and he said he didn't know anything about it as he'd never seen the purse or the money. But he remembered that Chrissie Jones, who sits next to him, had found a purse in her desk that wasn't hers and she'd handed it in to

Mr Faulkner. We must have put it in the wrong desk.'

'Of course, as soon as he realized Kenneth was really sorry for what he'd done.' It was Ida who spoke up now. 'And he came to tell his dad and me. I think that was a very brave thing to do, don't you, Miss Collins?' Ida leaned over to pat Kenneth's shoulder though he tried his best to bat her hand away.

Wendy paused, having no wish to intervene, and she was grateful she didn't have to respond because Kenneth was continuing his story. 'I never really meant to steal anything, it was only meant to be a joke, I didn't want you to think . . .' Kenneth glanced briefly at Wendy as silent tears made their way down his pink cheeks now. 'I thought David would hand it in and that would be an end to it.'

'We've always brought our boys up to tell the truth,' Ida said emphatically. 'You did the right thing coming to tell us. Isn't that right, Frank?'

Ida beamed in her husband's direction and tried to keep her voice light but Frank was still glowering. 'For goodness' sake, woman, you're making it sound like he did a good deed!' Frank said scornfully.

'Well, in one way he did.' Ida raised her brows. 'At least he owned up.'

'Aye, and he'll take his punishment an' all when we go to see the headmaster.'

Ida gasped, then her eyes filled. 'Don't you think he's been punished enough?' she said. 'He's been worried sick about it ever since it happened, haven't you, love?'

Kenneth nodded his head vigorously but he still refused to look Wendy in the eye. Wendy looked at him fearfully, knowing exactly what the headmaster's punishment would be, but there was nothing she could do. Thank goodness the incident was over – but the matter was now out of her hands.

Chapter 17

'I'll be glad when this Blackpool thing is over.' Wendy stretched her arms and legs as far as she could without falling off the chair and yawned. 'It's beginning to lose its appeal.'

'I'm not surprised,' Esther laughed, 'but at least the money business is all settled now and by this time tomorrow you'll be parading up and down Blackpool's prom like you've never been away, breathing in the fresh air and enjoying yourself.'

'I just hope I can relax enough to be able to do that.' Wendy sounded uncertain.

'You will, I promise,' Esther said. 'I bet by the morning you'll be looking forward to going.'

'You can hardly blame me for blowing hot and

cold, can you?' Wendy said. 'But at least I can laugh about the worst parts now.'

'You never know, play your cards right and you could end up sitting next to Richard all the way as well,' Esther said with a cheeky grin. 'Wouldn't that be a treat? The perfect chance to get to know him.' She looked knowingly in Wendy's direction, but before Wendy could respond there was a loud knock on the front door and Esther got up eagerly and went to answer it. 'Maybe that's him now, wanting to book the actual seat to make sure,' she whispered impishly.

Wendy heard several exclamations followed by girlish giggling and when Esther came back into the room she was followed by a young woman Wendy had never seen before.

'Come and meet Wendy, she's been sharing the house since Ada left.' Esther was speaking over her shoulder. 'This is Lily Longhurst, Wendy,' Esther announced with a wide smile. 'You've probably heard me talk about her, she's Martha's daughter.'

'We were at school together but we haven't seen each other for ages,' Lily said. 'Good to meet you, Wendy.'

Esther moved the cushions, making an extra place available on the couch and her friend sat down.

'I was away during the war in the women's land army, together with Ena's daughter,' Lily explained.

'We were posted down south and I sort of never came back.'

'It's lovely to see you again,' Esther sounded genuinely delighted. 'But what brings you back on this particular weekend when we've not seen you for so long?'

Lily looked embarrassed for a moment before she said, 'My boyfriend, Charlie, was coming home to visit his parents who live not far from here and he made me feel guilty that I hadn't visited my mum for ages, so I decided to come with him. I realized I don't have to spend the entire time with Mum so I thought I'd use the opportunity to pop in and say hello to some of my old friends.'

'That's lovely. It's really good to see you,' Esther said. 'You can come and keep me company tomorrow if you like,' she added without thinking.

Lily shifted uncomfortably. 'I'm afraid I can't do that,' she said. 'My mother has only gone and booked me in to go on some old peoples' outing. She is going to Blackpool for the day with a busload of old fogies and she thought it would be fun to drag me along too. Without asking me, of course, or else I'd have told her that it's the *last* place I want to be.'

Esther laughed at that. 'Don't say that to Wendy, she's one of the organizers.'

'Oops, sorry!' Lily said. 'Didn't mean to offend.'

'Don't worry, I'm not offended,' Wendy said, smiling. 'I prefer to think of it as a Coronation Street outing for all the neighbours, regardless of age. Esther's right, it's not an old peoples' trip at all. It's for anyone who lives round here. We're going to see the illuminations and I believe they used to organize a trip every year from the Street.'

'They certainly did,' Esther said. 'I remember going with them before the war and they were actually quite fun. Maybe you never came, Lily.' Esther sighed. 'Believe it or not, I'd have loved to go this time,' she said with regret. 'My young man's going,' she added, a wistful look crossing her face as she looked away.

Lily frowned. 'So why don't you go? You don't want to be leaving him on his own. I know I wouldn't want to miss an opportunity to have some fun.'

Esther explained the situation about Alice and Lily immediately looked contrite. 'Sorry,' Lily said, 'I didn't realize so much had changed around here. Last time I saw your mum she was up and about, still pretty active and mentally alert . . . ?' She posed this last more as a question than a statement.

'You don't have to worry, she's still all there with her lemon drops, isn't she, Esther?' It was Wendy who responded, though Esther nodded and grinned. 'It's more that she's concerned her heart might give out,' she added.

'I didn't mean to imply . . .' Lily left the remainder unsaid. 'And apologies to you, Wendy, I didn't mean to be rude about the trip; I'm sure you'll all have a great time. I know Blackpool can be a lot of fun so I only hope the weather holds. But Esther, tell me more about your young man. Are you two actually courting?'

'I wouldn't go that far, though I would say we've been stepping out. We see quite a bit of each other on my nights out because he's moved in locally as he works at the new garage.' Esther looked embarrassed as she explained about Arthur, trying not to build their friendship up to sound more than it was. 'He really wants to go on this trip. I don't think he's ever been to Blackpool,' she said finally, 'and naturally he says he'd like me to go with him, but under the circumstances I can't think of leaving Mum for the whole day and evening.' She spread her hands and shrugged but Lily didn't seem to be listening.

'He sounds quite special, this Arthur,' she said, frowning as she retraced a sudden thought. 'It really is a pity if that's the only thing that's stopping you . . .' She hesitated. 'But I've had an idea: why don't we swap places?'

'What do you mean?' Esther looked puzzled.

'I mean, you can take my ticket and go with Arthur, while me and Charlie can stay here and look after your mum without you having to worry.'

Esther looked uncertain. 'Do you really think that could work?' she said. 'No, I can't ask you to do that.'

'Why not? You'll be doing me a favour because that way I get to see Charlie. I haven't actually told Mum about him yet, you see. Besides, you didn't ask me, I'm offering. I know Alice, and hopefully she'll remember me. And I know all about having to be nice to mothers who are unnecessarily demanding, and so does Charlie. Wait till I tell him we can spend the whole day together!'

Wendy smiled when she heard that, remembering how she and Arthur had tried so hard to think of a way to make it possible for Esther to go, and here was Lily offering her the opportunity on a plate. She hadn't yet told Esther that Arthur had paid for a ticket for her to go.

'Imagine how pleased Arthur will be!' Wendy said with a sudden rush of excitement. 'Wait till you tell him, it will be a wonderful surprise.'

Esther still looked uncertain, then she looked at Wendy and then Lily and said decisively, 'All right, I'll go, thanks. That'll really be something to look forward to.' Then she smiled as a new thought came to her and said, 'And as Mum seems to like you so much, Wendy, I'll leave it to you to tell her about the day's arrangements!'

Chapter 18

The chara had been standing outside the Rovers Return since mid-morning and although it looked as if it had been specially cleaned for the occasion the driver gave the windows a final swipe with his chamois leather as he waited for his passengers. The first to arrive were Elsie and Wendy who had left their houses at almost the same time and strolled down the street together. Wendy was carrying her coat over her arm, in case it grew cool or wet towards evening, but now the air was mild for the time of year. With the sun shining brightly and the light fluffy clouds showing no threat of rain it promised to be a really pleasant day. Wendy relaxed as a small crowd began to assemble and she unconsciously scanned their faces, not even realizing that she was looking out for Richard.

Elsie produced the lists of all those who had signed up in advance and ticked off the names as people gradually began to board the bus while Wendy produced her neatly drawn-up accounting sheets to check the outstanding payments that still needed to be collected. There was a lot of chatter and good-natured laughter, and a sense of excited anticipation rippled through the group as the staff of the Rovers came to wave them all off.

Arthur and Esther strolled up together, having left Alice in the care of Lily and Charlie, and they stood grinning at each other incredulously, like cats anticipating a carton of cream. Wendy couldn't help noticing how closely they were standing next to each other, and when he thought no one was looking, Arthur squeezed Esther's hand and held on to it tightly.

Wendy watched as Bessie and Albert Tatlock climbed into their seats, making jokes about their oversized picnic basket that they parked beneath their feet, and through the sparkling windows she could see that Ida and Frank had also claimed seats together although they sat glaring into the distance, neither speaking to the other; their boys were sitting behind them, the only children to have come on the outing. When Ida stood up abruptly and made her way off the bus to talk to Wendy, Frank acted as though he hadn't even noticed.

'I wasn't sure if Kenneth or David were coming. I'd only listed them as provisional,' Wendy said as they stood together on the pavement.

Ida tutted. 'There was no way I was leaving them at home after what Kenneth did,' she said with a sigh, looking to where the two boys were already squabbling over who should sit next to the window. 'So I've come to settle up,' Ida said, 'hopefully before they kill each other.'

Wendy laughed.

'I insisted that they both came with us,' Ida said as she counted out the change into Wendy's hand, 'though needless to say Frank was against the idea.' Ida lowered her voice and Wendy couldn't help chuckling as she watched the boys continuing to tussle. 'He thought they should have stayed at home and we should have got someone to look after them,' Ida said, 'whereas I think it's a far more effective punishment for Kenneth to come with us.'

Wendy looked at her in surprise and raised her eyebrows like question marks.

'Instead of having his friend Lionel with him as we'd originally promised,' Ida explained, 'it'll be Kenneth's job to look after David all day and I'm sure he'll love that!' she said gleefully, with obvious sarcasm. 'But it will do him no harm to take some responsibility for a change – and Frank too, for that matter.'

Wendy looked at her startled.

'Oh yes,' Ida said, 'Frank's in for a big surprise if he did but know it.' At that, Ida giggled like a schoolgirl despite trying to keep a straight face. 'Because if he thinks I'm going to spend the day watching out for them, then he has another think coming. That's going to be *his* job today.' Ida chuckled. 'Only I haven't told *him* yet.'

'And where will you be?' Wendy asked.

'I'll be with you girls, enjoying myself, I hope,' Ida said.

Wendy stared at her. 'You mean Frank *really* doesn't know what you're planning?'

'Not yet, and I'm trusting you,' Ida said, her finger on her lips. 'I thought I'd save that little gem until we get there. I know I'm taking a bit of a risk because I'm banking on him not wanting to make a scene in public when he realizes, but I think it's worth the gamble. Wish me luck.' She held both her hands in the air with her fingers crossed and, with her eyes twinkling to match her smile, Ida reboarded the bus.

Ena Sharples had commandeered the two front seats, sliding across to sit by the window and parking her picnic basket under the aisle seat where she indicated that Minnie should sit. She directed Martha to sit behind them and Martha waited until Ida had reboarded before she too retraced her steps and got off the bus to speak to Wendy.

'I'm so glad our Lily was able to help out,' she said a little stiffly. 'Alice is obviously not strong enough to be able to make such a journey – though I see Esther's wasted no time getting herself otherwise entangled.' She gave a tight cough and a disparaging nod to where Arthur and Esther were engaged in a very private-looking conversation. 'Of course, Lily was really sorry not to be coming on the trip with us, but I told her she's probably done a really good deed helping out an old a friend like that.'

'It was very, very kind of her to offer.' Wendy hid a smile. 'Both Esther and I appreciate it. I'm sure you know how difficult it is for us to get out together.'

'I told her that,' Martha said. 'Of course, I'd have preferred she'd spent the day with me instead of being alone with Alice all day, but I'm sure she'll be fine.' And with a smug smile, Martha went back to her seat.

A steady stream of people arrived after that and Elsie ticked them off her list with a satisfied smile until there were only a few seats remaining.

'I've marked off two seats for me and George,' Elsie said to Wendy, 'but what about you, where are you going to sit?' She glanced down her list. 'I thought Richard was supposed to be coming.'

'Yes, he was,' Wendy said.

'Well, I haven't checked him off yet, but I suppose there's still time. Do you want me to put you down for two together?'

'I can't think what's happened to him,' Wendy said. 'He told me only the other day how much he was looking forward to it.' She felt the disappointment take root deep in the pit of her stomach.

'Oh no, apologies, I spoke too soon. Here he is now,' Elsie said and Wendy looked up with relief to finally see Richard striding down the street. She smiled at Elsie and made a signal that she should put two crosses on the last of the double seats. As he approached, she felt her heart beginning to race in anticipation at the thought that she would at last have the luxury of his company for two uninterrupted hours and she stepped forward to greet him. But then, to her horror, she saw a familiar figure pounding up the street behind him, breathlessly calling, 'Richard, wait for me, I'm coming too!'

Wendy stepped back and Denise Unwin stopped, panting heavily, while Richard turned to look behind him in surprise.

'I'm not too late, am I?' Denise was breathing hard, her intermittent breaths being expelled in short gasps.

'I didn't know you were coming,' Richard said politely. 'What made you think of it?'

'The lady at the Mission of Glad Tidings,' she said eventually when she got her breathing under control, 'Mrs Sharples. She mentioned after the service on Sunday that there were a few tickets going spare. Said I could pay you on the day, Wendy.' Denise cocked her head to one side and pulled her purse out of her handbag.

'Well, yes, you're in luck.' Elsie came over to join them. 'There are a couple of seats available,' she said and she took Denise's name and address. 'You can pay your money to Wendy.'

'I've never seen the illuminations,' Denise said as Wendy handed her a receipt, 'and as it wasn't raining I thought I would come. It seemed like a good opportunity for a fun day out.'

She beamed up at Richard as she said that and he looked at Wendy and raised his eyebrows as if to apologize.

They both hesitated for a fraction of a second, but Wendy could think of nothing to rescue the situation as Denise linked her arm through Richard's and, boarding the bus alongside him, led the way to the last of the double seats. Richard cast his eyes back towards Wendy and for a brief moment, she could have wept with frustration.

'What happened there, then?' Elsie asked quietly when Wendy was left on the pavement alone. 'From where I was standing it seemed you were a bit slow on the uptake, if you don't mind my saying.'

Wendy made a little shake of her head, unable to hide her disappointment.

'You know, if you fancy him, you'll really need to watch out for that one,' Elsie said. 'And don't say I didn't warn you. There's no doubt what *she's* after, so you'll need to get in there first, next time.' Elsie shook her head. 'I don't like the way she looks at him with those pleading puppy-dog eyes. She might as well have long floppy ears for him to tickle cos he seemed to fall for it!'

Wendy shoulders sagged resignedly and she didn't reply, though she couldn't help a smile at Elsie's comparison.

'I'm telling you, chuck,' Elsie said, 'if you've a mind to hang up your hat there, then you'll have to look lively.'

'Talking of hanging up your hat, where's George?' Wendy said, eager to change the subject and she was pleased when that made Elsie laugh.

'I hope he's not forgotten because he still owes me for the ticket,' Elsie said. 'I broke my golden rule and laid out the money when he asked me to.'

'Oh dear! Then it *would* be a shame if he didn't turn up,' Wendy said.

'I haven't seen him all week, come to think of it,' Elsie said. 'He said he'd probably be working in

Derbyshire, closer to home, so he reckoned it might not be worth coming to Weatherfield during the week, but let's hope he's not forgotten about today cos I can see the driver's chomping at the bit and won't want to hang about. He's already said that if we don't leave soon he can't promise that we'll be able to stick to our schedule.

Just then there was a loud shout and Wendy spotted George waving from the street corner at the far end of the road. But it wasn't the normally dapper young man that she saw, George looked as if he'd spent the night in his suit and she was shocked to see that he was weaving back and forth, doing a good imitation of a soft-shoe shuffle, occasionally tripping on the cobbles and singing noisily on breath that reeked of booze as he drew nearer.

Elsie pretended not to notice as she grabbed hold of George's hand and she laughed instead as she pushed him on board and signalled to the driver that the last passenger had arrived. They made their way slowly down the aisle, arguing loudly about which of them owed the other money, only moving on when the rest of the passengers urged them to keep their quarrel to themselves. Wendy trailed behind them, leaving the driver to check that the door was shut tightly, and as he cranked up the engine she made her way towards the back to sit on one of the long benches among a group of residents she barely knew, in what was the last of the vacant seats.

Chapter 19

The roads were quiet so they had a smooth journey and, despite the driver's warnings, managed to arrive in central Blackpool roughly on schedule. The driver parked the bus on a large piece of waste ground not far from Central Pier where there were already several other charas and coaches lined up down the middle and by the time he let them off it was close to dinner-time. Most of them had already eaten their sandwiches and were ready to look for a drink, the men in search of a pint while the women preferred to look for some little café or tearoom, the kind that they remembered from before the war.

'Make sure you take everything you need with you because I'll be locking her up,' the driver said while everyone stretched their legs and gathered up their belongings. 'You've got the whole day to do whatever you want but please make a note of where the bus is parked because we'll all need to meet back here no later than half past eight. I say that especially to the kiddies. If you do go off on your own, make sure you know where to meet up with your mum and dad later or else you'll have to ask for the Lost Children's Tent that's down on the beach. We'll need to be setting off promptly and won't want to waste time looking for you.' If you don't manage to see all the lights before we meet up again, don't fret, because we'll be taking a turn up and down the sea front to see owt you might have missed before we go home.'

'What time do the lights come on, please?' Minnie Caldwell asked, and this time Elsie replied.

'Don't worry, Mrs Caldwell,' she said, 'they come on about five-ish when it starts to get dark so you'll have plenty of time to see everything before then. But as the driver says, we'll need to leave here no later than half past eight if we don't want to be too late back. So, whatever you do,' Elsie raised her voice to make sure everyone could hear, 'don't any of you be late cos I promise you the driver says he'll leave you behind; and I for one believe him.'

There was a general buzz while everyone talked over the arrangements, who was going to meet who, where and what they would do if anyone got lost, although no one seemed to take seriously the driver's threat about leaving them behind. Eventually Elsie yelled above the hubbub, 'Have a good time everyone and we'll see you all back here, half past eight sharp!' And as the men began to disembark she added, 'All the women who fancy a cup of tea can stick with me cos Wendy's going to show us the best place in town.'

Wendy felt her cheeks colour. 'If it's still there,' she said, leading the way off the bus.

'And all the men ready for a pint can follow Frank,' Ida called, as she started down the steps behind Wendy, 'cos I'm sure he must know the finest pubs hereabouts,' and everyone but Frank laughed. 'Oh, and by the way, Frank . . .' Ida moved close to her husband and spoke softly and confidentially now, 'I'm relying on you to keep an eye out for the boys.' She gave him a beaming smile as they stood together at the bottom of the steps and she watched without comment as Frank's smile quickly faded.

'Don't look so worried,' Ida said light-heartedly, 'they'll mostly look after themselves. As you know, Kenneth can be very responsible when he puts his mind to it. Besides, I'll give them a few bob for the slot machines and maybe the crazy golf or whatever, so they'll be all right on their own for a bit. And I'm sure they'll be fine with a lemonade out in the pub garden when they're actually with you. Whichever way, you might want to check on them from time to time, and make sure that they don't eat too much candy floss.'

Frank looked at her, astonished. 'But you can't expect—' he started to say and Ida laughed. 'Well, I'm going off with the ladies and you can hardly expect boys of that age to hang around with their mummy all day, now can you? They'd never live it down.'

Wendy overheard and turned away, pressing her lips tightly together to stop herself giggling while Ida ruffled the boys' hair. 'Be good but enjoy yourselves lads,' she said to them, 'and make sure you stick with your dad cos he'll be watching out for you. In the meantime,' she added, taking Kenneth's hand, 'here's some coppers for the slot machines on the pier and make sure you share them with David.'

'Can we have some candy floss?' was the first thing she heard David say as Kenneth was counting out the pennies and halfpennies to see how much they had to spend.

'We'll see,' Kenneth said, 'but you can have this for now.' And she saw him give his brother a handful of farthings. 'We'll have some cockles and whelks and maybe some jellied eels later on, if you like.' Kenneth rubbed his hands together and licked his lips though David looked at him uncertainly.

Then they skipped off in the same direction as the men without bothering to turn or wave goodbye to Ida.

As Wendy stepped down from the coach she knew immediately she was within a stone's throw of the sea and tears came to her eyes as she breathed in deeply the familiar smells of her childhood. The air was fresh and salty with the tang of ozone that caught at the back of her throat as she filled her lungs, each inhalation bringing back a different memory of home and her family. This was what she had missed. She allowed herself several moments of nostalgia. She couldn't believe that she had stayed away so long. The gentle breeze was cool and refreshing without any strength to it and as she stepped away from the bus her eyes filled as she heard the sound of the waves lapping the sandy beach. She blinked hard as she gazed into the distance and she saw that Esther and Arthur had already peeled away from the main group, preferring to enjoy the day on their own.

She sighed as she watched them wander off together – and before they turned the corner to head towards the promenade she noticed that they were already holding hands. For a moment Wendy wished that Richard was with her, but she realized she hadn't seen him since they'd first set out. Her only consolation was that since they'd arrived, Richard had been ushered away to the pub by the men he played darts with at the Rovers, leaving Denise to hover uncertainly on the fringe of the ladies' group that hadn't yet departed. The rest of the passengers had already dispersed and Wendy was surprised to see Denise attach herself to Ida who was plainly with Bessie Tatlock, Ena, Minnie and Martha, as they began to drift away.

Elsie linked her arm through Wendy's as they watched the driver lock up the coach and walk purposefully away towards the narrow streets of terraced houses that seemed to have tumbled together behind the pier.

'Penny for them?' Elsie said. 'Or can I guess?'

Wendy gave an enigmatic shrug. 'I don't know, can you?' she said with a laugh.

Elsie gave her arm a squeeze. 'Never mind Richard for the moment. Now is not the time. I've had to let George go off too and I hope they don't bring him back in a worse state than he already is. I'm amazed he got here at all this morning cos he didn't remember that he owes me the money for the ticket.' She sighed. 'Never mind, no doubt we'll catch up with them later. In the meantime, just because he can't hold his liquor is no reason for us not to enjoy ourselves.'

'That's what we're here for,' Wendy said though

with a slight edge to her voice as she thought about Denise.

'First things first,' Elsie said. 'Let's go catch up with the others and then we can find this café that you've been telling us about. My stomach thinks my throat's been cut for want of a cuppa.' Elsie giggled. 'And then I suggest we go to the Tower while there's still plenty of daylight. I fully intend to go up to the top,' and she linked her arm through Wendy's, following her as she led the way to the Golden Mile between the North and South Piers.

Chapter 20

When they emerged onto the sea front from the café Wendy had taken them to after a welcome pot of tea, it was as if the freshness of the air had been overtaken by the more pungent smells of cooking. Elsie licked her finger and held it up in the air.

'What on earth are you doing?' Wendy laughed. 'Trying to guess what's on the menu? So far, I can smell at least three different types of seafood not to mention tripe and onions and fish and chips in batter. Anything else?'

'You daft ha'p'orth!' Elsie said. 'I'm checking the strength of the wind to see if it's safe to go up the Tower.'

'Don't worry, they won't let us up if the wind's too

strong,' Wendy said, 'though it is supposed to have a bit of a sway, you know, that's perfectly normal.'

'Hmm, I'm not so sure . . .' Elsie said.

'I'm more concerned about the colour of that sky.' Wendy looked up to see the blue disappearing as an ominous-looking greyness was rapidly replacing the original fluffy white puff balls of cloud.

'They do say that on a clear day you can see Liverpool and even the Isle of Man,' Elsie said.

'I know,' Wendy said, 'though I'm afraid I never have. And if this spreads any more you won't either, for the view from the top could be wiped out altogether.'

'Do you think we should tell the others where we're going, in case any of them wants to come with us?' Elsie said, indicating the rest of their group who were now some way ahead; 'Though I'm afraid that might mean that Richard's young lady would have to be included.'

Wendy frowned and turned sharply to stare at Elsie. 'What makes you call her that?'

'Sorry, I couldn't think of what else to call her. At least, not until you get off your backside and change things.' Elsie giggled mischievously. 'She certainly outmanoeuvred you this morning; the poor lad didn't know which way to turn.'

'Are you serious?' Wendy said somewhat haughtily, knowing inside that Elsie was goading her to do something, but not wanting to play along. 'I didn't think he found it too difficult to choose who to sit next to, at all. In fact, I'm beginning to change my mind about him.'

Elsie looked at her sceptically. 'We used to have a saying in our house when I was a kid about throwing out the baby with the bathwater. I hope you're not thinking of doing that,' Elsie said. 'I know you've been badly hurt in the past but think carefully before you do anything rash. I think you've got the makings of a good fella there and, whatever you might think, I'm telling you he fancies you.'

'Well, he's got a funny way of showing it, that's all I can say.' Wendy said, indignantly.

'You'll have to play your cards right, but whatever you do, you can't just give in,' Elsie said. Then she stopped and, cupping her hand around her mouth, called out, 'We're going this way!' She pointed towards the Tower as she shouted to the group up ahead who were about to turn the corner and disappear from view. 'We're going to go up the Tower if anyone's interested,' she yelled.

They all waved in acknowledgement but Ida and Denise were the only ones to make a move towards them, and she and Wendy slowed their pace to allow them to catch up.

'Do the men always stay separate from the women like this?' Denise was looking directly at Elsie as approached and she sounded disappointed.

Elsie shrugged. 'I suppose they do, though I've never really thought about it.'

'I've thought about it,' Ida said, 'and I can assure you that I wouldn't want it any other way.'

'Why's that?' asked Denise. 'I'd have thought it would be more fun sticking together.'

'But we *are* together.' Ida sounded incredulous. 'With our friends. And believe me, it's so much more fun *not* having to trail after our other halves as they prop up one bar after another.'

'And not having to listen to them moaning that we're walking too slowly or stopping too often when all we're trying to do is a spot of window shopping,' Elsie added.

'At least this way we all get to do what we want to do, wouldn't you agree, Elsie?' Ida said.

Elsie nodded heartily. 'But don't think you have to stick like glue to us, love,' she said looking directly at Denise. 'Feel free to go off on your own at any time you'd like. So long as you're back in good time for the chara to go home, the day's yours.'

Ida nodded her agreement. 'Like Ena and her cronies going off with Bessie Tatlock,' she said, and she looked about her even though it was obvious the others were nowhere to be seen. 'We all chose to go off in our separate ways.' She spread her hands as if to underline that she'd proved her point.

'Exactly,' Elsie said.

'For my part, I relish having a bit of independence from my husband,' Ida said, 'fond as I am of him.' She raised her eyebrows and gave Elsie a look. 'I can see my Frank any day of the week so why would I want to be with him all day when we're on an outing and I'd rather be with my friends?' And with that Ida laughed out loud.

Wendy had been to the Tower many times as a child and she had never tired of it. But recently there had been a gap of several years and she wondered if much had changed since her last visit.

'You get a proper view of the whole thing if you stand on the other side of the road,' she called out to the others and she almost skipped across the main road, grateful that the traffic was light. She wove her way over the cobbles and between the tramlines, carefully avoiding the trams that clanked along the front, heading south towards the Pleasure Beach and Squires Gate and north in the direction of Norbreck and Cleveleys. She barely noticed the strings of light bulbs that festooned the vehicles and lamp-posts or the huge storyboards speckled with light bulbs that stood beside the tracks and lined the pavements. They would come into their own later. For now, she stood on the promenade with her back to the sea and stared at the magnificent structure that stood before her on the opposite side of the road. She shielded her eyes from the residue of brightness as she stared skyward. There was no doubt the Victorian structure was an architectural masterpiece, with its four sturdy legs that formed the base and the three-storey redbrick frontage of the entertainment complex. Somehow it had managed to survive the war and, even more amazingly, it looked almost as good as new.

Wendy was suddenly overwhelmed by thoughts of her family and caught her breath as she remembered how she and her brother would pretend that the giant from Jack and the Beanstalk lived at the very top of the Tower, and each time they would beg their mum and dad to take them up in the lift to see him. For a moment Wendy believed she was holding on to her brother's hand and that it was her mother's eyes she was gazing into, then she realized that it was Elsie Tanner who had crossed the road with her and she quickly removed her hand from Elsie's arm with an embarrassed smile.

'When I was a little girl I used to think the top of the Tower actually pierced through the clouds and touched the sky on the other side,' Wendy said when her breathing had settled back to normal.

Elsie sighed. 'I only ever saw pictures of it at the cinema when they'd show holidaymakers enjoying themselves on the beach every summer. I didn't know what to make of it. I'd never seen anything quite so big. But we couldn't afford to come to places like this when I was a lass,' she said, her voice wistful. 'I never saw the sea till after I was wed and I went on my first Coronation Street outing. Ironic that my husband was in the navy during the war.'

The two stood in silence for a moment, wrapped up in their own memories.

'I always used to say that it was the closest I'd ever get to Paris,' Wendy said eventually and she gave a little laugh. 'Whenever we came here my brother and I used to pretend to talk French to each other, though it was rubbish really, neither of us had a clue . . .' She stopped and had to turn away as her eyes misted once more.

When they reached the Tower there were so many people – concerned-looking adults and overexcited children – milling about on the concourse that Ida immediately opted to join the queue for the next lift up to the top to escape the throngs before the area got too crowded. She could hear muted animal noises in the background, although she couldn't see where they were coming from, and she could hear a band playing what sounded like the last remaining bars of a repetitive chorus, followed by some fading applause.

'I'll come with you,' Denise volunteered, while Elsie said quickly, 'I think I'd rather have a look around here first. I want to soak up the atmosphere cos it feels like so much fun. I'll go up a bit later. I presume we have to pay?'

'You have to pay for everything separately, tickets are over there at the box office,' Wendy said. 'With all these people coming out I'd say it looks like we've missed the early performance of the circus, so that probably won't be on again until this evening

'I love a circus,' Elsie said, 'but I've not seen one for years. Is this one any good?'

'If the posters are anything to go by most things are pretty much as I remember them and they were always pretty good. They still seem to have a whole menagerie of animals, lots of acrobats, riders, and I see Charlie Cairoli who's brilliant is still the resident clown. From the looks of it, nothing much has changed since before the war!'

'To be honest,' Elsie said, 'I'm far more interested in seeing the ballroom. I love a spot of ballroom dancing and I've always dreamed of coming here.'

'That would be wonderful – all we have to do is to get tickets,' Wendy agreed.

'We're hardly dressed for a dance,' Elsie protested.

'I don't think that matters,' Wendy said. 'I think we can get tickets to go in and have a look around. Shall we do that?' Wendy suddenly felt quite excited. 'It's a long time since I've actually been inside that part.'

They got the lift to the third floor where it stopped near the entrance to the ballroom and Wendy pulled open the gilded doors and peered into the magnificently stylish space, full of elegance and charm, beckoning Elsie to follow her.

'Oh, wow! This is even more beautiful than I imagined,' Elsie said, her voice echoing as she let the door swing shut. 'It's amazing.' She inched forward past the ring of seating that bordered the dancing area until she was able to step gingerly onto the dance floor. Then, confidence growing, she took several bolder steps forwards. 'When they say it's well sprung they mean well sprung! It's like a mattress. Oh, I'd love to dance on here.'

'Dance or lie down and have a snooze?' Wendy asked, and they both burst out laughing. Elsie advanced into the auditorium which had several tiered levels of balconies and a huge dancing area that could double as a stage.

'Talk about glitz and glamour!' Elsie said. 'Have you ever seen anything like it?'

Wendy shook her head. 'When we were kids, if we went to a show, it would be one of those at the end-of-the-pier things, or at the Winter Gardens. Nothing so grand as this. Just look at those amazing chandeliers. Do you think they're real crystal?'

'I don't know,' Elsie said. 'I've never been anywhere like this before. I'm afraid it puts the Ritz in

Manchester in the shade and I'd always thought that was posh. I wish we had time to bring the others here. I think a trip might be called for to see a special show here.' Elsie was in awe.

'Well, it seems we can do that and we can bring our men, but the men can't come here without us,' Wendy said with a giggle. 'Do you see what it says up there?' She pointed to where a sign on one of the balconies read *Gentlemen may not dance unless with a lady* and Wendy spluttered with laughter as she read it out loud. 'How strange that it doesn't say anything about women not dancing unless with a gentleman.'

'They're obviously very particular about who they let in. I mean, look at this one,' Elsie said, pointing her finger further along the balcony. '*Disorderly conduct means immediate expulsion* – it sounds like they're pretty strict with certain rules at least.'

'I bet they don't let you in if they think you're dressed scruffily either,' Wendy said, 'even if they do say they don't have a dress code.'

'What, you mean like George today? I certainly won't be bringing him to a place like this unless he learns to behave. But I don't mind getting dressed up,' Elsie said. 'Any excuse, you know me. I could get Ida or Bessie to run me up a little something that's charming and elegant, like this whole place,' she said in a pseudo-posh voice. And she flung out her arms and did some fancy tapping steps and twirls as if she was a ballet dancer. Then she stopped and gazed about her. 'What are you looking at now, Wendy?'

'I was thinking that I don't recognize the name of the current resident dance band, do you? But look at that magnificent electric organ. Isn't that amazing? It's a Wurlitzer – they're very famous. Did you know this one was specially built for Reginald Dixon?'

'Who's he when he's at home?' Elsie asked.

'Him I do know. He was the regular organist here when I was a little girl, and from what it says over there he still is.'

'It looks twice the size of the organ I saw once in the Odeon cinema in Manchester.' Elsie's eyes were wide. 'And what are all these names?' she said. 'They seem to be dotted about all over the place.'

Wendy followed her gaze. 'I believe they're the names of classical composers. There's supposed to be sixteen of them, from what I remember reading.'

'Well,' Elsie said, 'all I can say is I'm really glad we came here; it was well worth the tanner for the ticket. It's an incredible place and I'm glad I've seen it. But perhaps we'd better go and see whether there's still a queue for the lift so that we can go to the top? We need to get up there while there's still enough daylight for it to be worthwhile.'

'Yes, you're right,' Wendy said. 'Though I could carry on looking around here for ages. But if we go now maybe this time I'll be lucky and we'll find the giant is at home.' She laughed as she pointed in the direction of the sky and she held the door ajar for Elsie.

Ida and Denise stepped out of the lift that had come down from the top and waved at Wendy and Elsie who were waiting to board it to ride back up.

'What's it like up there?' Elsie asked them eagerly. 'Was it worth a tanner?'

'Definitely,' Denise said. 'I'd happily pay another sixpence to go up again. I loved the sensation of it swaying back and forth.

Ida was less enthusiastic. 'For my money, it was very disappointing,' she admitted. 'On a day like this I'm afraid there's really very little to see, even though they tell you what to look for in every direction. But it was too overcast and there were only odd flashes of bright sunlight. I was hoping I might have seen Frank and the boys down on the pavement. The last time I saw the men they were disappearing into a pub but I didn't have the satisfaction of seeing them come out.'

'Never mind,' Elsie said, 'we've already paid our money and we might be able to see something. We only want to see the giant, anyway.' She said this with a laugh and both Ida and Denise looked puzzled.

'What giant?' Ida asked.

'It was nothing, just a private joke,' Elsie said, looking at Wendy and giggling.'

As the lift slowly rose all they could see was the intricate structure of tons of iron works until they alighted at the top onto the glass-panelled platform. By some miracle, when they reached the top the clouds separated for long enough for Wendy to point out the general direction of Fleetwood that lay to the north and the resort of Lytham St Annes that lay to the south, but it was disappointing that the clouds crowded in as she was trying to pinpoint the nearby beauty spots of the Trough of Bowland and the Lake District.

'When it's like this you can't even see the promenade or the Irish Sea and they're almost immediately beneath us if you can bear to look down,' Wendy said with a laugh, and that was when she realized that Elsie was not responding. 'Elsie, she said, 'are you all right?' Wendy went to shake her friend's arm, but she could see at a glance that Elsie's face had turned a pale shade of green.

'I can't bear to look anywhere and I certainly can't look down,' Elsie said, her voice suddenly thick. 'I need to get back to ground level as quickly as possible.' She took a deep breath. 'It's no wonder I've never tried to come up here before. I must have known what it would do to my stomach without having to actually test it out.'

'Oh dear.' Wendy was sympathetic. 'No, of course you mustn't look down if you're feeling sick. You'd be better off closing your eyes and holding on to my hand. I think the next lift will be going down very soon,' she said. Wendy grasped hold of Elsie with one hand while she rummaged in her bag for a handkerchief.

'I wish I hadn't had that cup of tea,' Elsie whispered, 'or eaten those humbug rock pillows so soon after my sandwiches.' She moaned softly and, grabbing the clean square of linen Wendy proffered, held it to her mouth.

'Never mind worrying about that now, don't even think about food. Just take very deep breaths,' Wendy whispered back while those who were standing nearby were obviously doing their best to take a step away.

Elsie clung on grimly, without speaking, and somehow they made it down to the ground floor without further incident. As the doors opened, Elsie rushed out onto the pavement, trying to avoid the crowds and doing her best not to run into the horses with their Victorian carriage attachments that were lined up by the kerb, waiting to sweep visitors off for a trot up and down the prom. She gulped in large lungsful of fresh air before she turned to Wendy.

'Well, that was a complete waste of money! I'm so sorry,' Elsie said when she was finally able to talk. 'I had no idea I was going to feel like that.'

Wendy shrugged. 'It's not important,' she said, 'so long as you're feeling better.'

'I'll be fine in a minute. I wish you could have stayed up there longer because I was so sure the giant was at home today,' Elsie quipped.

Wendy chuckled. 'We'll never know. But honestly, you don't have to worry about me,' she said, 'I've seen the sights before. It was you who so wanted to go.'

'I must say I'm feeling much better now that I'm back on solid ground,' Elsie said. 'Remind me never to try anything that involves being lifted even that much from the ground.' She indicated an inch between her index finger and thumb.

'Does that mean I won't be able to tempt you onto the Big Dipper?' Wendy said with a grin.

'I think I'll leave the entire Pleasure Beach alone for now, thank you very much. Though that doesn't have to stop you going. And maybe we can hunt out some of the others to go with you. But even thinking about it could make me throw up right now.'

'Sorry, I won't mention it again,' Wendy said. 'I don't want to spoil the rest of the day now, do I? At least the rain has held off, so maybe we should head north instead and see what else, or who else, we can find.'

Chapter 21

They strolled along at a leisurely pace, stopping to gaze longingly at the ladies' fashions that were displayed in several of the shop windows, even though the prices were out of their league.

'Wow!' Elsie said. 'Unless I come into some serious money soon, I think I'll stick with Bessie and Ida to supply my wardrobe.'

Wendy sighed. 'I was just thinking the same thing,' she said and they walked on.

Wendy paused briefly to stare into the large window of a sweet shop where a young lad was piling layers of sugar candy together which he then rolled down with the flat of his hand until the whole thing had been flattened to a manageable thickness. When it looked like one continuous pink sausage, he began to snip it carefully into measured lengths of saleable-sized sticks of rock, showing his audience how the word Blackpool appeared all the way through every stick before they were whipped away to be individually wrapped.

Elsie, however, wasn't interested in sweets and she walked on, lost in her own thoughts not realizing that Wendy was no longer with her until she heard her running to catch up.

'Do you fancy stopping for another cup of tea?' Elsie asked. 'I think I'm about ready to cope with that.'

'I'd love one, if you really think you're OK. Has your stomach settled?' Wendy asked warily.

'So long as I don't attempt to do anything too wild or exciting afterwards, I think I'll survive,' Elsie assured her.

'I wonder what happened to the others? They all seem to have disappeared,' Wendy said.

'Yes, I'm surprised we haven't bumped into anyone we know,' Elsie agreed.

They stopped outside an open-fronted shop where the window had been wound down, their attention caught by a man's voice ringing out what sounded like some kind of announcements.

'Kelly's eye, number one; rise and shine, twenty-nine; legs eleven.'

His voice was relentless and he paused only long enough between each number for the women sitting at the tables that filled the room to studiously mark off those that were on the cards laid out in front of them. Some only had one card and they looked fairly relaxed, but others had several carefully lined up and their eyes anxiously scanned every figure, looking more and more tense as each number was called.

'Gosh! I've not played bingo in ages,' Elsie said and stared into the room, fascinated.

'Fancy a go now?' Wendy asked. 'It's not much for a single card.'

'No thanks, I don't think so. Not right now at any rate,' Elsie said. Then she looked at Wendy. 'Did you used to play or is that another one of those "little differences" between us?' she asked as the man called out, 'Two fat ladies, eighty-eight; five oh, five oh and it's off to work we go' and Elsie almost doubled over with laughter.

Suddenly there was a shout of 'housey-housey' and Wendy thought she recognized the voice. She certainly recognized the face, for it was easy to pick out the tall figure of Denise Unwin as she stood up and waved her card in the air. Ida was sitting next to her, looking equally excited; Bessie Tatlock, who was on the other side of Denise, had an exasperated expression on her face as she whispered beneath her breath, 'I only had one more number to get!'

The caller sent someone over to scrutinize Denise's card and there was a sharp tension in the air among several of the contestants who also claimed to have 'only one more number to get'. Eventually the scrutineer nodded her approval and took the card away for final independent verification. It took several minutes but eventually Denise was handed a large envelope containing a crisp, white five-pound note that she was obliged to hold up to show to the other punters and she joined in the clapping that rippled through the room.

'Get your cards here, ladies, a brand-new game is about to begin,' the caller invited, beckoning to Elsie and Wendy, but Ida and Bessie had already stood up to leave and Denise soon followed them.

There was an awkward moment as they stood together outside and Wendy heard the caller's voice again, 'Eyes down for a knock at the door, number four, thirteen unlucky for some.'

'We didn't mean to break up your game – why don't you carry on?' Wendy apologized. 'We were looking for a café for a sit down and only saw you by chance.'

'I think we'd all had enough,' Bessie said, 'and we'd won as much as we were going to win, which in my case meant I got a card for a free go cos I filled in one line.'

'And I'm afraid I didn't win anything quite so grand

as a five-pound note either,' Ida said, 'and I didn't even get a free card although I had a single line as well. But I'd like you to share in what I did win, Elsie.' As she spoke, she whipped out a cheap black cowboy-style hat from behind her back and, with a chuckle, dropped it on top of Elsie's soft auburn curls.

'Yes, I'm right,' Ida said, stepping back to admire Elsie's new headgear. 'It suits you far better than it suits me. Please accept it with my compliments. And promise me you'll wear it for the rest of the day.'

'Well, thank you, Ida, I don't see any reason not to do that.' Elsie took it off her head to examine it. 'Or maybe I do,' she said and she laughed out loud when she saw that the bright yellow label on the front read, *Kiss me Quick*.

'I don't think my Frank would appreciate the humour if I dared to wear it, do you?' Ida said with a laugh.

'No, I can see how that might be pushing your luck,' Elsie said, putting the hat back on. 'But with my luck at the moment, George won't even notice I've got it on.'

'I've never won anything in my whole life before!' Denise was still excited by her monetary prize and she waved the five-pound note in front of Wendy as they made a U-turn and walked slowly back towards the Tower. 'And I've certainly never seen one of these before, have you?'

'What are you going to do with it?' Elsie asked innocently.

'I haven't decided yet,' Denise said. 'But it will have to be something special. I'll ask Richard, see what he thinks.'

'You could have a whole new wardrobe of clothes made by your very own dressmakers,' Ida joked.

'Now there's a thought.' Denise seemed to consider it. 'Or I could go on a splendid holiday.'

'Pity it's not quite enough to give up work and retire,' Elsie said with a giggle and Wendy laughed, for she'd been thinking the same thing but didn't like to say it.

They were having so much fun speculating as they continued along the prom that they hardly noticed it was slowly getting dark until they came to the Tower and realized that the beach front of the huge structure was already lit up. Neither did they notice the men in the increasing gloom until Albert Tatlock's familiar voice called out to them.

'You don't want to know us any more, is that it?' he shouted. 'And you can't even accuse us of being drunk – well, maybe some of us.'

He was sitting on a bench with the others clustered about him, deep in some serious discussion, while Frank Barlow was pacing back and forth on the pavement in front of them, frowning and looking extremely agitated.

'Thank goodness! Am I glad to see you, love, the boys have gone missing!' he called as soon as Ida came within hailing distance. Ida stared at him in disbelief as he grasped hold of her arm. 'We were just trying to decide where it was best to go look for them.'

'What do you mean, they've gone missing?' Ida snapped, all her earlier bravado gone. 'Didn't you set up a meeting place before you let them wander off on their own? Which way did they go?'

'Of course we agreed where we'd meet them, and I told them how to get there. I also told them the name of the pub we were going to end up at, if they missed us.' Frank sounded irritated as he pointed to the pub behind them. 'But we've been here half an hour already and they haven't shown up yet,' he ended miserably.

'They stuck with us for a bit and they came to the first pub we went to and sat out in the garden,' Albert Tatlock volunteered brightly, 'but they got fed up after a bit and I don't know which way they went after that.' His voice trailed off and he sat back, deflated.

'And you haven't seen them since?' Ida's face was pale as she confronted Frank while Bessie and Elsie squeezed her hands tight. Ida was doing her best to keep her voice calm but it was plain to hear that she was only partly succeeding.

'You know, half an hour late is not that long for kids getting involved in things like games or slot machines.' It was Richard who spoke up now and Wendy was impressed by how calm and authoritative his voice sounded as he faced the frantic parents.

'Our Kenneth is usually very particular about being punctual,' Frank said, shaking his head. 'And one good thing is that he doesn't panic easily.'

'Hmm . . .' Richard looked thoughtful, then he turned to Ida. 'Did they have some money on them?'

Ida nodded. 'I gave Kenneth some coppers for them to share on the slot machines, or anything else they might fancy, but it wasn't a lot. I mean, how long could it have lasted?'

'Hard to say.' It was Elsie who joined in now. 'If it was my Dennis, no time at all, but they might have lost track of time if they had a winning streak in the middle. I know my son would never let go until he'd ploughed every last farthing of his winnings back again.'

Ida smiled at her gratefully. 'I imagine Kenneth would do that too.'

'And if I know anything about him,' Wendy tried to reassure Ida, 'he'll take his responsibilities very seriously and he'll at least be looking after David, you wait and see.' But her concern grew when she saw Ida tearing up.

Richard's voice broke into the conversation once

more and it was noticeable how everyone listened, even Frank, this time.

'My suggestion would be that some of us go and look for them while the rest wait here in case they do turn up,' he said. 'They can't have gone too far, is my guess, and if we split up we could cover all the main spots where they're likely to be, let's say between here and the North Pier.'

'What about the Pleasure Beach?' Bessie asked. 'Isn't that what young lads like?'

'I doubt they'd have had enough money to have gone that far. Isn't that on the South Pier?' It was Richard who responded. 'Though we could try it later as a last resort if they still haven't turned up.'

Ida gasped when he said that. 'Do you really think . . . ?' She grew even paler.

'No, I don't,' Richard jumped in quickly. 'I happen to think Kenneth is far more sensible than to attempt going so far. I'm just trying to cover all the bases.'

'What about the police – shouldn't we be telling them?' Minnie Caldwell added her two penn'orth.

'Again, that's something we can do later, if necessary, but I don't honestly think it will come to that,' Richard said in his most reassuring voice. 'In the meantime, why don't we all check back here in . . . shall we say an hour? And we can review the situation then.'

Everyone nodded their agreement and they began to team up, mapping out the areas they would cover.

'Wendy, if you're willing, I think you and I should take a ride up to the arcade on the North Pier. I believe that's often a favourite spot for kids with a few pennies in their pocket,' Richard said.

'Of course, good idea,' Wendy said and looked around for Denise, expecting that she would no doubt want to join them. But for once she was nowhere in sight.

'Looking for your teacher friend?' Elsie asked as she and George prepared to set off searching on the other side of the road. George was now sporting Elsie's kiss-me-quick hat and looking as if his legs wouldn't be able to carry him very far, particularly as he kept insisting on sneaking quick kisses every few minutes, which Elsie pretended to protest.

'I wouldn't waste any time looking for – what's her name? Denise?' Elsie said. 'You probably didn't notice but she went off on her own earlier, in search of a fortune-teller she said, and I think she saw one in one of those little side streets we passed on our way back to the Tower. I only hope she doesn't hear too much bad stuff that she doesn't really want to hear.' Elsie giggled and Wendy gave her a sideways look of astonishment but didn't say anything.

'Hopefully our rescue mission is far more likely to resolve with a happy ending.' Richard grinned as he put his hand under Wendy's elbow to steer her in the right direction. 'Though I'm sorry you didn't win anything on the bingo or housey-housey or whatever it is they call it these days,' he said. 'I hear you were the only one.'

'That's only because I didn't play,' Wendy said, with a tease in her voice. 'I refuse to gamble even small amounts of my hard-earned money. When I've worked so hard to get it, I don't need to throw it away.'

Chapter 22

By the time they reached the northern end of the tram tracks, night had completely closed in, although it was almost impossible to be sure as the entire length of the promenade was ablaze with light that was brighter than sunshine. The tram they had been travelling on was festooned with bulbs that had been cleverly draped and sculpted to make it look like a pirate ship and when the driver hooted a warning to pedestrians as the double-decked vehicle trundled northwards along the front, it could almost have been a foghorn. They sat on the open-topped upper deck where all the children aboard were waving excitedly to the people on the pavement below and passed by lamp-posts studded with light bulbs and draped with fairy lights that had been fashioned into the shapes of birds, butterflies and all manner of animals, as well as illuminated flashing storyboards that gave life and movement to the much-loved characters from nursery rhymes and fairy tales that they depicted. The whole display looked even more spectacular than Wendy remembered from before the war.

They alighted at the North Shore and made their way to the pier where the first thing they were greeted by at the entrance was a larger-than-life mouse-like figure with a head that was permanently nodding and grinning, and arms that were constantly waving. Wendy thought the creature seemed more scary-looking than welcoming, but the children who clustered around it didn't seem to find it so.

Richard headed straight to the amusement arcade where almost every machine was in use and all that could be heard was the clink of copper on copper as the pennies rapidly disappeared forever through the slots or the less-frequent ping, ping, ping of winning coins being disgorged on the odd occasion that the player hit the jackpot and the machine paid out. It was mostly schoolchildren who were playing, totally engrossed while they still had sufficient pennies, banging on the side of their machine to persuade it to give out more when they won, and sighing when their money finally ran out. Richard approached a man in a dark-blue uniform who seemed to be monitoring the equipment to ask if he had seen two brothers looking as if they might be lost.

The man shook his head despite Richard doing his best to describe the boys and told him where he could find the Lost Children's Tent on the beach below.

'You never know, you might even find them there,' the man said with a laugh. 'And if not, you can report them missing.'

Unfortunately, it was the same story with everyone they approached as they made their way down the pier towards the theatre at the end; no one remembered seeing the boys during the course of the afternoon.

It wasn't until they came across Giuseppe's ice-cream stand that there was a glimmer of hope. They paused to drop a penny into the cap of the organ grinder while he was winding up his barrel organ with his monkey dancing across his shoulders and Richard asked Wendy if she fancied an ice cream. 'What about a 99? I think we deserve one.' And as he waited patiently for Giuseppe to bury the Cadbury's flake into the lightly whipped ice cream he asked once more about the boys.

'Yes, yes. I see two young boys. Maybe brothers,' the man said excitedly, his accent matching his Italian name. 'I remember well. They buy only one ice cream for two people,' he said with a shrug. 'I think no more money.' And he pointed back to the slot machines.

'Do you happen to know which way they went?' Richard asked hopefully but the man shook his head.

'I see littlest one. He bent over. Like this.' He demonstrated pretending to retch. 'Me think, "Poor boy, not very well." I want to help but many customers. I not leave the van. After people go away, I look again for boys, but . . .' He spread his palms 'Poof! Disappeared.'

'Thank you, that's very helpful,' Richard said, giving Wendy her 99.

'It sounds as though David was sick, in which case they can't have gone far,' Wendy said, as they turned away. 'Which direction shall we try first?'

'It would make sense to do what the man from the arcade recommended and try to find the Lost Children's Tent,' Richard suggested. 'Maybe they went there.'

Wendy followed him off the pier and down onto the beach below. The tent was situated just above the tideline and it was filled by a large table and rows of benches where several miserable-looking children sat, most of them being consoled by officious adults scribbling notes onto clipboards. There was a larger First Aid tent pegged into the sand only a few feet away where a lot more people were milling about and it was here that Wendy was delighted to hear Kenneth's voice.

'Miss, Miss!' he called, although it was David who

jumped off the bench and went running towards Wendy to give her a spontaneous hug.

'How did you know we were here?' Kenneth wanted to know.

'We didn't,' Richard said, and Wendy explained how they had come to find them.

Kenneth hung his head. 'We didn't miss the meeting with Dad and the others on purpose. I knew they'd be worried but I didn't know what to do,' he said, trying hard to keep his voice steady. 'I think David must have eaten too much,' he told Wendy as they made their way to the pier entrance to catch a tram back to the Tower. 'But I couldn't watch him all the time,' he said defensively. 'I suppose I shouldn't have let him have that ice cream.' Kenneth looked down at his shoes and he sounded so solemn Wendy almost wanted to laugh but she didn't, for she could see that he was distressed. 'He was bent right over the side of the pier and he was so sick I was frightened that he was going to fall off,' Kenneth went on. 'I couldn't leave him, even to get help. The Tower was a long way away and we didn't have enough money left for a tram.'

'I think you did the right thing coming here. It was a sensible thing to do,' Wendy said warmly, not sure how he would feel if she put her arm round him.

'It was good that you ended up in the right place,' Richard agreed.

'There was a lady on the pier, I think she was a nurse,' Kenneth said. 'She brought us here and managed to clean David up a bit once he stopped being sick. She seemed to think that someone might come looking for us, but I wasn't sure how anyone was going to know where we were.'

'You should have known your dad wouldn't wait long before organizing a search party,' Richard said with a laugh and he explained Frank had done just that. 'I take it you spent all your money at the amusement arcade?' he said.

Kenneth pulled out his empty pockets. 'I didn't want the coach to leave without us, but we were going to have to walk back,' he said.

'Well, you won't be late now,' Wendy said. 'They wouldn't dare leave without us, would they, Richard? But how are you feeling now, David?'

David looked down ruefully at the stained front of his T-shirt. 'I'm fine, thank you,' he replied, giving her a bright smile, and Wendy was pleased to see some colour seeping back into his cheeks.

'Feel fit enough to hop on a tram?' Richard asked. 'I think we need to get back as quickly as possible before your mother calls the police.'

Richard and Wendy arrived back at the Tower with the boys well before their hour was up and Ida ran to give all four of them a huge hug. Wendy was touched to see Frank for once welcome both of his sons without any accompanying scolding. The moment he saw that the boys were with them, he rushed forward to greet them, genuinely delighted to see them both safe and sound. He seemed to have forgotten his earlier anger.

'Oh, thank goodness you're safe!' Tears were streaming from Ida's eyes. 'Where were they? How did you find them?' She was bubbling with questions, although she didn't pause long enough to listen to any of the answers.

The boys did tell their story eventually, over and over as each of the other search parties returned empty-handed. Everyone was relieved and delighted that the story did at least have a happy ending, even if they hadn't been the rescuers, but Wendy and Richard used the retelling as an excuse to slip away, promising to meet up with the others later, as previously agreed, at the car park.

'Well, I don't know about you but that little adventure has made me quite hungry,' Richard said when they were clear of the rest of the group. 'And as there's plenty of time before we have to get back, would you fancy taking a stroll in the other direction to see the lights on the South Shore? We could head towards the South Pier and see how far we get. Maybe pick up some fish and chips on the way?'

'That would be lovely,' Wendy said, 'but you know,

I was wondering what's happened to Denise?' She spoke tentatively, not sure what Richard's reaction would be. 'I hope she hasn't got lost.'

Richard shrugged and Wendy was surprised that he didn't show more concern when she told him when she had last seen Denise. 'Why would she want to have her fortune told?' was all he said.

'I'm not quite sure,' Wendy said, 'I was just getting a bit concerned.'

'Oh, I wouldn't waste too much energy worrying about her,' Richard said, with a twinkle in his eyes. 'I'm quite sure she'd have found a way of finding *us* if she'd really wanted to.' He chuckled. 'She's never had trouble doing that before.'

Wendy turned to him in surprise.

'It's one thing looking out for two minors, even if they aren't technically our responsibility, but she's an adult and quite capable of looking after herself,' Richard said. 'And in case you haven't noticed, she's always had an uncanny knack of doing just that and latching on to others whether she's wanted or not.' He looked at Wendy meaningfully and she felt her face flush.

'We'll no doubt meet up with her later – she knows the time and place where we all have to be.' With this he smiled and held out his arm for her to link. Wendy smiled and put her own arm through his.

Chapter 23

Wendy wondered if she might have misinterpreted Richard's seemingly tolerant behaviour towards Denise, because his feelings towards her were clearly apparent now, even though he had never even hinted at them before.

They began to walk in the direction of the Pleasure Beach, which had never been Wendy's favourite place, but she had to admit that it looked far more spectacular at night than it did during the day. Every section and mechanical part was lit up with different-coloured lights, so that the whole park area looked as if it was a constantly shifting fairyland. Some of the brightly coloured bulbs were perpetual, while others flashed on and off in ever-varying rhythms, creating an endless display of patterns, images and tableaux, depicting well-known fairy stories. The larger the attraction, the more impressive its illumination seemed, and structures like the Big Dipper and the Ferris wheel, not to mention the flying helicopters and the swing boats, flashed and sparkled against the black-velvet night sky and seemed to fly in all directions, as if they were at the heart of a never-ending fireworks display.

It might have been Wendy's imagination, but the combination of food smells among the restaurants that were concentrated along the Golden Mile was not as attractive as the smells emanating from the more individual eateries that were strung out in the direction of the South Shore and the fish and chips shops, in particular, brought back so many memories that were impossible to ignore. All Wendy could think of was walking home with Andrew along the sea front and suddenly her heart began pumping so fast she wondered if she would be able to eat. But she was surprisingly hungry and although she couldn't get Andrew out of her mind, she made no objection when Richard suggested they stop at a bright-looking café, decorated from floor to ceiling with elaborate Victorian tiles.

The proprietor was cleaning the fryer, straining off the scraps of batter left over from previously fried fish, and when Richard gave their order and he tossed two tails of freshly battered cod into the newly sizzling fat, they looked instantly appetizing. He immersed a basketful of half-cooked chips so that they could become crisp and golden and the whole exercise seemed to take only minutes.

Wendy watched eagerly as the proprietor made up a parcel for each of them: a small paper cup containing mushy peas and a wooden fork to eat them with, a white paper bag full of the newly cooked chips that he had scooped out as soon as they were done, and a chunky piece of freshly fried battered cod for each of them. He dredged salt and a sprinkling of vinegar over each of the packages, leaving Richard and Wendy to add their own ketchup or brown sauce before quickly wrapping each meal into a double-page spread of yesterday's *Blackpool Gazette*. Wendy suddenly felt awkward as Richard paid for them and brushed her hand aside when she tried to offer to pay her share.

'My treat,' he said. 'A sort of thank you for your part in organizing the day. The illuminations certainly are stunning and well worth a visit and I've really enjoyed myself. I can see why they're so popular; it doesn't matter if you're a child or an adult, the whole display is very impressive.'

'It looks very different, seeing the lights from street level, of course,' Wendy said, 'instead of from the pier or on the top deck of a tram.' She was not sure why she should feel so pleased that he had enjoyed the day, but somehow she was aware of wanting to hang on to his praise about her home town.

'You can certainly see all the characters from a different angle down here, and you realize how enormous some of them are,' Richard said. 'I can see why it must have been an interesting place to grow up in. What made you leave?'

Wendy was silent for several minutes and Richard apologized. 'I'm sorry, if you'd rather not talk about it I'll understand.'

'N-no, it's not that. It's probably time I did talk about it,' she said, thinking of Elsie's advice. 'But . . . it's hard.'

'And I've been crass and insensitive, blurting out about it in the middle of the street. Look, why don't we find a café or a milk bar or something where we can have a cup of tea? At least that will be a bit more private, and if you want to talk about it that will be up to you.'

Wendy nodded, responding to his thoughtfulness. 'And maybe you can tell me about what happened to you during the war,' she plucked up the courage to say.

'I don't usually like to talk about the war,' Richard said when they had finished their fish and chips and were settling down in the corner of a small café with a large pot of tea and a jug of milk with the luxury of a separate bowl filled with cubes of sugar.

'Did you really have such a bad time?' Wendy asked. 'I'm afraid I was being equally thoughtless, expecting you to want to talk about it.'

'I don't imagine it was any worse a time than anyone else had,' Richard said. 'Let's face it, we all had our lives turned upside down and suffered losses we'd rather not think about.'

'That's true,' Wendy said. 'I thought losing my family to a badly timed bomb was bad enough . . .' She had to pause when her voice cracked so that it was a minute or two before she was able to continue. 'The last thing I needed was to be taken in by a scoundrel who took advantage of my youth and my naiveté . . .' And as she told him about Andrew and how he had betrayed her trust, Richard didn't interrupt. 'I was lucky that at least that little episode didn't ruin anyone else's life but mine, although I never did learn what happened to his real wife and family and whether they ever found out about me . . .'

A silence fell between them once more and eventually Wendy said, 'If you don't mind my asking, did you lose anyone in the bombing? I know it was particularly heavy down south, or would you rather not talk about it?'

'I'll tell you my story,' Richard said, not looking

at her. 'Though it has a certain stark irony to it. I'd been embroiled in the war from the beginning, shipped off first to the Mediterranean and then to Africa as soon as the fronts opened up. It was tough, no question about that, and it was hard to keep going.'

'But you had no choice?' Wendy said.

'No, we didn't. And all you can think about when you're in a situation like that is survival. How you can stay alive so that you can come home in one piece to your loved ones.' He hesitated. 'It never seriously crosses your mind that they are in as much danger as you and that they might not be here when you get back.' He stopped and stared off into space for so long that Wendy wondered if she had made a mistake expecting him to talk about it or if she should intervene with another question. She said nothing and eventually he said, 'Apart from my family, I'd left behind my fiancée, Susanne.' He stopped again and this time he wiped the back of his hand across his forehead and turned to look at her. 'We were engaged before the war started and when it did, she wanted to get married right away.'

'But I take it you didn't?' Wendy prompted.

'I didn't want her to have to cope with the dreadful reality of being a young widow.' He took a deep breath. 'That had happened to one of my grandmothers in the Great War.' He gave an ironic smile.

'So instead I became a widower without ever having been married.' He fixed his gaze on her but Wendy had to look away.

'A bomb?' she said, desperately wanting to reach out to touch his hand, though not daring to.

'Some leftover ammunition dumped from a German plane that was on its way home after a London bombing raid. The whole street copped for it.' He bowed his head as he spoke. 'She didn't have a chance.'

'It must have been very difficult, trying to start again when you came back,' Wendy said softly when Richard looked as if he had composed himself again. 'What made you become a teacher?'

Richard shrugged. 'The government was desperate, grants were available . . . and it seemed a better option than the suicide I'd frankly been contemplating,' he said starkly, though it sounded as if he was trying to put a jocular tone to his voice. 'I didn't think Susanne would really have wanted me to do that.'

This time Wendy didn't know how to respond and she shivered as Richard heaved a shuddering sigh. Then his mouth twisted into an ironic smile. 'As I'm sure I've said before, everyone has a story, and that includes me.'

He suddenly looked down at his wrist watch. 'Oh, my goodness! Have you seen the time? We'd better make our way back to the bus,' he said 'or we'll be left behind. I didn't realize we'd been sitting here for so long. I completely lost track of the time.' Then he grinned. 'I know you don't like running, but we might have to if we're to make it back in time.'

Wendy laughed. 'Well, I can hardly afford to miss the chara and neither can you; we'd be the laughing stock.'

They left the café and set off walking at a fast pace and Wendy was glad that Richard made no attempt to engage in further conversation. Her head was spinning and she needed to digest what she had already heard. Richard was right, she thought, everyone did have a story to tell. And Elsie had been right to suggest giving him a chance to tell his and taking the time to get to know him rather than prejudging and jumping to hasty conclusions. She also said a silent thank you to Denise, who had left them alone, as that had given her the chance to get to know him better. Wendy couldn't help smiling, curious to know if the young teacher had discovered that there was going to be more to her future than meeting a tall, dark stranger and going on a long journey.

They were approaching the Tower when Wendy heard a shout and she looked up to see Ena Sharples and Martha Longhurst gesticulating and calling, not to her or Richard, but to Minnie Caldwell, who was wandering across the road in a world of her own, paying no heed to the fact that she was crossing the tramlines. They were trying to warn her because she didn't seem to have heard an approaching tram. Admittedly it was lit up to look more like a galleon tossing on the high seas than a tram routed on the Blackpool promenade, but Minnie should have heard it as it clanked slowly towards her. Wendy watched in horror as Ena stepped off the pavement and tried to grab hold of her friend's arm in an attempt to pull her away from the tracks, but Minnie didn't move and it was impossible to tell if the driver had seen her or not. When Ena made contact with her arm, Minnie seemed to freeze to the spot and it took several moments for her to realize that the tram was clattering towards her. When she did, she shook her head as if in an attempt to waken up and tried to take a step back, but her shoe somehow became wedged in between the metal rails and she couldn't move. She suddenly looked about her in panic and began to wail.

'Stop the tram!' Ena shouted. 'Somebody stop the tram!' Then she stretched into a star shape for a moment, waving her arms wildly at the driver.

No one could be sure whether the driver had seen Ena, for although the tram was only travelling slowly, at first it showed no signs of stopping. Richard immediately understood the danger. He flew across the road in front of the tram, wildly waving his arms at the driver, paying little attention to the rest of the motor traffic which, because of the illuminations, was also slow-moving. Then, while Ena held on to Minnie's arm, he began to manipulate Minnie's foot until he was able to release it from her shoe. Without thinking, he pushed Minnie out of harm's way and into Ena's arms and the shock of the sudden movement forced Minnie to finally react positively and she took a step backwards onto the pavement. Richard, to Wendy's horror, continued trying to disentangle the offending shoe amidst the squeal of metal on metal as the driver applied the brakes.

Wendy was shocked and stood as though locked into position as she tried to make sense of what she had just witnessed then realized that Richard had somehow managed to stride clear and avoid being hit by the tram, holding the shoe high in triumph. Heart still racing, she was relieved to see that he was not only able to move freely on the pavement but that Minnie was moving too, if somewhat more slowly, as Ena and Martha guided her to a nearby bench.

Wendy followed Richard across the road to where Ena and her friends had gathered and heard Minnie insisting, 'I'm fine, there's really no need to fuss. Nothing happened.'

'It's only thanks to Miss Collins's young man here that you're still in one piece,' Ena said indignantly, glaring at Minnie. 'You could have been killed. As it is, you've probably broken your ankle. I told you before we set off that those silly shoes were no good for walking about in all day.'

Minnie gasped and for a moment looked as if she was going to answer back but all the breath suddenly seemed to be forced out of her and she collapsed backwards, tears trickling from underneath her closed eyelids.

'At the very least you need to say thank you to that splendid young man.' Ena jerked her thumb towards Richard. 'I reckon he saved your life.' she said.

Wendy was surprised to hear Ena speak about Richard in such glowing terms and couldn't describe the frisson she'd felt when Ena referred to him as 'Miss Collins's young man'. She looked at him and smiled, but he didn't seem to think he'd done anything remarkable.

'I'd say that's a bit on the dramatic side, Ena, wouldn't you?' Martha suddenly intervened, standing stoutly by Minnie's side. 'Though I'm sure she needs to be grateful, there was no real harm done.'

Ena tutted. 'Well, how would you describe what happened?' Ena turned on Martha. 'If he hadn't acted so promptly I hate to think what might have happened.' Ena shuddered. 'Thank goodness the tram driver was able to stop in time.' She turned in the direction of the driver but the pirate ship tram had started up again and had gone sailing off down the promenade.

'But my shoe! Look what's happened to my shoe,' Minnie wailed.

'Never mind that, be glad it's not your foot that got squashed like that,' Ena snapped. 'Though I'm not sure even now that you'll be able to walk on it.'

'Course I can walk on it,' Minnie said dismissively. 'I'm fine, I'm telling you.' But as she tentatively put her foot flat to the ground she winced with the pain and had to draw it back again. After a few more moments of trying to put her foot to the ground and then withdrawing it, Minnie began to whimper. 'I don't think I can do it.'

'Now why doesn't that surprise me?' Ena said with sarcastic emphasis.

Richard looked at his watch again, then back at Minnie. 'We're going to have to make some decisions,' he said, 'as we can't afford to miss the chara home.' They all turned to look at him as if they had forgotten where they were.

'I think the best thing would be for me to go back to the meeting place as quickly as possible. Everyone should be back by now and I can ask our driver if he'd be willing to come and pick you up and take you to the hospital.'

'I don't need the hospital!' Minnie still sounded scornful.

'Why not? It'll cost you nowt,' Ena said. 'And how else are you to know if summat's broken or not?'

Ena gave a pitying 'tut' as Minnie's tears began to trickle once more.

'But folks will be wanting to get back home,' Minnie cried.

'Then they'll have to wait, won't they?' Ena said firmly.

'At least if we get to the bus there'll be people to help. If you can't manage to hop on we'll be able to carry you between us, at least as far as the front seat,' Richard said, trying to take the sting out of the awkward moment.

'That seems like a really sensible plan, lad,' Ena said. 'Mrs Longhurst and me will stay with her here till you can come and fetch us all. And *I'll* thank you for your quick reactions, even if she doesn't.' She lowered her voice. 'She's no idea how close a shave that was, but maybe that's for the best.'

'Why don't I come with you, Richard?' Wendy volunteered. 'There's nothing more I can do here.'

'Good idea!' Richard said, and the two set off walking swiftly towards the car park in the hope that the chara had not left without them.

Wendy was not surprised to find they were the last two to return, apart from the missing trio, and everybody cheered ironically as they climbed aboard and stopped to have a quick word with the driver.

'But what's happened to Mrs Sharples and her crew? Are they not with you?' Elsie was sitting at the front with George, cradling a clipboard, marking a tick against the list of names as each person returned to the coach. She rolled her eyes heavenwards as she looked at the three empty seats that had been left vacant for Ena and her friends at the front but said nothing to Richard who was making his way towards the back. Wendy, looking after him, saw Richard settle into a single seat several spaces removed from where Denise was sitting alone. She caught Denise's eye and wondered why the younger girl seemed to give her a lowering look.

'I don't know,' Elsie sighed, 'there's always someone who can't keep to schedule no matter what you threaten them with, but I must admit I didn't expect that one to be Mrs Sharples.'

Before she could say more, Wendy jumped in to explain what had happened to poor Minnie, and Elsie was immediately contrite.

'Goodness, what a thing to happen!' Elsie said, 'I'm sure no one will mind being a bit late home under those circumstances. We must get poor Mrs Caldwell sorted.' Elsie turned to address her words to the bus at large as she explained the situation and everyone sympathized and nodded with understanding. 'Hopefully we won't have to be at the hospital for very long,' Elsie said, 'but I trust we are all agreed that that's what we should do?'

The driver had agreed to make the detour and he

got out to crank the engine so that they could set off to take Minnie to Casualty without further ado.

No one objected to Ena staying behind to accompany Minnie into the Casualty department of the General Hospital and all were prepared to delay their departure until Minnie's leg had been X-rayed and the doctors had decided what needed to be done. Wendy acted as liaison, reporting Minnie's progress back to the passengers on the bus and no one raised any objections to arriving home much later than they had originally planned – especially not the young Barlow boys. If anything, they were excited at the thought of being allowed to go to bed very much later than usual and it was all Ida could do to contain them and stop them annoying the other passengers as they ran up and down the aisle shouting, 'We're going to be up all night. We're not going to bed tonight at all!' until Frank had to threaten them with a spanking if they didn't behave.

To everyone's relief, Wendy was soon able to report that Minnie seemed to have a clean ankle break that didn't warrant an overnight stay, but she might have to wait some time before they could strap it up properly so that she could be moved.

'A plaster cast, a strong cup of tea and some aspirin,' was what the doctor had told Ena and, as Wendy went to relay the news to everyone on the bus, a cheer went up.

Richard was waiting for her, as she approached the coach, and as they climbed back on board she caught sight of Denise who was sitting on her own. She cast a glance in their direction and Wendy could see that she was annoyed that Richard had chosen to be with her instead, but Wendy could also see hurt and embarrassment in her face too.

She turned to Richard, 'Why don't you sit with Denise on the way back?' she suggested.

He looked at her quizzically. 'I'd rather sit with you.'

She smiled, 'I know, but there's no need to be unkind, and it's only for a little while.'

Richard didn't look so sure, but he shrugged. 'If you think it's the right thing to do.'

She squeezed his hand. 'I do.'

'Hurry up in front, gerra move on!' someone shouted from behind then, so Richard quickly took his seat, and now Denise had a truly smug look on her face, but this time Wendy didn't mind.

She had hoped that the two of them might be able to sit together on the homeward journey and that they might have been able to continue the conversation that she had enjoyed so much earlier. It had felt good to be able to open up so freely to a young man for the first time in many years and she had hoped that Richard might have felt the same about talking to her, but she didn't feel the need to make Denise look stupid to do so, despite what she thought about her. It wouldn't have been fair and would have got everyone gossiping.

When Elsie got up to make an announcement Wendy was glad to be distracted from thinking about Richard and Denise, and she sat on one of the seats near the front of the coach to let Elsie take the floor as she held her hands up for silence.

'OK, ladies and gents, let's be having your attention, if you please,' Elsie said. 'It's time for some decisions to be made about how we should best fill the waiting time. I'm reliably informed, thanks to Wendy here, that we'll have at least a couple of hours to fill before Minnie can be discharged from the hospital and we can come back to pick her up. I take it we're all agreed that we're prepared to wait for her?' She paused, and no one contradicted her. 'So, all we have to do then is to decide what we would like to do with the time.'

There was a buzz of conversation so she held her arms up once more. 'Thanks for your cooperation, by the way. I know it's not nice for any of us to think of getting back so much later than we'd planned, but I'm sure it's even less nice for Minnie.' At that, there were mumblings of agreement and much accompanying head nodding. 'And the last thing we want to do is to make Minnie feel guilty that she's held us up, so let's see if we can put that time to good use.'

'Are we going to do a circuit of the entire promenade so that we can see the full extent of the illuminations?' Albert Tatlock shouted his question above the general hubbub and everyone at least stopped talking to listen. 'I bet not everyone's been able to walk that far. There still seemed lots to see and it was one of the things on the original programme, as I recall.'

'You're quite right, Albert,' Elsie said, 'and the driver says we should do that first before we move on. In fact, he's ready to go now if everyone's happy with that.'

There was an instant show of hands and it seemed everyone was in favour.

'After that, I don't know about you lot, but I'll be about ready for a drink.' This time it was Frank Barlow who spoke up and his suggestion was greeted by cheers and whooping noises and shouts of 'Hear! Hear!'

'I take it that means everyone is in agreement with our second suggestion?' Elsie beamed with relief as a shout of 'Yes!' went up from everyone and she turned to Wendy. 'Sorry to put you on the spot, love,' she said, 'but as a one-time resident of Blackpool perhaps you could recommend somewhere half decent for us to go for a drink? Somewhere that's not too far from here, of course.'

Wendy had not expected the question and was

taken aback, hesitating for a moment or two. 'I don't know a great deal about pubs,' she said eventually, 'but the first place that comes to mind – in fact the *only* place that comes to mind,' she added with a laugh, 'is the Rose and Crown on River Street, which is very close to Central Pier.' She glanced at all the eager faces that were swivelled in her direction but no one showed any signs of recognition when she named the only pub she really knew.

'Anyone who remembers Ada Hayes from number 5 . . .' Wendy paused and tried looking directly at Esther now, but she was engrossed in a conversation with Arthur and didn't seem to be listening to Wendy so Wendy looked away. 'Well, for those of you who don't know, Ada was a teacher,' she began, 'and she was billeted at the Rose and Crown here in Blackpool for a short while during the war when she was evacuated here with most of the Bessie Street School kids.'

Albert Tatlock suddenly signalled that not only did he remember their Coronation Street neighbour Ada, but that he remembered now that he and Bessie had once visited her there at the pub during the war when they had come to Blackpool to see their evacuated daughter Beattie in Lytham St Annes. Wendy was grateful to hear from him. 'I don't know if the original landlady is still there, Mrs Ellis,' Wendy said, 'but she was really very nice and I'm sure she'd make us welcome if we tell her who we are.'

'Thanks, Wendy, that sounds like a splendid idea,' Elsie said. 'So, unless anyone has any objections or any better suggestions, I vote we head there as soon as we've seen as much of the illuminations as we want.'

There was a moment's silence then great shouts of general agreement. 'Let's be off then!' 'What are we waiting for?' 'Let's get these illuminations out of the way!' and 'Why aren't we there yet?' And Wendy was delighted to note that Frank Barlow looked as pleased as anyone.

Chapter 24

They didn't have to tell the driver to cruise slowly up and down the promenade, he was obviously an old hand and they were able to see things they had missed as they'd walked about or had only seen in daylight when they didn't look very special. It was at this time of night that Blackpool was at its best, when everything was lit up and moving, and they could appreciate the full extent of all the tableaux. The illuminations seemed to go on for miles and Wendy felt that she now understood why they were so famous, enticing people to travel huge distances to see them. There seemed to be something for everyone, from the youngest to the oldest, and everyone from Coronation Street made all the right approving noises as they admired the variety of images and scenes depicting children's characters such as Snow White and the Seven Dwarfs, and the more adult themes of the rotating blades of a huge windmill and rows of high-kicking dancing girls whose legs flashed up and down. The Barlow boys were particularly excited to see trams dressed up to look like the engines and carriages of an American railroad train, or a stagecoach and horses that looked as if they were galloping by, looking exactly like the wagons that they had seen in Western films in the cinema.

When Elsie eventually sensed that interest was satiated and energy was beginning to flag, she suggested that maybe it was time to move on and head for the pub, and when no one complained, Wendy told the driver to turn off the main road and she then directed him through the side streets until he pulled up outside the pub on River Street close to Central Pier.

The windows at the Rose and Crown were lit up too, although they looked more like a Christmas tree than late summer illuminations, but nobody minded because they looked bright and inviting as they flickered and flashed and continued the theme of light. Inside, the pub was not so bright and, if anything, it looked like it would have benefitted from a lick of paint. But Wendy was greeted warmly by Mrs Ellis the landlady, who claimed that she did indeed remember her and Ada.

'It's lovely to see you again,' Mrs Ellis exclaimed

when the two had exchanged greetings, 'but my goodness me, how many people have you brought with you?' Everyone disembarked the bus and they kept on coming until they were all packed inside the pub. 'Not that I'm not delighted to have such a full house,' she said, 'but . . .' She looked overwhelmed for a moment and hesitated as though unwilling to confess that she didn't know whether they could actually accommodate so many people all at once. 'To be honest with you, we don't usually encourage coach parties,' she said with an apologetic look, but when Wendy explained the circumstances of their dilemma, she was instantly sympathetic.

'Oh, what the heck!' she said, throwing her arms in to the air, 'we'll manage somehow,' and she called in the extra hands who had been on a break in her own living quarters to come and help cope with the rush on the bar.

'I'm afraid we've two young lads with us as well, will that matter?' Wendy apologized, 'or do we have to leave them on the bus? Their parents are with us and the boys usually go into the garden if we're stopping at a pub. They're very well-behaved.'

Mrs Ellis laughed. 'Don't worry, we won't make them do that at this hour of night, at this time of year. They're the least of our worries, but maybe they could start off in my kitchen with some lemonade until we see if we can find them a bit of space.'

'This was a good choice, Wendy.' Elsie came and patted her on the back. 'Despite it being so crowded. Let me get George to buy you a drink for saving the day. He owes me some money and that might be the best way of getting it back.'

Wendy laughed. 'There wasn't much choice. I'm afraid it really is the only pub I know in Blackpool.'

'Yes, but they're bending over backwards to accommodate us when they could have sent us packing, so that gets a gold star in my book.'

The staff worked valiantly to serve the newcomers as quickly and smoothly as possible and none of the visitors minded that there was little room to sit down.

'We'll be sitting for a good couple of hours once we get on the road,' Albert said, as he propped up one corner of the bar, much as he did at the Rovers Return, 'so it's not a bad thing to stretch our legs now.'

'It would be good to stretch our arms as well while we're at it,' Frank said. 'I'd suggest a game of darts but I don't see a board.'

'That's because it's in use in the lounge bar tonight,' one of the young barmaids said as she pulled a half of lager for Wendy.

'That's all right then, perhaps we can go in there to join them,' Frank said.

'I'm afraid that won't be possible tonight,' Mrs Ellis said in a voice that sounded not unlike Annie

Walker when she was trying to assert herself, as she came over to join the conversation. Frank looked at her, puzzled.

'It's ladies' night tonight,' she said, 'and we always move the dartboard into the other bar. We have a permanent oche fixed in there for these special occasions and any women are free to play.'

'So what about the men?' Frank grumbled.

'We've no objections to any menfolk going to cheer their women on,' Mrs Ellis said, 'but they're only allowed in to watch if there's room. Women always take priority on ladies' night.'

Frank looked disappointed. He'd fancied playing a game or two.

'There was supposed to be some sort of competition going on in there tonight that might have been worth watching,' Mrs Ellis said, 'but I'm afraid the other team have cried off so it won't be happening.'

'You're all right.' Frank sounded relieved. He didn't want to tell her that he had made a point of never watching any of the Weatherfield women in the Snug at the Rovers play, and he had no intentions of watching women play now.

'Unless, of course, you'd like to put up a Weatherfield ladies' team to play against us?' Mrs Ellis said, turning to Wendy. 'I'm sure we'd manage to squeeze in a few extra spectators if any of the men wanted to watch them.'

Wendy looked at Elsie, the designated team captain of the Rovers ladies' team, and laughed when she saw she was rubbing her hands together at the prospect.

'How about it, Weatherfield ladies?' Elsie said, nodding towards Ida and Bessie. 'What do you say? It certainly sounds like a proposition to me, though for once in my life I have to say it's a shame that Ena Sharples isn't here. And where's Esther? We can't play without her.' She looked around the room.

'Esther's over here, Elsie, so you need look no further for your star!' a man's voice shouted and, without warning, Arthur lifted Esther high in the air.

'Arthur! Stop it! Put me down!' Esther squealed as she tried to bat him away.

'Go on, love, you *must* play, it will be a treat to watch,' Arthur said as he put her down gently and Elsie reached out and grabbed hold of Esther's hand, drawing her together with Ida and Bessie into what she liked to call a players' huddle.

Wendy smiled. Esther was very lucky to have found a special man like Arthur for there was no question that he adored her. He hadn't taken his eyes off her whenever they were together, his gaze full of pride and admiration, and she'd certainly found her niche playing darts.

'The four of us usually play together at home so we'll be happy to play Weatherfield versus Blackpool if you've got some spare darts,' Elsie said to Mrs Ellis as all four stood up straight once more and Wendy's eyebrows rose as she glanced over towards Frank, wondering what he would make of that.

'Knock 'em for six!' Arthur shouted as Mrs Ellis handed them some darts and led the way to the other bar to introduce them to the Blackpool team.

Elsie looked down and sighed when she saw the bunch of cheap, wooden-bodied darts with bedraggled feathers that the landlady had given her. 'What are we supposed to do with these?' she whispered to Bessie.

'You know what they say, beggars can't be choosers,' Bessie said with a chuckle. 'We'll have to show them just what we *can* do.'

With that, Elsie squeezed her hand, plastered on a smile, and went to shake hands with the home side's captain.

Chapter 25

Kenneth and David Barlow had finished the glasses of lemonade that Frank had bought for them when they'd first arrived and were getting restless. They were tired of sitting in the Rose and Crown kitchen on their own with nothing to do.

'I know, why don't we sneak into the bar?' Kenneth suggested. 'It's so crowded in there I bet no one would notice us with all that shouting and name-calling.'

'Good idea!' David agreed. 'We could at least find out what's going on. Why should the grown-ups have all the fun?'

When they emerged gingerly from behind the draught curtain that covered the door leading into the hallway, they were surprised to find the public bar was half-empty and that the main body of noise now seemed to be coming from behind a door marked Lounge Bar. No one seemed to be paying attention to either of them and so David opened it stealthily and peered inside.

'I can't see anything but legs,' he whispered. 'It looks more like a forest. You're bigger than me – come and tell me what you can see,' and he pulled Kenneth inside after him.

It looked like it would be impossible to introduce even one more person into the overcrowded bar, but somehow the boys managed to squeeze through between all the legs.

'Almost everyone from the bus must be in here,' Kenneth whispered back when he was finally able to take a full breath, 'but there's loads of people I've never seen before. It seems there's a darts game going on with the locals.'

'Is Dad playing?' David wanted to know. 'Who's he with?'

Kenneth stood on tiptoe, straining to see. 'No,' he reported, sounding astonished, 'it's Mum who's playing with Mrs Tatlock and Mrs Tanner and I can just see Esther Hayes is with them.'

'So where's Dad?' David sounded puzzled.

'Would you believe Dad's watching and he's actually cheering them on!' Kenneth had to stand down for a moment to catch his breath but David wouldn't let it go.

'Who's winning?' David whispered insistently.

'I don't know, I can't see the chalk board,' Kenneth shot back and, as he tried to manoeuvre himself into a more comfortable position, he realized he was stuck and would probably remain so until a significant part of the crowd shifted forwards and made some room.

The Weatherfield team had had no practice playing ladies from other pubs and, hoping that they might have a better chance of winning, Elsie had opted to play fours, the best of three. It was agreed that they would start on a 301 and would start and finish on a double. The two captains then took aim at the bull's eye to see which team would start the game and Elsie, as Weatherfield's captain, was thrilled when she managed to throw nearer to the target as it meant that the Weatherfield team would have the advantage of throwing first. They began slowly and no one said anything as they gradually racked up points. They seemed to be fairly evenly matched and Elsie was delighted to see that all four were playing solidly throughout.

The evening seemed to fly by and they were still level-pegging as they were coming to the end of the third and deciding game. Elsie looked at the scores on the chalk board, trying not to get too excited when she realized that they might even be able to win. Naturally, when deciding the order of play she had kept the best till last and she felt a surge of hope thinking that they would now be looking to Esther for the critical final throw. Ida had managed a good throw, scoring sixty, with surprising encouragement from Frank, but now the tension was mounting as the Weatherfield team needed only seventy-eight to win; it would all be down to Esther. They were relying on her to throw at least an eighteen. The tension in the packed room was electric and Elsie wanted to hide her face behind her hands as Esther, who had thrown an eighteen and a twenty with her first two darts, prepared to take her final throw. The room went quiet as she stepped up to the oche, her eyes half closing as she concentrated and took aim. Even Arthur was silent, though Elsie could see he was willing Esther on. Then a shout went up as the dart landed on the double twenty. Weatherfield had won!

Arthur couldn't wait to embrace Esther. He was as excited as a child, and the watching crowd of chara passengers rushed forward to offer their congratulations.

'What a great way to end the day!' Esther said smiling.

'So long as your name's not Minnie Caldwell,' Elsie quipped.

'Thank goodness for Lily Longhurst, is all I can

say, or you wouldn't be here,' Wendy said and she gave Esther an extra hug.

The bonhomie was infectious; everyone seemed to be hugging everyone else after play had ended and they began to unwind from the tension of the game.

'Wasn't she brilliant?' Arthur said, lifting Esther off her feet once more.

'I don't know who to congratulate first,' Wendy said as she hugged each of the team in turn.

'I've never heard Frank Barlow being so enthusiastic about women playing darts before,' Albert Tatlock said as he and Bessie came to join the group.

'That's because he never has!' Elsie said.

'Well, I don't know what made him want to watch this time, but he must have liked what he saw. I'm so pleased for Ida,' Wendy said as an aside, 'but I wonder what it was made him change his mind?'

'Obviously it was the standard of play,' Albert said and there was a twinkle in his eye as he added, 'Once he realized that they weren't exactly going to be an immediate threat to any of us back at the Rovers. Isn't that right, Frank?' he added quickly as Frank joined them.

'I must admit, credit where it's due,' Frank said as he came up behind Ida and caught her unawares in a rare public embrace. 'You weren't half bad, and I mean all four of you,' he said, looking a little bashful.

'I told you, you didn't know what you were

missing,' a delighted Ida wagged her finger, pretending to admonish her husband.

Only the Rose and Crown players were looking a little dumbfounded. They confessed they were not used to losing but they took their defeat in good spirit, shaking hands and congratulating the visitors and, as losers, offering the conventional free drinks to all the Weatherfield team. As she took their orders the captain of the locals said to Elsie, 'Next time you're passing you must call in for a return match. Only I promise we'll beat you hollow,' she said with a good-natured laugh.

They got their orders in, just in the nick of time for the landlady was shouting that it was time for the last round, and Elsie checked the clock and realized it was high time they were heading back to the hospital. The crowd had begun to thin as people took their final drinks back to the public bar and seats in both rooms were now plentiful.

Wendy, who had been on the lookout for Richard, hoped she might at last be able to share some of the fun with him, despite Denise and when she felt the strength of a man's arms seize her in a playful hold she thought for a moment that it must be him. But she began to doubt it when she became aware of the outline of his hand on her backside through the flimsy material of her skirt and he began to pull her towards him. She reacted angrily then, and swivelled around, hitting out at what she assumed must be a stranger as she tried to force him to release his grip.

'I would never have thought a darts match could be so exciting,' he said and Wendy froze at the sound of a familiar voice, unable to believe what she was seeing. She felt sick and her heart began to pound in her chest. How had she thought she could ever forget him? She was looking into a pair of deep navy eyes which were staring at her with the look of pure lust that she had once mistaken for love.

She wasn't sure if her jaw had actually dropped open, but even as he said, 'How lovely to see you. I never expected to come across you in the Rose and Crown again,' she felt incapable of replying.

'Is everything all right?' Another voice she recognized joined in the fray as she desperately tried to gather her thoughts. 'Is this man bothering you?' Richard asked, his eyes quickly scanning the situation.

'Not at all,' the man answered before Wendy could make any comprehensible sound. 'We're very old friends, aren't we, Wendy? Though we haven't seen each other for a while.' He put out his hand, which Richard ignored, and said, 'My name is Andrew.'

'I think I might learn to play darts if it makes one so popular.'

Wendy stiffened as Denise came bounding over to join them and she thought she saw Richard tense too.

'Surely someone as pretty as you doesn't need to play those kind of games in order to get a man's attention?' Andrew said with a treacly smile and Wendy was shocked to see Denise gaze into his eyes and part her lips as if in anticipation of a kiss.

Wendy felt sickened by Andrew's open flirtatiousness and felt even worse seeing Denise's response to it. Had she behaved like that once? Had she been as naïve as Denise appeared now? Wendy felt the bile rise in her throat and knew she had to get away.

'Excuse me,' she said, 'but I have to go and check something with the driver for the return journey,' and she ran out of the bar, ignoring everyone who tried to speak to her.

She hadn't realized that Richard had followed her out to the car park and she was surprised how pleased she was to hear him calling her name a minute later.

'I'm over here by the chara,' she responded. She was sitting on one of the wide coach steps as Richard came over to join her.

'Was that . . . ?' He jerked his thumb in the direction of the bar. 'Was that who I thought it was?' he ended diplomatically.

'Yes, I'm afraid it was. Though I can hardly believe it. He was the last person—'

'I must admit I was a bit concerned because you looked pretty well shaken,' Richard said.

'I had no idea he'd come back to Blackpool.'

Wendy frowned. 'He must be living close to where he used to live when I first knew him, if this is his local,' she said.

'Unless he never left,' Richard said softly and Wendy looked startled. Had she once more made assumptions that had been without foundation?

Richard sat down beside her on the step. 'If there's anything else you want to tell me . . .' he said and Wendy smiled at him gratefully.

'It was quite a shock, suddenly meeting him like that after all this time,' Wendy said. 'But maybe that's what was needed to make me realize that I really am not in love with him any more.'

'I know it's a bit trite, but they do say time is a great healer,' Richard said, and although she continued to stare down at her feet Wendy could sense that he was looking at her intently.

After a moment's silence Richard put his arm round her. Wendy looked up, surprised by his move, but she didn't object and her heart had begun beating so fast she hardly dared to budge. Then she snuggled into the warmth of his coat and she could feel that his heart was pounding too. They sat for several moments like that then Wendy heard Elsie shouting to everyone and they quickly pulled apart.

'Time to go,' Wendy said. 'It sounds like Elsie's rounding everyone up and I'd hate them to be delayed getting to the hospital on our account.'

She didn't really want to break the mood, but she stood up as she saw people swarming across the car park towards them and she busily brushed out the creases in her skirt as the driver appeared and opened up the bus.

'I presume we don't have to sit in the same seats as before?' Richard said as they climbed aboard and he surveyed the seats that Elsie had hastily set aside for Minnie, Ena and Martha.

'I don't think so; not now,' Wendy said.

'Do you reckon there'll be room for one more up front?' Richard said, giving her hand a sudden squeeze. 'I didn't really enjoy sitting so far back.' He glanced meaningfully up the aisle to where he had been sitting with Denise, who was now laughing and chatting with the other passengers towards the rear. 'Could you bear for me to come and sit next to you on the way home?' he asked with a knowing smile. 'I'm sure Denise is enjoying herself, and I think you and I have rather a lot to talk about . . .'

'With any luck Mrs Caldwell will be ready for us by the time we get to the hospital and hopefully there'll be no more delays,' Elsie said. She was breathing hard as she climbed back on board.

'You don't have to take on all the worries for everyone.' Wendy laughed. 'But having said that, where's George?'

'Oh, he's probably still in there somewhere.' Elsie sounded exasperated as she indicated the back door of the Rose and Crown where the last of the exiting stragglers were slowly wandering through. 'I don't know what got into him, but for some reason he couldn't tear himself away from the bar tonight. Maybe he feels guilty because he still owes me money and he's afraid to face me.

'Talking of tearing himself away from the bar, the one I'm more concerned about is the driver,' Wendy said, 'I don't know how well he can hold his liquor but I hope he doesn't think he's got to make up for lost time by racing against the clock.

'I wouldn't worry too much,' Elsie said, 'I'm sure he knows these roads like the back of his hand by now, if that's what you're worried about.'

'I don't think getting lost is the problem,' Wendy said, 'I'm more concerned about whether he's actually fit to drive at all. Goodness knows how much he's been drinking since we stopped off, and he was still knocking them back when Mrs Ellis called time.'

'Don't worry, I'm sure everything will be fine,' Elsie tried to reassure Wendy as they ushered everyone aboard and the driver started the engine and began to pull away from his parking spot. At that moment George came running across the car park, waving his hands like a drowning man, but to Wendy's horror the driver speeded up as if he hadn't seen him. Wendy and several of the other passengers were shouting for him to stop, but it wasn't until Richard threatened to grab hold of the steering wheel that he finally did apply the brakes to pick George up.

It took some time for Wendy to calm down and she was thankful there was no further incident as they drove off to the hospital. Fortunately, Minnie was ready and waiting for them as they pulled into the deserted car park and Ena and Martha were able to push her in her temporary wheelchair directly out onto the forecourt and right up to the door of the bus. Minnie's leg was encased in a white plaster-of-Paris pot, though it was plain that it had only recently set and that she wouldn't be able to put any weight on it, not even to hop across the small apron of asphalt and on to the steps. But that wasn't necessary for several of the men rushed out to carry her on board and a great cheer went up as they carefully lifted her up the steps and onto the front seats, where she sat sideways on with the bad leg elevated onto the seat beside her. She still looked pale and shaken and her eyes were glazed from the effects of the painkillers, so she asked Ena Sharples to convey her thanks to everyone for their patience. Ena took it upon herself to add that Mrs Caldwell would hopefully be able to fall asleep and, as she was otherwise unscathed, no more assistance would be required until they reached home when she would appreciate if they could help her to alight.

Once Minnie was safely on board, Wendy felt she could relax and she settled down into the double seat she was sharing with Richard, wondering just what it was that he wanted to talk about. She couldn't help a little smile as she remembered the look on Denise's face when she realized she was being relegated to a single seat near the back. Wendy was just enjoying the floating feeling that usually preceded her actually drifting off to sleep when there was a sudden jolt and it felt as though the whole bus had been picked up and shaken. Everyone was disturbed and Wendy jumped up, convinced once more that the driver must be drunk. It took a few moments for her to realize that the driver was outside, trying desperately to turn the crank handle so that the engine could spark and engage, but he wasn't having much success.

'Silly bugger! Doesn't he know there must be something wrong if it's not picked up by now?'

Wendy looked up and realized it was Arthur talking when she saw his shock of red hair coming down the aisle and disappearing out into the night. Others had obviously got off too for she heard arguing and angry shouts outside the window, followed by yelled instructions and a lot of swearing. A few minutes later the driver came back on board.

'Ladies and gents,' he articulated carefully, 'I'm sorry to have to tell you that we have a slight problem.'

'Another one?' Everyone groaned. 'Haven't we had enough?' 'All I want to do is get home.' 'I'm ready for my bed now, not a night in a hospital car park.'

Wendy was amazed how quickly the mood had flipped as it suddenly became obvious that everyone was tired and close to the edge of their patience.

'However!' The driver held up his hand dramatically. 'We're in luck! It seems we have our own personal mechanic on board and he is actually dealing with the problem right now so that hopefully we will soon be on the road and on our way home.'

There was a collective sigh of relief.

Wendy, who was in the seat by the window, was watching carefully and she reported progress to Richard and the others who were seated nearby as the engine bonnet was lifted and she saw Arthur whip a clean white handkerchief out from his pocket and begin wiping down some of the engine parts.

'I bet it's the electrics that have got wet, what with them huge waves that come crashing onto the prom and all that salty sea air,' George said, trying to appear knowledgeable even though he was slurring his words.

'And how would you know that?' Elsie sounded scornful.

'Cos I've had to drive a car or two in my time. Goes with the job.' George preened, but Elsie raised her eyebrows to demonstrate her disbelief.

Suddenly there was another dramatic jolt and the driver, still standing by the door, almost fell over as the whole vehicle shuddered once more. But this time the engine finally sparked into life and a huge cheer went up from all the passengers.

'Well!' the driver said, dusting himself down, 'that sounds very much to me like the sweet note of success. I don't think we'll be spending the night in the hospital car park after all,' and he slid back gratefully into the driver's seat.

'Three cheers for our favourite mechanic! Three cheers for Arthur!' the shout went up as the top of his red head appeared on the chara steps. Arthur shrugged and blushed and tried to make nothing of it as he worked his way back down the aisle to where he'd been sitting with Esther, but the cheers followed him for quite some time as they hailed him the hero of the hour.

The incident seemed to have injected a sudden fresh burst of energy into everyone and the air of euphoria had not yet worn off. To Wendy's relief, this time the driver checked to ensure all the passengers were safely aboard and she felt reassured by Arthur's promise that the engine would continue to run smoothly all the way back to Weatherfield.

Everyone began to relax once more, but Albert Tatlock seemed determined to launch into a sing-song and he and Bessie began to sing, encouraging everyone else to join in. They began heartily enough with 'We'll Meet Again', quickly followed by 'Pack up Your Troubles', but not everyone knew all the words to that and the singing soon began to fizzle out. When it was reduced to tuneless soft murmurings, Albert didn't try to revive it and Ida and Frank were pleased when the singing stopped, for they were using the damped-down atmosphere to talk together quietly and amiably, something Ida felt they had not done for a very long time.

'Did you really enjoy the darts match?' Ida asked, for she had been truly amazed by Frank's reaction and wondered what had caused the sudden change. 'Go on, tell me. You can be honest.'

'You did well, I *did* tell you,' Frank said almost grudgingly, 'and you know I'd be the first to say if it was otherwise. Why? Did you not believe me?'

'Well, you never believed before that I could play and you took every opportunity to tell me that,' she said. 'I bet I'm as good as you any day of the week,' she added, but this time her tone was teasing.

'Now let's not go overboard,' Frank said and he gave her a hug as they both laughed. 'Anyway. Here. I've bought you summat,' he said disentangling himself. 'I was going to give it to you anyway to make up for all that trouble with the boys this afternoon. But you may as well have it to celebrate your darts success . . .' He hesitated. 'I know I've not always been very nice to you of late . . .'

'No, you haven't,' Ida agreed, 'but I'll forgive you,' she said, smiling, and she gave his arm a squeeze as he handed her the small package wrapped in tissue paper. She opened the tiny box to find a silver charm, a miniature model of Blackpool Tower on a fine silver chain sitting on a velvet cushion.

'I thought it would be a reminder of our first day out in a very long time, a day that in the end turned out well,' Frank said, looking bashful as he tried not to meet her gaze.

'It's lovely, my love. Very thoughtful and much appreciated,' Ida said. 'I'll treasure it.' And she squeezed his hand. 'Here, put it on for me, I want to show it off right away,' she said, fingering the pendant self-consciously as he did so. Then she stretched to give him a peck on the cheek before she snuggled up against him, letting him wrap his arms around her so that they could both sleep. But before she did so she looked across the aisle to Kenneth and David who, not five minutes before had been admonished for racing up and down and making too much noise, and were now propped up against each other, heads touching, fast asleep. She nudged Frank and pointed and they both smiled, remembering their sons' loudly stated determination to stay awake until they got home.

Soon the level of conversation throughout the chara had been reduced to murmurings, overtaken only by the sound of gentle snoring. Minnie and Ena raised the decibel level of the latter every now and then as if they were in a competition and Richard, too, made contented snorting noises, his arms wrapped affectionately around Wendy as they slept.

And no one awoke until the brakes screeched across the Coronation Street cobbles and the passengers tumbled out of the chara, barely registering their surroundings, calling only, 'Night-night.' 'Sleep well!' 'See you tomorrow!' as they stumbled off to bed.

Wendy and Esther opened the door to number 5 gingerly and were not surprised to find Lily spread-eagled across the couch.

'Think we can leave her there?' Esther asked. 'I can't bring myself to wake her up to go home at this hour of the morning.'

Wendy yawned and stretched. 'Nah! Let's leave her there. I think she'll be out till morning,' she said.

'I'm off too,' Esther said, 'though I'd better look in on Mum, I suppose, after I've got my nightie on.'

'I'd say it was a very successful outing, wouldn't you?' Wendy said, grinning as she began to climb the stairs.

'Very successful indeed,' Esther agreed, a dreamlike look drifting over her face.

'So, what are you looking so smug about?' Wendy inquired.

'Smug? Me? I don't think that's the right word.' She paused. 'Happy, maybe,' and she stopped on the stairs and twisted one of her curls about her finger.

Wendy stopped behind her. 'Are you going to share it, whatever *it* is?' she said.

Esther smiled. 'It was just as I was getting off the bus,' she said, suddenly diffident. 'Arthur asked me to marry him and I said I would think about it overnight.' The words came out in a rush and Wendy practically fell down the stairs when Esther abruptly turned round to give her a hug.

Wendy stared at her friend, delighted, not able at first to take in that the reticent young man with the flaming hair had actually plucked up the courage to pop the question.

'I think I'm going to say yes,' Esther said and Wendy was suddenly awake.

'I should hope you are!' Wendy exclaimed. 'You'd be mad not to.' Then she giggled. 'Just think, you'll have your very own tame mechanic in case you ever get a motorcar!' And Esther joined in the laughter as they went into the bedroom where Wendy fell across the bed without even bothering to undress.

'And how was your day?' she thought she heard Esther say but she was too tired to reply. She smiled broadly as she fell into an exhausted sleep because she knew it wasn't Andrew she would be dreaming about for the remainder of the night, it was Richard – and that would make the whole day worthwhile.

It was close to Christmas before the Blackpool Group as they became known at the Rovers were able to meet up again to reminisce and they laughed and joked together as they regaled each other with their 'best memories', and 'funniest incidents' of the day.

'No doubt about it, it was one of the best,' Ida said as she fingered the silver charm that she wore around her neck. 'A day to remember. We really must do it again next year.'

'Next year not being so very far away,' Ena Sharples reminded her.

'It was very special, you winning that darts game like you did.' Minnie Caldwell was walking short distances now that she had graduated onto crutches and she'd made a special effort to be included in the reunion.

'It certainly had a happy ending for me and Esther,' Wendy said, reaching out her hand towards Richard.

'But I must admit, Elsie, I thought you might have

fancied finally divorcing Arnold and making it a trio of engagements to come out of that day,' Esther said.

'What, and spoil the party?' Elsie laughed. 'I think you and Arthur, and Wendy and Richard have both got good 'uns there and I think you should each be allowed to have your special day without me butting in. I've had my day in the sun – it was just a pity it clouded over so soon.'

'But what about you and George? I thought you'd be game to have at least one more go,' Wendy said. 'Though we don't seem to see him around much lately.'

Elsie laughed. 'Nah! He was fun while he lasted – but if I put my mind to it I can do better than that.'

'Shall we not bother inviting him to next year's illuminations, then?' Wendy said.

'Certainly not! He still hasn't paid me for the ticket I got for him for the last one. But let's put that behind us and have a toast to the future instead.' They all raised their glasses and without prompting shouted in harmony: 'To Blackpool, and to Coronation Street!'

Acknowledgements

Little did I think when I acknowledged those who had helped and supported me through the process of writing the first two books I produced during the Covid 19-related lockdown that I would soon be signing off on a third lockdown book. Travel may have been curtailed during the pandemic but thankfully there were no such restrictions on creative imaginings or on childhood memories, all of which were freely available to be safely bundled up and revisited with no threat to life or limb. During this past year, some of the restraints due to Covid have been lifted and we are, at least, once again able to move about more freely within the four countries of Great Britain if not overseas; and thanks to regular meetings for work purposes and social chit-chat, through the likes of Zoom, Skype, Facetime and WhatsApp, I have been able to maintain my regular writing schedule.

I would like to acknowledge all those who have helped me in the production of this book *We'll Meet Again* which once more, with special thanks to ITV, features Coronation Street favourites of yesteryear. Thanks go to Shirley Patton and Dominic Khouri for their invaluable help and knowledge.

I would like to thank my two special Kates – my editor Kate Bradley, Editorial Director at HarperCollins and my agent Kate Nash of the Kate Nash Literary Agency, for without their continued help, support, guidance and encouragement there would be no Maggie Sullivan books. I have missed the parties and the face-to-face contact we used to enjoy, and hopefully will again soon, but we have found other ways to keep going during all the difficult times and they have helped to keep me going. Thanks also go to my third special Kate (Kathryn Finlay) who has provided friendship and actual sustenance when required.

I am, as ever, indebted to my fellow Romantic Novelists' Association members, for their help and support, in particular award-winning writers Sue Moorcroft and Christina Courtenay (Pia Fenton). I have so looked forward each week to our regular cyber chats and I have enjoyed being able to meet up with them once again in person. I look forward to further writing treats and retreats together in the coming year! Special thanks also go to Ann Parker and Jannet Wright for always being at the end of a telephone line or internet connection with writerly – and non-writerly – advice and I will be much relieved when, unlike December 2020, there will be a permanent re-instatement of Christmas!

I am extremely grateful for the meticulously detailed research and information gathered so quickly and completely by Trevor Moorcroft, as he has helped to make certain sections of this book come alive. Special thanks also to Bryan Martin for coaching me in the finer points of darts! Thanks, too, for the Blackpool-related nuggets from childhood that were suggested by Hazel Kay and the late Julie Leibrich.

During the pandemic it has been a difficult time for everyone, but for me the Covid writing experience would have been very different without the friendship, love and support from all my friends and family – a special thank you to you all.

Maggie Sullivan

Discover Maggie Sullivan's Our Street at War series with her heart-warming story, *The Postmistress*.

Read on to enjoy the first chapter.

Chapter 1

Greenhill, Spring 1939

'Looks like we're definitely headed for war if what's writ in these papers is to be believed,' a gruff voice said.

The shop bell tinkled as Vicky Parrott pushed open the front door of the Post Office that gave onto Greenhill's narrow High Street and she stood for a moment on the doorstep looking to see who had spoken. The Post Office was wedged between Boardman's newsagent, tobacco and confectionery shop and Thompson's the butcher shop and, as Vicky looked up, it was Lawrence Boardman who was coming towards her waving the *Daily Express*.

'Here y'are,' he said. 'I kept your copy back as the delivery boy was late in this morning. Thought you might want to read it over your first cup of coffee.'

'I had that a while since, but thanks. I know my dad will want to see it.' Vicky stepped outside and took the paper from him. She couldn't help a groan escaping as she scanned the dramatic pictures accompanying the front-page stories. The outlook did indeed seem very grim.

The Great War had had such a devastating effect on the small Lancashire town, and on the Parrott family in particular, that she couldn't bear to acknowledge that hostilities might be starting up again. Wasn't that supposed to have been the war to end all wars?

Vicky wasn't religious in any way. How could she keep the faith after all that had happened to her and her family? Nevertheless, she found herself unconsciously offering up a prayer to whatever gods there might be that the reporters' predictions would come to nothing. She glanced across the road to where the river continued to glide silently behind the rusted railings, looking for all the world as if nothing were amiss. And indeed, when she looked in one direction it really did seem as if nothing had changed, for all she saw was the peaceful scene of the schoolhouse with clusters of carefree children chasing each other around the playground. It was only when she turned to look in the other direction and her eyes focussed on the old cotton mill in the distance that she was reminded that it had recently been turned into a munitions factory, manufacturing ammunition and important parts for hand weapons and shells.

She shook her head to rid it of the unwelcome images that were suddenly crowding in and she tried to hang on to the stillness she usually enjoyed at this hour of the morning, the peace and quiet of those few splendid minutes before the daily bustle began. At least the High Street looked peaceful. She imagined Greenhill was like any other Lancashire mill town, with its cobbled streets that would soon be thronging with shoppers and the gentle smoke that curled from the distant chimneys so that they looked like they had been etched onto the backdrop of the craggy moorland hills. The only hint of war was an army recruitment poster in a shop window and her lips quivered with a fanciful smile as she thought of what Dot Pritchard had always been so fond of pointing out. Kindly Dot, who for ten years before her marriage had been such an important part of Vicky's life, had only been a young lass herself when she had taken on the task of looking after Vicky and her little brother Henry after their mother had died from Spanish flu. Dear Dot, who at the age of eighteen had so willingly taken on the potentially arduous role of substitute mother, showing them nothing but love. Vicky could hear her voice now.

'It might all look harmless,' she used to say, 'but we've no way of knowing what goes on behind them closed doors.' She'd have a knowing look on her face and she'd tap the side of her nose and this had always made Vicky laugh as her imagination went into overdrive.

This morning, apart from the newsagent, there was no one about but the dairyman, Billy Pritchard, Dot's father. The street was quiet save for the occasional whinny from his old horse while Billy was busy delivering fresh pints of milk to each doorstep, just as he always did. Meanwhile, the work-weary nag scented the air, plopping yet another steaming pat of fertiliser onto the cobblestones.

'Ne'er mind eh, Pretty Polly?' Lawrence Boardman brought Vicky out of her reverie as he handed her the newspaper. 'You know what they say, while there's life . . .' He turned his face skyward. 'And looking on the bright side, it might well be another sunny day.'

Vicky cringed at his use of the soubriquet. She was far too old at twenty-five to be referred to as 'Pretty Polly' even as a tease; it was a childhood nickname that harked back to her early days at the old schoolhouse and she thought it should be left there. The only person she hadn't minded using it after she left school was Stan . . . She stopped. There was no time for such memories now. It was a new morning and she needed to face it brightly, as she tried to do most mornings. She pasted what she hoped looked like a patient smile onto her face as she turned to go inside. 'Thanks for the paper,' she said and the doorbell jangled once more as she went back into the Post Office.

'Victoria, is that you?' The familiar rasp of her father's voice, followed by a throaty cough, greeted her as she lifted the counter and went through to the small living room behind the shop front, calling, 'Yes, it's only me, Dad!'

But the room was empty. None of the clutter on the small table had been disturbed. Only a disembodied voice wheezed over the banisters from the top of the stairs. 'Who was that in the shop? Why have you opened up so early? I haven't had my breakfast yet.'

Vicky rolled her grey eyes heavenward, an ironic smile tugging at her lips as she stood in front of the mirror over the fireplace where she had left all her kirby grips the previous night. She pulled her long dark hair off her face, gathering as best she could the wispy tendrils that seemed determined to escape and, sweeping them round her fingers, deftly pinned it all into a neat bun at the nape of her neck. She tried to pinch a bit of colour into her cheeks and succeeded in highlighting the high cheekbones that she was always being told were her best feature. At least the world hadn't stopped turning and her father was his usual irascible self.

'There's nowt to fret over, Dad. It was only me checking the weather,' Vicky said, disguising a sigh as she tossed the newspaper onto the table, knocking her father's favourite pipe to the floor. It hadn't had any tobacco in it since his lungs had been so badly damaged by mustard gas in the Great War but he liked to suck on it – like a baby's dummy, she always said – and she couldn't get him to part with it. She tutted as she bent to pick it up, fortunately still in one piece. She stared down at the grim front-page headlines again with the gruesome pictures of tanks and soldiers on the march and she groaned. Here they were, talking about a new war, while she was still dealing with the consequences of the old one. Life was so unfair.

'I've already put the water up and Mr Boardman next door's sent in the paper,' she shouted up to where she could see her father on the small landing at the top of the stairs. 'Shall I mash you some tea?' But the only response she got was the sound of more coughing followed by the slam of his bedroom door.

The tiny gong on the pretty clock on the mantelpiece that had once belonged to her mother pinged nine times and, on the final stroke, Vicky stepped into the Post Office, just as she always did. She pulled up the blind on the front door and swung the 'closed' sign round to read 'open'. Dr Roger Buckley was already on the step, as he was most mornings, the first customer of the day. If she was honest, she looked forward to seeing him though she wouldn't have dreamt of saying so. He was a good-looking man with a high forehead, a strong, smoothly shaven chin, and a perfectly chiselled nose, she considered him to be like an early-morning tonic, and she knew from the admiring glances his velvet-brown eyes and dark slicked-back hair drew from most of the women in the neighbourhood, that she wasn't the only one who thought so. The village's most eligible bachelor, some said, though in fact he was a widower with a child and Vicky liked him best when he dropped in to the Post Office at the weekend with his little daughter, Julie. If she had time, Vicky would stop and chat to the bright six-year-old and, if she wasn't busy, she'd let her wind the date stamp to the correct reading then press it into the ink pad before she stamped it onto any piece of scrap paper she could find. Julie was like a ray of sunshine, Vicky thought, though talking to her sometimes made Vicky tearful, thinking of things in her own life that might have been . . .